# DUNIA

## STEVE MWASE

Arizona USA

# DUNIA

Published by Cactus Rain Publishing, LLC
San Tan Valley, Arizona, USA
www.CactusRainPublishing.com


ISBN 978-0-9829181-5-9 Paperback
ISBN 978-0-9829181-9-7 eBook


Cover Design by Dennis McLain

Published November 1, 2014
Printed in the United States of America

# DUNIA

## STEVE MWASE

*You've always told stories
of what happened generations before your birth
with a first-hand voice.
How do you come across them?*

**What if I told you that I was part of them?**

# Terminology

**AC:** Army commander (Top commander of the southern army).

**ACID:** Aggressive Chronic Immune Disease (Disease that killed the southern leader).

**AMAG:** Analogy Man and God (Study Ingrid girl took at college in the Northern State).

**Antis:** Smaller weapons developed by the north to counter their sophisticated military weapons.

**AWOL:** Absent without official leave (Military acronym for absent soldiers).

**Bikoyi:** Undergarment worn by women in the south.

**Cicotaf:** Commander-in-chief of the armed forces (Political leader of the Southern State in military circles).

**CoS:** Chief of Staff (Second in command in the southern army).

**CV:** Curriculum Vitae (Resumes of northern immigrants to the southerners).

**Dunia-roulette:** Deadly game played secretly in northern clubs.

**EPIC:** Eden People's Illegal Centre (Prostitute district in the capital of the Northern State).

**FB, RB:** Forward Brigade, Rear Brigade (Units of the northern army in war).

**GFA:** General Fox Airbase (Only airport in the Southern State constructed by the north for STEITU project).

**GOA:** God's Own Army (Official name of the southern army).

**Gomasi:** Robe-like garments worn by women in the south.

**JCAS, ACos, MCos, LCoS:** Joint Chief of Staff, Air Chief of Staff, Marine Chief of Staff, Land Chief of Staff (Northern Army top military appointments).

**Lukiko:** House of Assembly in the Southern State.

**Mareto:** Mixed blood in the language of the south.

**MC:** Master of Ceremony (Head of marriage function in the south).

**NEDO:** Northern Ecological Dunia Order (Rocket; lethal weapon).

**ODOS:** One Dunia One State (Codename for operation order by President Savage to his army commander).

**PP:** Philanthropy Party (Political party for the God-loving people of the north).

**STEITU:** School Trial Excursion into the Unknown (Trip project for northern students to the south).

**Synod:** Assembly of top religious leaders.

**Twege:** Words to Ease God's Expressions; anagram; "Let us learn" in the southern dialect.

**VIPs:** Very Important Persons (southern political delegation during its visit to the northern state).

**WAC:** White Academy College (College in the Northern State intended for whites).

**Wolokoso:** Gossip.

# DUNIA

**STEVE MWASE**

# Chapter 1

Thousands of years ago the earth shook violently, and after many days thick smoke gushed out of a wide crater in the centre of Dunia. The smog darkened the land and suffocated nearly every living thing. Day and night became inseparable. Then flames soared out of the crater, setting the earth ablaze. The choking smell of scorched matter that was left behind lasted a very long while.

With the passage of time, however, came heavy rains, and after it, sunlight returned to Dunia. The broken earth filled and became a body of water, which divided the land into two parts.

Years later, people returned and continued to call both halves of the land Dunia, until a mythical man appeared.

=

At sunset a man climbed on top of a steep rock on the island of Dusampeal in the middle of the body of water. With the sun to his back, he stretched his left arm sideways, punched the air and announced, 'This is north.' He repeated the same drill with his right arm and added, 'This is south.'

The man remained standing in a crucified position until a giant cross, which reflected his posture, planted itself in front of him. On its surface were carved the words 'South' and 'North,' just as he had indicated.

Later, when politics became the Alpha and Omega, the north became known as Northern State and the other as Southern State. Generations later still, the island of Dusampeal came to be referred to as Directionland.

=

After some time the two societies became distinct races. Contrasting tongues emerged as the two peoples began to call similar things by different words. The occupants of Dunia developed variations in skin tone that became more pronounced with their location. Those in the south had darker skin, whereas their cousins in the north were light skinned. Those in the north saw their noses sharpen and their skin become hairier; the noses of their cousins in the south remained flat and wide, and their skin had little or no hair.

Since all records had been consumed by the inferno, there were contradictory versions of what happened to Dunia. Artists had their theories, which were known as folk tales. Believers quoting from Scripture talked of times past and future; the verse 'God made man in his own image,' made them denounce the idea of having personal names. However, scientists were the ones who came up with a plausible explanation. While referring to the incident as secondary only to the 'Big Bang,' which they explained as the very beginning of all life, the earth scientists said that the south was located directly under the sun and the north was away from the hottest star known to mankind, and this was the source of their differences.

=

Giant cold-blooded meat eaters marauding across the south found man to be an easy prey, which forced humans to change their way of life. People began to live in communities and develop the art of defense. As these predators and prey multiplied in number, so rose their demand for space. Southerners began to search for food outside their fortifications, where they came face-to-face with predators. The hunter became the hunted after many deadly sorties between man and beast. As their fortifications were overrun by predators, man's defense inevitably evolved into attack, making him the master of the jungle. With the seasonal rains nourishing the ground, life in the south returned to its former glory before the eruption that tore Dunia in two.

Things were completely different in the north, where the villain was not a creature. The north was cold most of the year, requiring its inhabitants to stay inside or crowd around bonfires for warmth. Inevitably the demands of nature forced them to venture out for food. Yet there was not much food to find, and people were plunged into starvation.

During the time of year when the land in the north warmed, everything was in plenty. 'The current manages the future' became the people's philosophy, and with it they became natural strategists. When the warm season grew increasingly shorter, the inhabitants lost hope, and belief in God became nonexistent. Long ago, the northerners abandoned the ways of their ancestors and acquired personal names, whereas, in the south, people continued without names, but their religion changed.

# Chapter 2

For generations the north was locked in a bizarre cycle of harsh weather. Yet, northerners would not dare immigrate to the south where they knew the natives as cannibals. The theory was so deep rooted in the northern society that a lesson was introduced in the school curriculum, which warned against visiting the south. However, those who dared the voyage came back with stories of wonderful weather and plentiful food.

Improving the northern weather became the pinnacle of scientific research. Study after study worked on ways of warming the land until one scientist, Dr. Spider, announced a breakthrough. 'Warm air rises because it is light,' began Spider, a junior lecturer at a renowned school of science. 'The air in our atmosphere is cold and it is heavy. If we can create air passages from the south, warm air will fill our space.'

Dr. Spider made himself a name, and his idea was immediately implemented by the state. By the time Dr. Spider's project was due for testing, the weather changed unexpectedly. The temperature rose by a couple of degrees, which was completely unexpected. There was an argument among the scientific community whether to go forward with the test.

Their dialogue broke down when Dr. Spider insisted that the test had to be done, come what may, even though there had been no calculations made for the effect of this temperature change. On day four of the deliberations, in a room at the college where the project was being discussed, the head of meteorology science called an end to the debate with the statement, 'Science is test and not argument.'

Dr. Spider raised his voice to challenge. Booing rang across the hall. It took awhile for silence to return. Another doctor, well respected, said that the very test might work against them, because the atmosphere was as warm as the one they were planning to import. A sample test with similar conditions of south and north of Dunia was done, and the results were questionable.

After six months, the scientists felt the weather was conducive to conduct an aerial test. A canister as big as a minibus packed with rare gases rose vertically into space, and it unexpectedly made a U-turn. It landed in the middle of the test compound as the edgy scientists ran in every direction for cover. One scientist, the one who made the prediction of the test working against them, died in the inferno that was ignited by hydrogen, the gas which powered the rocket. The project was suspended, and the state gave the public no reason why.

It was after one month when word of fire at the test site started to go around. Then weeks later, with the cold intensifying, the demanding public expounded their views on the project: The state had to abandon the project because all knowledgeable scientists on the matter were killed in the inferno.

The state did not take the public criticism lightly and rushed the project again without the proper research to correct the previous problem. The north fired rockets at the south that were designed to split open the moment they came in contact with warm air. Because proper tests had never been done, the rockets were unknowingly packed with deadly matter.

As a result, women in the south began to produce babies with diverse disabilities; some were born without limbs, and some twins had their vital organs conjoined. Most of the children died in infancy.

Not knowing what was killing their babies, the people in the south assumed it was a curse from God, because in their view, they had turned away from Him. Although they still felt His presence since the most highly regarded people in their society were witchdoctors. Being referred to as the chiefs of the land, these witchdoctors said they were the ones to be consulted about the abnormal births.

The chiefs called upon spirits in darkened shrines by shaking instruments that sounded like tins containing small stones. These spirits, which were known as clan ghosts, appeared, but they said that abnormally born babies were extremely evil spirits, and that the senior ghosts, Grande, had to be consulted in their case.

After a long period of chanting in the dark, there was heard erratic knocking and kicking on the shrine entrance, followed by a feeble voice.

'I thought so,' it spoke.

'We're happy to see you, Grande,' replied everyone at the shrine.

'This evil spirit again?' said the feeble voice.

'Yes, Grande,' responded the witchdoctor who was the shrine keeper.

'Let's get to it. I am needed across the high seas.'

'Yes, Grande, but your children here need your intercession,' said the shrine keeper, whom the ghosts simply called 'Keeper.'

'Lucky to still be alive.' He looked around, 'I can see the spirit in his home is very strong. Have you told him what to do?'

'Not yet, Grande,' the keeper answered.

'Do you want me to do your job for you?'

The keeper apologized, 'I am sorry, Grande.'

Grande raised its voice in reply: 'Sorry when my people die, is that it?'

There was silence.

'I won't be repeating this: Take two red cockerel, two she goats with goatees – one black and the other spotted – and a heifer with two teats. Do you understand?'

'But, Grande, the heifer will be hard to find,' intoned the grandchildren.

'Ask the keeper, otherwise the clan should prepare itself a row of graves, and you probably won't like that, grandchildren.'

The consulting party answered shakily, 'Oh no, we would not, Grande.'

'Now, I have to cross the high seas,' said the feeble voice and the door rattled again. Silence returned to the dark shrine.

After the shrine keeper, who looked tired, stretched himself to the breaking point outside the shrine, he said, 'You must bring the sacrifices very soon. You also heard what Grande said – worse could follow.'

# Chapter 3

Shrine rituals could not stop the anarchy in the north. Those in charge were preparing to fire the most deadly rocket the region had made. Its name, Lethal Weapon, caused uproar in the Millennium where the people's representatives, called deputies, sat. After days of haggling, the rocket was renamed Northern Ecological Dunia Order, NEDO. A radio announcement was made to the nation soon after agreeing what the weapon should be called:

It is two days until the launch of the NEDO rocket. This historic operation that shall change the cause of our suffering will take place at the shore closest to the southern mainland. It will be televised live, and the day itself will be a national public holiday.

=

Barbara was new to the Millennium, having only been inducted three months prior. She had vowed to form her own opinions and be a good deputy, since it was an honour for her and her family that she had been chosen.

Religious believers in the Millennium, known by the term, 'the God-loving people,' were inflamed by the announcement and called on the other deputies to overturn the imminent launch. Their cries were so loud that the Speaker was forced to recall the House to discuss the matter.

Quoting from the Scriptures, the believers advised the House to remember how precious man was. The secular deputies, on the other hand, used the term 'human' instead of man, and regarded those from the south as sub-human.

Barbara listened closely throughout every Millennium session. She took notes and studied them at night in her bed. Though she tried to remain neutral, she developed a keen respect for

Ingrid Savage, the wife of the leader of the Northern State, and listened even closer to what she said.

Mr. Humane Savage, the leader of Northern State, though not a spiritual man, had read the Scriptures thoroughly and was proficient at using his understanding of it in his arguments to the deputies.

'Gentlemen,' he began amid silence, 'it is not the first time we've had to kill nature for our survival. We've done it in the past, and shall continue doing so if we are to live a happy and long life in this land of double opportunities. The vision that led us to be superior to others was given by the creator, was it not? For He said, 'Go and rule over others,' so it is not by mistake that we reign. Even so, we either do this or perish. God wouldn't want to see His creation perish, would He? Besides, God helps those who help themselves. In such a scenario, the only issue is our survival; for God and our creativity!'

Murmurs rose from the deputies and their concern soon became apparent. In his speech, Mr. Savage had not addressed the females, he had said 'gentlemen,' although 'Ladies first' was the usual opening phrase in the Millennium. Members who acted contrarily to that command had to appear before the Millennium corona at the end of the session.

Mr. Savage realised his mistake. Before the session ended, Savage talked at length of how the situation had affected his inner thinking. He blamed his inexcusable utterance on what he called elements in disagreement with reality. He talked of how he loved his family, turned and faced the direction of his wife and asked her to tell the ladies in the Millennium what sort of husband he really was, but he wasn't silent long enough for her to speak.

The northern leader talked quite a lot, and yet nothing seemed to be on the subject being discussed. He was not talking about one subject. He talked about leadership, marriage, family, faith, children, and so on and so forth. But little could Savage do. The law was clear, so when the session ended, the sergeant at arms asked him to appear before the corona.

'Your plea has come to my desk,' the corona told Savage.

'Yes, my lord,' replied Savage.

'I shall, however, not make a ruling on your utterance now.' With a wave of his hand, he dismissed Mr. Savage.

=

Later that day Savage behaved unusually at home. Never would he serve his wife at table, and yet today, he not only served her, but he fed her like a baby.

This was the time when they had separated bedrooms after the wife learned of her husband's affair with his secretary.

Savage, who had made no plea against the alleged affair, entered his wife's bedroom to sleep for the night.

The question from his wife, Ingrid Savage, was how dare he? Knowing the law about gender, doom is what she saw and heard from her husband. Sharing the room with her unfaithful husband was out. She walked out and left him alone.

'Forgive me, I beg,' said Savage on his knees with his hands clinched and shaking. Ingrid neither spoke nor stopped. She spent that night in her daughter's room.

=

A week later, the corona served Mr. Savage with the sermon. 'It shouldn't be you, our leader, of all people! And since the first lady was just in, I ask you to choose between resignation and divorce,' the corona told Savage.

Savage's fears of the worst outcome had been calmed by his legal advisor. The lawyer told Savage that divorce would not necessarily lead to impeachment. Angry to avenge his wife's uncompromised denial made Savage choose divorce.

The nation was in shock, but not the first lady, as she had known all along that her husband wished to leave her. Mr. Savage and his aide started to keep together like pigeons. The leader's mannerisms provoked media attention in a society that viewed divorce with contempt. Newspapers ran articles criticizing the leader on a daily basis, all the while talk shows on radio and television satirized him. Savage changed from somebody to nobody.

It was payback time from the God-loving people who had filed a protest against NEDO. With many signatures appended to this petition, the Speaker recalled the Millennium to discuss the matter. The debate was the hottest since the issue of firing rockets on the south began.

'Why was technology that was meant to better lives being used to maim?' became the theme from the deputies. Believers lamented loudly about what the launches were doing to innocent babies in the south. One of them, an elderly woman, stood in the Millennium and said, 'Abnormal births, caused by our rockets, are driving poor babies to their deaths. How long will we stand aside and watch?' She was almost crying as she spoke.

Savage noticed something in reaching back for the arm of her chair, the old woman touched Barbara's arm. Automatically, Barbara reached to aid her to her seat. In that moment, Barbara's neutrality went out the window. The old woman smiled at Barbara with a great deal of calm and wisdom. Barbara connected physically with another and realized the human aspect of the situation. Without making a stir, she resumed her note taking. Savage noticed her note taking for the first time. No other deputy had even taken notes. Though she tried to remain neutral, she was expecting a baby with a man from the Southern State of Dunia, and whatever was said meant a lot to her unborn child.

Savage was unable to respond, but one of his supporters voiced a chilling challenge: 'Surely, honorable members,' the secular legislator began in a humble tone, 'this is not about our leader. Imagine what could happen to us here if a worse tyrant cropped up over there.'

# Chapter 4

Barbara heard the doorbell to her apartment early one morning. Thinking it was her man, she grabbed her gown and rushed to let him in because the weather had turned cold.

'Good morning, madam. Can you let us in?' said a tall man who worked with the secret service bureau at the Millennium.

'Sorry, I am still in bed,' responded Barbara.

The man reached for the pocket of his jacket and showed the deputy his identity card. Barbara ignored the protocol and tried to shut the door. The man grabbed it.

'What about this?' he said, as he handed the deputy an official warrant authorizing a search of her house.

Freezing from the cold air entering her house, she did not bother to check the document. She helplessly stepped back.

The two men briskly followed her inside. The last one to enter closed the door behind him and walked straight to the only bedroom, grabbed the bedding, and tossed them across the room.

She asked what they were searching for.

The men said nothing and continued to move things in the house like a whirlwind.

Finally, the tall agent shouted, 'Where is he?'

Barbara took a deep breath, put a hand on her protruding stomach and asked the man whom he meant.

'Your lover boy, madam,' the agent answered.

Barbara, sitting in the only arm chair in her apartment, said nothing back. The agents began to collect all of the documents in the house.

'Can you please tell me what all this is about?' she pleaded.

'You saw the warrant, didn't you, madam?'

Glancing at it, Barbara said, 'Yes, of course, but it does not specify anything.'

'They normally don't, do they, Madam Lawmaker?' said the one who had been silent.

After a grueling hour the agents left with almost nothing. The hand written notes they had interest in turned out to be of no use to them since they were written in her own form of shorthand. She had written them in a distorted way so that only she understood what they actually meant. When the agents asked what was written on them, she said it was a series of formulas about the cosmos, a private study she claimed to be undertaking.

As soon as the agents left her house she closed her eyes and said a quick prayer. She then burnt all of the remaining notes in her possession. Her effort to reach the father of her unborn child in the south and warn him about what had happened was frantic.

Mr. Savage knew Barbara would file a case of harassment against the state in the constitutional court. It was he who ordered for the warrant to search the deputy's house, and it was he to stand in the dock. This was not going to be as easy because of the blunder of utterance he had made in the House which offended gender. His lawyer had told him that this was a criminal offence, and impeachment was the most likely scenario. He thought of asking his ex-wife, whom women deputies respected, to talk to Barbara, but he found doing it hard. So, he approached the deputy who told him that Barbara was passing what the Millennium discussed to the south through her boyfriend. They carefully hatched a plan to frame Barbara, and a new warrant to search her house was issued.

The new search found a document detailing plans to launch deadly attacks in the south. Also found was a note, signed by Barbara, asking for her man to destroy all evidence relating to the Millennium minutes she had passed over. It also urged him to go into hiding. The Criminal Investigating Desk attached to the Millennium couldn't wait to take legal action against Barbara.

In court Barbara denied any link to the evidence produced against her. After a long trot, where a signature expert proved that it was Barbara's signature on the note, her lawyer asked for the crucial exhibit to be fingerprinted. The prosecution team approached the judge and whispered to him.

'Well, my dear learned friend, let it be my duty to remind you that electronic evidence is only admissible in establishing true parentage in our justice system,' the judge told the defense.

'My lord, a well-respected person representing part of the nation's population is being wrongly accused. Her life and that of her unborn child are at the peril, and if we have a way to vindicate her, let's use it.' The defense lawyer spoke his last words while facing the jury.

The jury returned with 'No verdict reached.' The judge asked whether they could reach it if they were given more time. Their spokesperson said that it was unlikely. The judge discharged them and announced a mistrial.

Savage showed outright discomfort about the court's failure to convict Barbara. In the days that followed he pleaded with the Millennium to have deputy Barbara censured. The Speaker argued that the evidence found in the deputy's house put the state in irrevocable danger, and as lawmakers, it was their duty to make sure the danger was reversed.

He used many metaphors to convince the House in vain until he employed one for games. Weather had condemned field games to near extinction, and the national snooker tournament had just concluded. The player favored to win it made a silly mistake that allowed an underdog to come to the table in the final frame and won the game. Most deputes were snooker enthusiasts and they saw the game live.

'My fellow citizens,' began Savage. 'There is no doubt we are the ones in play at the table, and the south is anxiously watching until we make a foul. Just imagine the lives of those we represent in the event of a silly mistake, ladies and gentlemen.'

There was total silence in the Millennium after Savage's short speech.

After recess, a prerogative which paved way for the matter to be heard in an open session passed unanimously. Those in favour of having Deputy Barbara removed from the Millennium won. As a gesture of what the House Speaker called consolation, Barbara would not face further court battles with the state. She was instead asked to locate her man and turn him in, to face justice for stealing state secrets from a people's deputy, while disguised as a lover boy.

Barbara took the Millennium decision lightly. She was six weeks away from giving birth, and it was then that deputies got their maternity leave. She only continued to hope that her man would not be apprehended. She knew of a northerner who had built a school in the south, and she gave a message to him to deliver to her man. Could he have received the message in time?

On her last visit to the antenatal clinic, Barbara learned what would change her life forever. The doctor told her that she would have a cancelling with two ladies. She asked why, but the gynecologist smiled and told her that it was not to do with the condition of her child. What was it then? She asked herself and waited anxiously.

The two women introduced themselves as soon as she took a seat in front of them. Barbara's heart hastened. She knew one of them, a member of the state childcare unit where orphaned children, and those whose parents were deemed irresponsible, were incarcerated. She wanted to walk away, but there was no energy in her legs. She kept looking at the women.

Eventually it was unbearable. 'May I have a short call?' she asked and got up. The women wanted to give her a hand. She shrugged them off, but soon realized she was overreacting and humbly told them that she was fine. It was the last time they saw her. With only handy belongings, she was in a hurry to get to the fatherland of her unborn baby, to the Southern State.

# Chapter 5

The northern God-loving people did not accept the theory of southerners being cannibals. To them people in the south were sane and pure like those in the north. The missionaries immigrated to the south, and while there began to spread the word of their God.

Shrine keepers had a huge impact on the southern society, which made understanding northerners difficult. Terms like demons, devils, and ghosts were associated with the light-skinned religious immigrants. The situation was so hostile that in a bid to protect themselves, the God-loving people constructed strong living structures which they lit with gasoline generators.

Night and day looked the same in their camps, which made southerners excited and curious about their magic. Fear weaned as natives changed from foes to fans. The God-loving missionaries began to move around in self-powered wheeled cars. Simplicity, love, and kindness is how southerners could identify the people they understood only by body language, because neither spoke the other's language completely.

God-loving northerners used their places of worship to teach eager southerners the language of the north. As time passed, the God-loving people gave gifts of transistor radios to their hosts in the south. Eventually it was via these gadgets that southerners learned the north had been firing rockets responsible for their sufferings.

People in the south rushed into the streets, yelling with their hands on top of their heads. Seeing their earnings under threat, the shrine keepers warned of Grandees punishing those preaching a different cause of the abnormal births.

But the people had been changed remarkably by the sacrifices they had made. Many had sold everything, including their land, to pay the ghostly demands, and they were now poor and homeless. Here was a chance to stop the practices of the witchdoctors.

Using their powers as chiefs and keepers of the shrines, the witch doctors demanded that their subjects be quiet. With the people having nothing more to lose, the row between chiefs and locals descended into civil disorder. Speaking on the matter, the ruler of the land, a man who became what he was through inheritance, outlawed all fifty-two chiefs in his domain.

His order was like a parent silencing a fight between two unequally matched sons by punishing the one who was stronger. Just as it often happened in a brotherly fight, so the people's anger flared, and they burned the shrines to ashes. The state began to descend into social unrest since the chiefs were clan leaders and the shrines represented clan symbols, or clan totems, as they were called.

A few weeks later the ruler appointed new chiefs whom he called elders. With those appointments, order fully restored, a demonstration was well attended throughout the south, during which flocks of people living in areas close to the northern border waved black flags bearing the symbol of a human skull. While chanting, 'Death to the killers,' the demonstration, which slowly spread throughout the south, saw people fill roads, treetops, and roofs.

# Chapter 6

Unlike the leadership arrangement in the north, Southern State did not have a public political House. Its ruler, in his own right, made the decisions he deemed fit as ruler. His system was slowly but surely moving away from the comfort zone of the people. The mindset of the population was changing. Many people had sneaked into the technologically advanced north to search for a higher standard of living. When they returned, it became intolerable for them to stay long at home.

The southerners who visited the north experienced promising relationships with others they met there, and the outcome was a racial lyric: dark-skinned men found light-skinned women soft bodied and attractive, while the latter found the former dominant and sexually exciting. In contrast, light-skinned men could be heard vowing how hot they found darker women who, in turn, had made a song praising the loving behaviour of the paler men. Thus, skin of mixed color began to emerge throughout Dunia, beginning first in the market places of the coastal areas of trade.

Meanwhile, a public demonstration had definitely told the ruler something, especially as many people had carried placards with his face and title scribbled on them. He sent messengers to assemble his newly appointed elders at his mansion house. After seven days, all fifty-two men had arrived and were treated with a fine banquet.

Dressed in the most decorated outfit that any southerner had seen, the ruler used the right cliché to open the meeting. 'My fellow, God-fearing people,' he announced, 'I have called you here to tell you of the danger of extinction we face.'

Ensconced in the best splendor of their lives, with the most delicious food and drink set before them, the elders, who had been chosen for their faith, knew they were present at God's calling, and they applauded their ruler.

He continued, 'I would have called you days ago, but the people's reaction towards the aggressor made me think that you were among our beloved people, sending the right message across. Stop the Millennium!'

His listeners acknowledged the words nervously.

'By the way, do you know that the top aggressor has lost his wife in this and is now living with a prostitute?' the ruler asked.

The elders looked at one another.

'Now, my people, this is the kind of person who wants to rule over us! Are we God-fearing people to be led by an adulterer? To this, my people, I say no!'

There was a murmur around the room.

In an attempt to change the subject, he asked, 'I believe all of us here have lost a relative in these attacks. Am I wrong?'

There was uproar from the elders at these words.

'Now they are going to demolish our places of worship!' the ruler added, to which cries of 'no, no, no' came from the audience like weaver birds. It took some time for calm to return. When it did, he continued, 'It is for this that I have called you here. I know we cannot match the aggressor, but we can make a mark and make him rethink, during which time we can decide what to do. Of course, with their evil and sinful intention of leveling the places of God to the ground, my people, we stand to win.'

The following morning the ruler's most favored son came to see him. The boy knew him to be callous to anyone who told him something negative when he was not in good spirits. Studying his father, who was thinking about what he called 'The evil facing Dunia,' the son saw that he was not in the best of moods, so he chatted instead with his youngest brother, who was always at the ruler's side.

Though he had twenty offspring, the majority of the populace expected their ruler to have more. But if he were to produce another child, he would have violated the local maxim of a man having only ten boys and ten girls, which was based on ten toes and ten fingers. More importantly, any father who did not have the same number of sons and daughters was thought to have wronged God.

The heir son had news from the north for his father. He had learned from a young man of almost the same age as the ruler's son who had recently returned from the north and was working at the school. Although the young man was a porter, his skill of writing in shorthand made the school authorities ask him to give shorthand lessons to a selected group of students. The ruler's son and heir apparent was among the selected group. Unlike his father, the ruler's son wanted to learn what goes on in the north, which made him take the shorthand writing seriously.

Today he wanted to read the news from the booklet he was carrying, but symbols he was unable to decipher confronted him whenever he tried reading. He turned the page upside down, thinking that perhaps he would understand it better that way, but the text only became more perplexing. Losing courage, the boy panted and fidgeted. Swallowing a mouthful of saliva, he checked the script again, yet it was still puzzling. Finally, he became anxious, unable to guess what was to come next.

His father had a lot of confidence in the boy, to the level of anointing him heir to the throne. People asked secretly why this particular son had been chosen. The ruler was aware of these concerns and often mentioned how this unique son had the brains to repay the aggressor. While the public would have asked how, this society regarded people of influence as anointed by God and thus questioning them was morally wrong.

The heir's courage returned when he saw the ruler relax. 'We have some news, Father,' he began. 'The Millennium met recently and decided to expand its authority to cover the whole of Dunia.'

'What news? You said what?' asked the ruler, looking puzzled.

The son trembled, but managed to open the booklet and locate the relevant sentences. He tried to figure out the story, but did not recognize the words, so he closed the booklet and tried to explain.

Meanwhile, his father had sobered. 'Let me see,' he said, stretching his hand out.

'Not the usual one, Father.'

'Well, all the same, I'll take a look,' insisted the old man, still holding out his hand.

With little that could be done in such a situation, the son handed over the booklet. Seeing his father flick through it like a child going through a book of pictures, the boy reached out to show him the page in question.

The father glanced at the shorthand writing and sneered. Tossing the booklet back at his heir, he asked, 'What exactly does the evil Millennium say?'

'Very sad news, Father,' the boy replied. 'Just like that, they want us out.'

The ruler held his chin in his hand. Although he could not read the language of the north very well, he could understand with some degree of difficulty when it was read out slowly and carefully. Readers who could get him to understand the little he did were singularly few, including this heir of his.

The ruler would bang his table most of the time if a reader said a word using the northern accent. He wanted words to be said with a lazy and somewhat archaic pronunciation, and he accepted neither gurgling nor incorrect breathing; only coherent words, which he barked repeatedly. Yet this peculiarity was not the ruler's alone. Most southerners of equal age had a similar weakness.

In this case he was angrily asking questions in order to understand the news fully. His son asked if he could summon his friend who had written the words in the booklet. The ruler nodded his head, and when the young man entered the room he invited him to his private seat.

'Yes, my lord?' asked the youth before sitting.

The ruler impatiently told him never to call him lord.

'It is how it is with those known to have a better understanding of life, Father,' replied his son with a bow.

The father shook his head in disapproval, and with a trembling hand he asked the newcomer to speak. The young man made a dry cough as he began to read out the message in the booklet.

Raising his head, the ruler looked the youth in the face and interrupted, 'Where did you get those words?'

The young man could not find the appropriate words to answer him with, so the son replied for him, 'It has to do with the writing ahead of us, Father.'

After the young man had read out the news, the ruler absentmindedly asked him what it was about.

'The Millennium has resolved to expand their power of authority to us here,' he replied.

'Treacherous!' cried out the ruler, and immediately sent his successor son to call the head of security.

An unusually tall man, weighing quite enough to permit his height, walked into the room and raised his hand twice. His legwork was like that of a recruit soldier being introduced to foot drill.

'We have some unfortunate news,' began the ruler, who then paused for a moment before continuing, 'But I want you to see to it that it does not cause evil, understand?' He said the last word louder than the rest.

The head of security, commonly known as chief, tightened his entire body and in the process gave out a loud fart. The two young men who were watching put their hands over their mouths, too late for the heir son whose laughter escaped through his fingers.

After a moment's silence, the ruler pointed a finger at the young man who had not laughed and barked, 'I want him around.'

'You mean to be with him?' asked the chief, his hand trembling while pointing a nimble finger at the heir.

'No, I mean here, with me all the time,' the ruler roared. He looked at his son, before turning back to ask the chief and the young man to leave.

'How did you happen to please the ruler that much?' the chief confidently asked the young man the moment they were outside the building.

'I have been to the north on a number of occasions, and I know how to handle such elite.'

'How do you get there so often?'

The young man looked the chief in the face. 'Well, they entertain those of us willing to pick up their ways of life.'

'What do you mean? I don't understand you.'

The young man took some time to respond. 'I have a girlfriend from there.'

'Where do you live?' asked the chief. 'You don't mean she's living with you, do you? Can I maybe, ha, I mean, meet her?'

The young man, after looking on momentarily, only replied, 'Anyway, that's why I said I'm there often. If you will excuse me, sir, I should be going.'

The head of security rushed back to the ruler. 'Please, sir,' he begged with a bow, 'the young man you want near you has big connections with the aggressor. His girlfriend comes from there and, according to him, she is a senior politician!' The man spoke while gasping for breath.

The ruler asked him to sit. 'Yes, my son has been telling me all about him,' he spoke, observing the roof. 'According to him, the young man is very bright indeed.' He then looked at his chief and raised his voice. 'You know what? I am going to make him my advisor.'

The chief observed the heir before even acknowledging his master's decision, which made the son smile. The ruler asked the chief to make sure his new advisor was given a place to live inside his palace. 'He is to stay as near to my son and me as possible,' he added.

'Yes, sir,' replied the chief before taking his leave. Halfway across the room, he looked back. 'Sorry, sir,' he murmured with a turnabout. The man continued to rotate. His aim should have been to salute, which he did not. Instead, he left without making any meaningful departure. The heir son looked at his father in amusement as the father looked at his son.

# Chapter 7

The young man was to begin his job of advisor by meeting with the family of the ruler. Seated in his chair, surrounded by all his children and four wives, the ruler asked him to relate what he called 'the hills and valleys' of his life.

The young man began by clearing his throat. 'Well, my lord,' he started and then bowed. He then put his hand over his mouth as he felt his body tremble.

The ruler raised his hand, somewhat lazily, to signal for him to go ahead.

Nervously, the young man ran his eyes around his audience and started again. 'I am a man who has seen what beats me in age,' he said. 'I've been to the other side, and I'm convinced I know the ways of those people as much as any one of them.'

There was a murmur from the women, who knew the ruler hated people with acquaintances in the north, which he called the devil's hideout. To their surprise the ruler just nodded, and asked the young man to continue. Tension in the room eased, but not for long, because the ruler soon asked the young man to explain how he had obtained the minutes of the Millennium – the words that had been written in his son's booklet.

Appearing to have regained his confidence, he replied, 'I know how disturbing it seems, but anyway, it's a long story.'

'Tell us, we have all the time for you,' said Ruler.

Continuing, the young man mentioned that someone close to him was a representative of the Millennium, to which some people whispered to one another. The ruler grimaced a little, but soon gave a hand gesture for silence.

'My lord, these people are generations ahead of us,' the speaker continued. 'In the north there is what those people call disc writing. As you talk, what you say is put on a shiny, thin plate, which they call a compact disc. It is then placed in a bigger apparatus with a glass screen called a computer, which, according to our ways, would best be called a television. Then everything is repeated just as the person had said it. You can even watch yourself talking, just as it was. This computer system is just like you thinking... your brain; well, actually your memory.' The young man had been tapping his head while trying to explain. 'And that is how I got this message, my lord,' he added.

The room was thrown into complete silence. The ruler did not allow the family to remain long in their amazement. Reaching for the young man's shoulder, he announced, 'From now on he is part of the family, and I will be addressed as Lord Ruler.'

The now lord ruler recalled the elders whom he regarded as his trusted ambassadors to the people. The gathering assembled in its former location, with everyone wondering why it had been recalled so soon. With his young advisor by his side, the ruler raised a hand before the gathering. There was a loud heckle in response.

The mere raising of a hand should not have provoked such a mood, thought the ruler. There was only one thing to explain it: the aggressor's evil and sinful intention of leveling the places of God to the ground, which he reported in their last meeting, had not been executed.

'I've called you, people of God, to let you know what I've come to learn from this young man,' said the ruler, killing the ecstasy of the audience. Laying a hand on the young man's shoulder, he asked him to tell the gathering what he knew about Northern State.

Although the congregation waited patiently to learn what was going on in the 'wonder-world,' as they called it, many thought they were seeing a different ruler from the one they knew. His acceptance of a man associated with the aggressor was something they had not expected. The crowd began to wonder what kind of message such a young man might have, but these were men who trusted in patience, which to them was a virtue they interpreted as the mother of hope. They waited amid calm and humbleness.

'My lord,' began the young man.

The sound of booing overwhelmed the gathering and everyone observed their ruler, who looked unmoved. There was a stiff breeze over the entire audience as the assembled people moved their heads to the left and right slowly.

'People of God, gathered around to listen to me,' said the young man.

His second statement made the audience draw their necks up higher, as if to see whether it was the same person who spoke.

'God created man as a creature of creative creation,' continued the speaker, who paused when he saw the vulgar expressions being charmed into smiles. 'That is the motto of the people of the other part of Dunia. It is only a human being that they haven't managed to create, but they are probably on track to make one. Their creatures talk, think and plan beyond what we can only imagine. Maybe this is the time to ask ourselves why we aren't like them,' he suggested.

There was total silence.

The young man continued, 'The answer is as strong as it is simple, gentlemen. God loves us and gave us enough to live. Our brothers from the north didn't get that chance. They strive to live so much that they have toiled to over-live. But, even then, they have wicked people at the top who seek to offend nature most of the time; people who have no respect for us. It is on this point that we should collectively fight the aggressor. But how do we fight him? We do it by resembling him in creativity. We need to work and work hard, and work now!'

After listening to the young man's speech, the gathered people considered what he had said, and they now began to understand why their ruler could not challenge the said word of Lord, which they knew to represent their creator. After all, some of them had heard of men in the Northern State sharing titles with God.

Meanwhile, the ruler sent the crowd off after a prayer, led by the young man, who concluded it by saying, 'Lord Almighty, we ask you to show courage and determination to the lord, our ruler, so that he may tackle the matters that lay ahead.'

# Chapter 8

The Millennium launch strategy had changed. A version called 'New Target,' referred to as 'the ruler and his interests,' made many deputies feel for the south, especially as most of them had a vested interest there. It was the place they hoped to immigrate to in case the bad weather persisted.

Many knew the undeveloped south would welcome them as developers or investors, which they knew was only a matter of time. Therefore, the idea of pushing through a piece of legislation designed to attack Southern State's infrastructure was unthinkable to them. Savage's ex-wife, also a deputy in the House, had joined the opposition, along with a sizable number of legislators.

However, researchers had just concluded a new report: 'Only launches of rockets can make Northern State have better weather. A telescopic test, performed after there were no launches for a week, has revealed a lot of cloud over the north, and further investigation has exposed a thick layer due to cover the sky. Visibility will be reduced to near invisibility and temperatures will drop remarkably. The situation will bring about untreatable illnesses and death!'

According to the researchers, the climate was changing faster than they had imagined, with currents of strong wind from the south causing much more havoc than originally thought. They called the constant change all kinds of names, and spoke of the wind gaining a lot of punch in the course of crossing the vast expanse of water between north and south. Terms such as whirlwind, storm, hurricane and tornado were created.

The deputies asked what should be done, to which the researchers answered simply, 'It is nature of our making!'

Imagining how the creator had made Dunia and given it to the people under similar submission, the God-loving people kept pushing for a humane way out of the crisis, but they did not get much response beyond rejection and abandonment. When they insisted, they were branded traitors who wanted to sell a prosperous, wealthy nation into oppression and poverty. They reacted by quitting the Millennium.

Bills began to flow freely in the Millennium after the departure of the God-loving people. Grounds were being found for bouncing back NEDO, with the Millennium tailoring the entire approach to the people in Southern State as being under criminal rule. Terms like dictator, despot and tyrant were used.

Among the new bills was one regarding defense, which came with terms such as military. Some deputies did not understand why it was necessary to form an army. In their view the ruler of Southern State was not a big enough threat to require such an organization.

Savage stopped to explain himself since the God-loving deputies left the Millennium. 'Just go and encourage young men to do military training, my dear deputies,' was his humble answer.

The deputies went off to start their campaign, but something lingered in their heads every step of the way. One historian on military matters, who was covertly invited to address the Millennium, had said that military training was the toughest of human endeavors. The man was explaining why when Savage cut him short with the words, 'Just take a good approach, my fellow statespersons.'

Most of the deputies knew the young people would welcome the experience and would be eager for the adventure, but they were not sure how the parents of the young people would react. Trials were carried out and the public asked more questions than even expected. Most puzzling of all was how to explain, without beating about the bush, the difference between army and military. It was then that the deputies regretted their leader not allowing the historian to finish his speech about the army.

There was tension in the House all right, but that was due to naivety; Savage should also have known. Some of the deputies who were strong supporters of the leader tried to replace the notorious terms; army and military with defense and security. Yet, what the public conceived was the art of switching words around and about. People knew the army becomes military in its defense and security undertakings. To them this was the same brutal institution, which was meant to turn humans into killing machines. However, the deputies did not give up arguing that, 'This particular army will provide security against the violent surging waters and offer swift evacuations.'

Promises of hefty rewards for men who performed the best, along with weekly payments of large sums of money to those who preferred to serve, were made. But youths were not recruited in the numbers required. It provoked the first passage of a bill in the Millennium about militarism: Military training was to be a must for every man between the ages of eighteen and twenty-four.

The nation began to wonder who might be behind the management of the army. Savage was not knowledgeable regarding military affairs, and the people who were had been excommunicated ever since the north switched from being a monarchy to a democracy more than a century ago.

The constitution had been revised time and time again, with successive leaders wanting to bring back the army. Their attempts had always been in vain, as there was never an enemy to defend against. However, with the state experiencing the worst weather conditions in living memory, people became unmindful.

The issue of the state using the climate as an excuse to get what it wanted made people talk about an army using slang words that only they understood. They called it 'wolokoso,' meaning gossip, and at other times they called it 'katemba,' meaning drama.

But there was one man who had been spoken about in the recent past for having replicated an army. A lot had been said about him in the private press but, of course, nowhere in the state media. The issue at hand was to find out about this man since he was the only candidate for the job.

The man's persona came to the perusal of the House. In his late teens he had managed to build an army that was under his command using a screen gadget that reportedly resembled a computer. Choosing to call the members of his army holograms, he went ahead and constructed a chamber in which he put them, renaming them robots. These robots could fight against each other, and either win or lose the battle. The man did this for many years as a hobby.

After a while, having become obsessed with his idea, the man wanted to present a show in the national arena. The manager of the arena contacted the authorities, who deemed the subject serious and told the state leader. This being the time when the south began its crusade of seceding from the north, the leader saw the army as a good deed.

The man's chamber was opened up to the politicians, who viewed his proposal with mixed feelings, because a regular army could not be formed according to the constitution. Regardless, the leader secretly decorated the man, who was in his early twenties at the time.

Not many prominent politicians had learned the man's real name, let alone met him. Soon afterwards he pushed the Millennium to amend the constitution, whereby the army was accepted as a state institution, headed and directed by the leader.

Savage, desperately wanting someone to manage his new army, made a shocking pronouncement to the nation: 'General Shroud Rough Fox, I, Humane Savage, the leader and commander in chief of Dunia Modern Army, do, by the Millennium Amendment Act 001 of our constitution, hereby appoint you as the commander of our army, for God and our creativity.'

During this announcement the people heard their leader use titles outside the ordinary, and they would have questioned it bitterly had they not been curious to know more about the man appointed. Standing more than six hands high and weighing well over fifteen stone, with a moustache that had never seen a razor, Shroud Rough Fox, aged about sixty, became an army general with four stars and the head of Northern State Modern Army.

In the Millennium it was agreed that the army personnel would be called servicemen, eligible for promotion and a higher salary after delivering good service. Decision making designed to endanger the state and disobeying commands from superiors would qualify a serviceman for dismissal from the army in disgrace. As an act of honor, guns would be fired when a serviceman was being interred. Criticism of such expensive measures that would force the public to pay extra money on every item they bought became common. Savage anticipated the political damage, because he deployed his trusted deputies and political cadres to satisfy the taxpayers.

By the end of the first year a well-trained army had been born in Northern State. Upon commissioning it, Savage made a stunning announcement to the people: 'We cannot stand dictators next door. Actually, he can best be called tyrant.'

When a pressman asked what could be done to a separate sister state with a right to exist, Savage answered that the 'chocolate people,' who were by now a separate race, had reunited Dunia as one state.

# Chapter 9

Almost one month since attaining the position of advisor to the ruler, the young man was in his room when the chief knocked on the door, entered and announced, 'You have a visitor.'

The young man was shocked, since he had not expected anyone to visit him in the lord ruler's luxurious mansion, which the locals called 'Lubiri,' meaning palace.

When he asked who it was, the chief replied with a sneer, 'A woman from the other side,' before leaving and slamming the door behind him.

Advisor's heart leapt, not because he was pleased that his woman had come at last, but in fear that his lord might take him for a traitor and kill him. However, upon recalling how the ruler had treated him during the family meeting, he gained courage and went to meet his visitor.

Barbara was heavily pregnant and due to have her baby soon. It shocked Advisor that she had traveled in such a condition to a place where medical attention was insufficient. The heir son was the first to welcome the light-skinned woman with the words, 'Feel at home,' and the couple sighed with relief as he led the way to where his father sat in waiting.

The lord ruler, looking rather surprised, invited Barbara to take a chair near him. She sank into it, giving a deep breath as her left hand caressed her enormous belly.

The son took the young advisor aside and asked him, 'Why should she come in such a condition?'

'That's the same question I'm asking myself,' he replied.

'Maybe you should take her aside and find out why!'

Without replying, Advisor rose and asked the ruler to excuse them. The ruler remained silent, as if the young man was talking to himself, so the heir son burst forth that the couple needed to be given time alone first. The ruler nodded.

After walking a distance, and well aware that he and Barbara were out of earshot from the others in the room, the young man asked her, 'What brings you here in such a condition?'

'It's a long story, but congratulations! I thought they were kidding. Anyway, I had to pay the price.'

'What do you mean, Barbara?'

'I lost my seat as deputy and I am no longer a citizen of Northern State,' she explained.

'But why, my dear?' he asked.

'Because of this, you are enemy number one of Northern State. They call you a terrorist and you became all of that because of me, according to the Millennium.'

'Come on! Damn the Millennium!'

'Yes. And there are pictures of you all over the state with a big reward offered.'

'How did you manage to cross over then?' asked Advisor.

'They gave me a choice – stay there in prison or take you to them to answer charges of espionage.'

'What does that mean?'

Barbara replied, 'Spying on the north for the benefit of here.'

'Are you willing to do that?'

'What do you think?' she asked with a smile.

The arrival of Barbara coincided with a banquet in the mansion as one of the ruler's daughters was marking her eighteenth birthday. It was during this function that girls became engaged, using the occasion to find a future spouse.

Young bachelors would start the party by running in a circle around the girls. After some time each girl picked a boy she preferred, and led him into the center to the very spot from which she had been observing the boys. The girls then made the outer circle and sang songs praising their chosen bachelors.

Traditionally, the girls wore nothing over their chests. Their singing was accompanied by a special dance, which made their budding breasts nod vigorously, sending strong signals to the bachelors. Inevitably, the scent of the half-naked girls, who had spent days smearing their bodies with ghee, drifted over to the boys, who immediately turned to face them.

The senior drummer would jump from drum to drum, seeking the maddest beat. Boys would then start to dance 'maada,' which required them to shake their chests with vigor. After a time, the bandmaster would signal for them to slow the beat down, and then the bride would throw a handkerchief on her chosen groom. The drums would peak again as the new couple disappeared from the arena, marking the end of the open ceremony. The strength of the scent left behind would determine the performance of the night and the luck of the new couple in their marriage.

Although tonight's function kept with the tradition of being conducted when the moon was full, there were no other girls to accompany the mansion daughter. Her parents could not say it publicly, but they hoped their daughter would choose the young advisor. The mother had spoken to the girl about it, and, although eager, she was unable to make any romantic gestures towards her man-to-be, so Advisor was unaware of her interest.

The girl's mother had prepared a room in the mansion for the couple, and guests had arrived in large numbers. Such an audience had never been seen before. Everyone would be counting the full moons from now, because nine of them, or nine months if you wish, had to see the bride with a newborn. Circumstances to the contrary were regarded as a bad omen. Such relationships were doomed not to last, which actually did happen in many cases.

Barbara, seated next to her man, regarded the proceedings as somewhat primitive, but, knowing this was where her child belonged, she tried to think positively. After all, she had come to the south to live, so she felt obliged to learn rather than criticize or simply stare.

It was now time for the bride to show up and the audience became anxious. Unfortunately, she could not appear. With the many invited guests frequently checking their wristwatches, the mother went to find out what was delaying her daughter. Loud wailing followed, for the girl's body was found hanging above her bed, in the centre of which lay a note scrabbled in shaky writing.

Sounding somber, the ruler asked Barbara, 'Why have you caused this to my daughter?'

Confused and not knowing how to answer, Barbara collapsed. Advisor stooped down to check on her and he cried out for help as Barbara was gasping for air.

After blaming Advisor for her daughter's death, the mother called for lightning to strike Barbara. The ruler thought of reacting to his woman's utterance, but guilt prevented him. It was he who introduced the young man into the family.

Earlier, when the young man talked of having someone, the ruler had seen things differently. At the time he had wondered what someone from another race could possibly give him. The old man had known Advisor was a wanted man in the north and that he was here to make a new beginning in life. He also thought the 'someone close' that the young man mentioned during his interview, whether a lover or not, was a matter of history, as there was no way he could return to the north; nor could the ruler imagine the friend coming to live in the south.

Although the ruler had not known his daughter's chosen spouse, he had regarded everything Advisor said as wisdom, and for him marrying his daughter would be importing wisdom into his family. For a moment the ruler felt like giving in to what his household was clamoring. The mother of the dead girl ahead of the entire house was yelling, calling upon God to take Barbara's life during her labor.

'Come and help her to a private room,' the ruler commanded, and maids rushed and took Barbara away. Moments later, a newborn baby was heard crying. As if putting the tragedy behind him, the ruler remarked, 'A girl is gone, and a girl has come.'

# Chapter 10

Exactly forty days after the death of the daughter of the Southern State ruler, a day to mark her funeral was observed.

After seeing off the many guests who had come to attend the ceremony, which was believed to send the spirit of the dead into heaven, the note found on her bed was read to the family.

He has someone, moreover of a superior race. No, Mama, we got it all wrong. Neither you nor me are to blame, but let our custom bear the curse.

The father had something to add at the somber meeting: 'Let it be a lesson to all – never is a girl to go into a bridal ceremony without meeting the man or at least his parents.'

Would the ruler's ruling bring comfort to Barbara? However many times she asked her man if he'd had anything to do with the dead girl, Advisor's answer was always the truth – No, please.

Yet the mansion residents treated Barbara in a way which made her feel abandoned and guilty. The woman began to see the words, she died because of you, everywhere she looked. Time came when her man's scent was like that of rotten meat. Maggots became the only thing she could see and sense all over his body. This is when she felt her man had had an affair with the dead girl, but he did not want to tell her the truth.

So terrified, the poor woman could not even trust her own shadow, and she spent days meditating, asking for forgiveness. God answered her prayer by pointing to what had come out of this supposed guilt.

Barbara's baby brought a great meaning to her life, and the chocolate-colored infant was as light as she was. But bearing a child without a name was tormenting Barbara like an evil spirit.

As if realizing for the first time how apart the two states were in thought and culture, she began to see a lot of emptiness around.

For an innocent baby to suffer due to the resolve of a tradition was something she could not bear. Barbara could sit down and abuse the situation with all sorts of negative adjectives, such as barbaric, archaic and immoral, yet no sooner had she done so than she would call back her words. Her feelings became more powerful, however, as she began to feel increasingly devastated about having a child without a name.

At times, Barbara accepted the inevitable and chose to modify her daughter's color description with which locals had nicknamed her. She tried to modify Chocolate to Choco, Choka, Choky or Chokei, yet nothing really pleased her. There was a time when she felt happy with Chokie, but then someone often came and called the child Chocolate. It was then that calling people the color of their skins, which was an insult where she came from, hit her hardest. Advisor was unable to sleep that day as Barbara spent all his sleeping time trying to convince him that they should name the child secretly, but he was fearful in case her tongue slipped in public.

It became too much for Barbara and she decided to approach the ruler for a solution. 'My lord,' she began, kneeling down, which was something she was doing for the first time in her life. 'Since I am Barbara and you accepted to call me so, I beg you to allow my child to bear a name.'

The ruler sneered and categorically said no.

Barbara stopped eating that day. I'd rather starve to death than see an innocent creature go through all this, she thought. Yet, after she had not consumed anything for several days, she looked at her child and pity filled her heart. Barbara decided to go for a walk to the marketplace. It was at the market that she met someone who recognized her and called her by her name. Not believing her ears, she turned around to see a light-skinned woman with whom she had served in the Millennium.

Neither of the two women could believe that moment in time. Acting on instinct and according to their own culture, they embraced each other with kisses. Their 'embarrassing' conduct attracted a crowd, which seemed to be enjoying their looks rather than their talk, and the numbers grew with time. Barbara became frightened and asked Esther to leave the place.

'No, I can't,' Esther replied.

'But why, don't you fear the crowd?'

God-loving Esther looked at Barbara and told her, 'Look, I'm here to bring the word of God to these people. It's true they know their creator, but they fear him instead of loving him. I have been holding a crusade over there.' She pointed to an open space in the centre of the marketplace. Lowering her hand, she continued, 'It's good on market days because the people are many, and I have harvested quite a number.'

'But the people don't have names, so how do you refer to them?' Barbara asked.

'It's not an issue of names,' Esther answered.

'What then?'

'Listen, my sister,' Esther began somberly, 'you were not born with a name, were you? Then, put these people in that picture when the land was under one culture and when we, too, did not have names. Our ancestors thought just as these people whom you see here believe now. Maybe you've forgotten what made us change the tradition. It was collective tasks. I'm convinced these people here will also accept names eventually. We should lead them to do one task together in the same place and at the same time, say, a choir or tug-of-war. Identifying with one another, and yet needing support from each other, will inevitably force them to bear names, as his or her identification will increasingly become cumbersome and misleading to them.'

The two women exchanged addresses and hoped to meet again.

The road spread out like a mirage in front of Barbara all the way back to the mansion. The expanse of a struggling world met her eyes in all directions. It was broad daylight, yet she was afraid of her surroundings. 'Savage,' Barbara cried out, 'how can you possibly think you face a challenge from such a society?'

She wanted to say more, but something caught her throat. It was anger. That was when she knew she was talking about the human absurdity that she shouldn't be part of. She raised her hands and swung her head to the left and right, and her steps began to fail. 'The traditions of the past must have been uncouth,' she told herself.

People began to close in around Barbara. Realizing that she was acting abnormally, she tried to concentrate on something else. For some time she could think of nothing else until she remembered Esther's story, whose strong campaign for her political party caused her to flee her motherland.

According to Savage, Esther was the campaign machine behind the Philanthropy Party. So, for him to win, she had to go away, and very far at that. One night his supporters visited her home and gave her cash and everything else that was necessary, and told her to build a new life elsewhere, as she was a threat to the state. They advised her to go to the south and help the people there to love and understand God. After remembering that story, Barbara began to feel pessimistic about Esther, wondering if she might still be working for Savage and whether she could be trusted.

Still confused when she reached home, Barbara found her child crying, rushed and picked her up. By now, the woman had decided against starvation and went to the kitchen where she drank a full ladle of cold water. With her baby strapped to her chest, she embarked on preparing something simple to eat. Barbara felt happy to have passed her first hurdle. As a person who believed in the Holy Book, the refusal of food was an evil thing, because the creator had placed her among plenty to nourish her. She praised herself for not having told Esther about it, as her friend would have seen her as an evil person.

Barbara closed her eyes and held a silent prayer. Afterwards, her mind led her into her real life and she saw the many obstacles that she had crossed. Bridging the past and present was more disturbing than her head could handle. Life had been too complicated, all the way from her school days to her political career, and until the present day. She vowed to help the people she represented in the Millennium, and yet she hadn't even had time to say goodbye to them.

Even the task that had brought her to the south had not been fully realized, but how could she turn in the father of her child? How would she tell her daughter when she grew up? Her sickening thoughts turned into happiness when her baby began to suckle. The infant then began to feel her mother's face with her soft, beautiful fingers. Barbara began to cry.

—

People close to the ruler kept asking why the young man, who was with a light-skinned woman, should continue to enjoy mansion benefits. It was worse for the mother of the dead girl, who cried whenever she saw Barbara. All of this made Advisor consider sending his woman away, but the outside world was not that friendly, either. People thought light-skinned people, who had problems similar to their own, were evil and cursed by God.

The fact that Barbara lived in the most luxurious house in the land made people think more positively about her. No one would dare to call her a curse, but her going to live locally would change all that, and might even be dangerous.

Advisor's mind was consumed by the matter, and he began to have sleepless nights. He also lost a lot of weight, which prompted his friend, the heir son, to ask him what the matter was. At first Advisor was not sure whether to tell, but remembering that the dead girl was not his friend's full sibling, he had a rethink. The next time the son approached him, he decided to talk. 'I don't know, but it is top secret,' he said.

Seeing fear in his friend's eyes, the heir son reached for his hand and led him to his room, where he thought it would be safer. But before he could utter a full sentence, his child awoke with a loud cry, which also woke Barbara. Advisor fell silent and asked the heir son to go to another room, but Barbara asked them to remain and offered to leave instead.

'Are you against her listening?' asked the heir son.

'Well, not quite, but...' Before Advisor could finish, Barbara was already on her way towards the door with her child. 'No, please remain, Mama Chokie,' he asked, his voice shaking.

Barbara stopped to listen, but the way her man addressed her made the woman feel sick and disgusted. The various names that her child could have had overwhelmed her mind. Unable to stand it, she started calling them out rapidly: 'Ingrid, Flavia, Blander, Dissent, Mary, Elizabeth, Gladys, Victoria, Susan, Peace, Grace, Helen, Camilla...'

'This is what I'm about to talk to him about. Please, I beg,' said Advisor.

As Barbara sat, he began his ordeal. With speech varying between fear and confidence, and really just beating about the bush, Advisor tried to explain how he felt. All along, Barbara and the heir son moved their heads like lizards. Finally, Advisor was compelled to mention that the child was in extreme danger in the mansion.

'I don't think so,' replied the heir son, looking rather perplexed.

'Yes, it is true,' began Advisor. 'The mother who lost a daughter is all out to harm her.'

'No, I don't...'

Barbara interrupted him, 'But I think so, too. If not, then give my child a name. I will have rested and my child will have rested too. Imagine the child doesn't sleep at night? What in God's name do you people think?'

When they were inside, the young man burst forth. With the woman shedding tears, the heir son asked her to take it easy, and he promised to talk to his father.

# Chapter 11

The army in the north came with many flying objects it called jets, which unleashed mayhem on the people. They were very noisy and caused panic, and even claimed the lives of the infirm during their daily maneuvers. The population could not bear it and demanded an explanation, but there wasn't one beyond 'defense jet fighters.' When people asked what that really meant, the next answer was that they were fast moving objects used to secure space with stealth and precision, in deterrence of enemy attack.

With the hearts of the infirm failing as a result of too much loud rumbling from the skies, the population was shocked as to why its custodian, the state, had placed more value on speculative security than the health of its people.

For some time the authorities appeared to be lost for words until Savage came up with the following statement: 'Space technology will claim the lives of innocents, who will become martyrs in changing the weather conditions; but make no mistake, the ruler in the south is a big stumbling block to our advancement.'

The leader's words made the public consider what freedom really meant, and the feeling that they had won it centuries ago vanished like steam from a plate of hot soup.

The servicemen had acquired the common name of soldiers. This went without saying for the Holy Book spoke of it, so it was not a new term to people's ears. However, this brought something else to mind – that these were not the type of soldiers specified by the Scriptures. Instead, these men seemed to be above the law, and judging by their public behavior, they were using drugs.

To add insult to injury, parents became afraid of their own sons in the army. As if to let people know exactly what they were, the soldiers always carried devices that could go off with a deafening noise. These caused senseless casualties, yet the men continued to carry them in 'self-defense.' Needless to say, their homecoming on leave was unwanted.

As if the people of the state had not had their fair share of mayhem, huge ugly-looking vehicles began to appear on the streets, which were always packed with soldiers wearing clothes that made them look like a jungle. The answer was that they were 'on patrol.'

As the atmosphere in the state became increasingly tense, the Millennium kept coming up with excuses, until, finally, the state announced it was fighting terrorism. This was another new term that required thorough clarification; but with a few incidents of unexplained devices going off in public places, the authorities did not have to give long explanations to make people understand. Talking while emphasizing only nouns and verbs, the authorities said, 'Listen, learn, lay low... house, home, hear...' Painful policies thus found soft ground and privacy became a thing of the past.

In the meantime the deputies in the Millennium who were opposed to Savage's leadership tried to gather momentum. They could not understand why a peaceful state had to go through all this simply because of a 'tyrant' who had never shown any sign of aggression. 'Instead, we're aggressive,' they told the House, probably to answer the cries of the people who had voted for them. There was a lasting division within the Millennium, and an early election was sought.

It was during that campaign that the God-loving people called for Savage to be voted out of office. Their campaign slogan was 'People, we don't have a dictator or a tyrant apart from Savage,' and it appeared to win over many minds. Society was realizing, to a remarkable degree, the importance of God, their creator.

Savage was fast to create a deterrent that used yet another new trick. With only two months until the election date, the tax on goods was abolished and salaries doubled. A fifty percent wage increment was promised, effective from the date that would see the winning candidate being sworn into office. However, it would only happen if Savage was the man to return.

As it would be the biggest wage increase since time immemorial, the people nicknamed it the 'Savage-big-deal.' Not wanting to attract attention in a state that was becoming increasingly desperate to hang onto power, the people rebranded it 'Bids'. Nevertheless, the God-loving people had a better yield. The houses of God were often full, spreading the gospel of getting their tyrant out of office. It was the wrong strategy, because when it reached Savage's ears, these places were declared terrorist havens.

When the God-loving people, who had formed themselves under the political name of Philanthropy Party-PP, tried to deny the charge and asked for evidence, people on TV screens across the state admitted to being terrorists, sent by the PP to assassinate Savage and his allies. Whether these people were genuine in their claims, enough had been done to throw the PP into a bottomless pit. Even their supporters came out cursing their representatives for using God's houses to deliver evil. The PP's appeals fell on deaf ears, leaving the organization no option but to stop campaigning and drop out of the race.

Meanwhile, Savage had played his crisis cards well. He no longer went out in public places with the maid that had sparked his divorce, and he realized that things had begun to go wrong for him ever since breaking up with his wife. The local saying 'Behind every strong man is a strong woman,' began to haunt him. In his view, Ingrid was the right woman for him. She, too, was eager to pardon her husband. So, when Savage asked her to come back to him, it was like telling a cat to guard against menacing mice.

Ingrid's affidavit to reunite with her husband saw a lot of opposition from her political party, the PP. Surprisingly, however, the judge took no time in accepting the Savages' appeal, ruling that it saved his court the difficulty of having to judge which parent should take custody of their child, since both stood an equal chance. It was learned a little later that the Savages had promised Justice Trots something money could not buy if he delivered a judgment that reflected their wishes. Ingrid, who had not dropped the name Savage after the divorce, could not wait to start campaigning loudly on her husband's behalf.

'People must always learn how to forgive, although forgetting is a natural weakness,' was the phrase that the first lady was to use throughout the campaign.

In the end, Savage won with a landslide, so he returned to office for the next ten years, although many could foresee him reigning for yet another term.

# Chapter 12

Savage had formed a new government, and it was time for him to reward the judge that reunited him with his wife. As promised, the man got something that money could not buy; he was made minister of justice. Some people, especially PP dropouts, made cynical remarks about the appointment, and their concern spread among the populace, who were equally asking what Justice Trots could deliver. The public still called the Savage reunion a saga that had ended in a sham, but now they had a more interesting event to analyze.

Savage had appointed his wife as minister for religious affairs, and public concern over it attained high levels. The phrase 'a democracy shouldn't work that way' became the common talk. Although many people viewed what Savage did as a dynastic gesture, other critics applauded it, claiming that their leader needed someone with a religious consciousness close. By now the population had known Savage as a man who acted contrary to the ways of God, despite knowing them.

Savage rubbished the politicians who saw politics as an integral part of religion. He was disturbed by faith whenever he saw people perish under natural circumstances, wondering whether they should pray or fight for their survival. With the Millennium now made up of only his newly formed Northern Republican Party and an army growing from military might to scientific repute, Savage's dream of changing Dunia was rapidly turning into a reality.

The first sitting of the Millennium passed a bill that named the leadership of the Southern State as 'enemy number one'. There would be a sustained air campaign until the southern leadership agreed to  laws implemented  by the Millennium. Many people doubted the will to achieve this objective. When Savage gave General Fox an operation order code named 'One Dunia One State-ODOS,' which he did not inform the Millennium about until the very last moment it became clear that Dunia was on the brink of what it had evaded for generations: war was looming.

Panic was commonplace because Dunia had experienced devastating war before, ending in armies being outlawed on her soil. The story of what happened was so pathetic that it was banned from the school curriculum – the subject about death of man, vegetation, and animals always left students traumatized. That is why the post-war generation had resolved to remove the word army from general use. Even words like 'fight' and 'conflict' were only beginning to return in common use.

Savage knew the history of his land better than most. In his appeal to the House and state, ODOS would wage its campaign differently. The deaths witnessed since the army had been banned in Dunia would not happen again, he emphasized. Instead, ODOS would confront the enemy with precision, and no man would have to confront another.

General Fox was instructed to assemble a force within weeks and bring the authority of the Southern State to its knees. It was not made clear what would happen to the leader of Southern State, which the Millennium preferred to call Disputed State. Rumor had it that Fox would remain in the south as supreme commander until an administration was sent in.

The current events were not in line with what Savage had promised during his election campaign. Some politicians in the Millennium were horrified and tried to question their leader, but Savage always had an answer that would throw the House into praising him as being the right man to rule.

It did not last long. The people of Northern State woke to something they had never seen before. The streets were filled with all manner of clumsy-looking, ugly vehicles. As the old lost their breath in a chase to nowhere in particular, children scattered all over the place, yelling and running to God-knows-where.

The military vehicles that moved in long convoys towards the south were quite enormous and deadly looking, yet inside were human beings disguised as wild beasts. Their parents could not imagine them being the children they had given birth to; neither could their siblings imagine they were seeing their brothers, with whom they had chatted and gossiped only recently.

'So this is the army?!' people could be heard murmuring amid whistling.

# Chapter 13

As reports arrived of a great army moving towards them, the Southern State ruler was meeting some God-loving people who had paid him a visit. They were discussing, among other things, the importance of loving God and emulating what he did for mankind.

Although the people of the south knew of the creator, very few knew that he had written anything. As such, it was very difficult to convince them that the Holy Book was a book from God. Whenever the God-loving people tried to correct themselves that it was actually God's disciples who used his words to write it, their listeners only got more confused.

The issue of language was now the irony, and yet no one in the group was competent in it. Esther said she had a contact staying with a native speaker at the ruler's mansion, and Barbara's concerns about her friend completely disappeared when five God-loving people visited her. Barbara asked her man to arrange for them to meet with the lord ruler. The assembly was, however, brought to a close as soon as it began when Advisor arrived and whispered something to the ruler.

'I'm sorry, but we have to stop. Your people can't do this to me!' said the ruler, rising from his chair.

The God-loving people looked at one another in confusion. Barbara rushed to have a word with her partner, who told her the whole story. Then she went back to her colleagues, who called one another sister or brother, and told them of the eminent attack.

Meanwhile, the lord asked Advisor to sound the alarm, which gathered all the faithful. When everyone had assembled, the lord ruler asked all able-bodied men to help to protect the state from the looming invasion. Some dismissed it as the usual gossip from their leader, but Advisor made them understand the seriousness of the matter. The people then dispersed to spread the word among the population. The lord ruler dispatched the chief of security with his guards to get people into service and send them to any vulnerable locations.

The first attack by Fox's forces would be launched after crossing the body of water at the narrowest point. The military vehicles to support the troops on the ground were unable to cross the water mass. The operation commander gave the order to pull back as soon as the leading battle tank, that was designed to float, sunk instead. He gave the order for the troops to withdraw to higher ground, overlooking the shoreline, and radioed General Fox.

'My logistics cannot cross the water obstacle, sir,' he said.

Every officer and man knew the operation had to be aborted. The order from Fox was to stay and wait for further orders.

A helicopter was heard approaching at sunset. A male figure with a telescope dangling down his neck came out and struggled with wind made by the chopper blades.

It was General Fox. He ignored the salute and began to peruse the horizon with his telescope. The ridgeline ahead was coated with rainbow colors. It was already dusk, but the horizon clearly showed it was still broad daylight across in the south. Many meandering features looking like rivers and pathways ended into the valley below.

'Very beautiful,' Fox commented as he lowered the telescope.

'Yes, of course, sir,' the operation commander answered.

'Good, now I want to see,' Fox looking bullish said.

'See what?' The commander asked.

'Prove it,' Fox yelled.

The commander gave a hand signal to the tank commander. Within only minutes one tank headed for the waters and it disappeared under the water table. After about five minutes, Fox dressed himself in a sheepish grin. He seemed like he was saying 'sorry' quietly until he left, entered his helicopter and took off.

The next day, guided air-to-surface missiles, which could only be fired with authorization from the commander in chief, destroyed part of the ruler's mansion. The strike missed its primary target, but claimed a number of casualties: a boy and a girl died, while a woman sustained spinal damage. Barbara and her child sustained severe limb injuries, but Advisor was unhurt.

Lying on her bed in agony, Barbara tried to speak, but the people around her did not understand, so they called her partner, who moved close to listen.

'People should go underground,' Barbara told him in a faint voice.

At that moment Advisor remembered a book that she had often read to him. It was about a group of people who were overpowered in a fight and went underground. Their attackers thought the war was won, only to be ambushed, and after a brief battle the defenders repossessed their land. However, the story, written by one Wolf, spoke of something that took many years of hard work to achieve.

Advisor asked himself whether the same could really work in the present situation, but, nevertheless, he searched for the book in order to go over it. Being a man who preferred shorthand to longhand, the story would, of course, take him quite a long time to read. It was after turning many pages that he remembered what readers had to do to understand the entire story in a short time. So he turned to the back cover where he read: A classic tale that could leave one in limbo as to whether it is fiction or non-fiction...

The book blurb gave mixed signals, whereas the young man's hope was to find out whether the story was real. Still, it was a tale similar to the crisis at hand. Having no other advice to give Lord Ruler, who was eagerly demanding some, the youth decided to tell the story that unfolded inside the pages.

It took quite a time to get the embattled leader to understand his advisor's strategy. Yet when he seemed to comprehend it, he asked, 'How can you dare to think that we can take on such a long-term strategy now?'

'My lord, it's the only option we have,' Advisor replied. 'These people beat us by far in nearly everything, but they won't expect us to have the wisdom of taking cover under the earth. Remember, my lord, that the creator made nature to help man in need. I believe the earth can hide us away from this savage aggression.'

After some thought, the ruler called the elders together. The people assembled and their ruler delivered the news that a great army from Northern State was on its way to attack them. Reminiscent of the story about leveling the places of worship, which had not happened, the gathering did not take the report seriously. They thought their leader only wanted to draw their attention for sympathy. But one thing the ruler had learned of late was to give time to anyone who was speaking. He had learned the art of listening and judging later.

The moment of listening was as it should be – quiet. After some time spent listening to various speakers, the elders began to visualize some element of truth in the matter. Recalling the damage caused by rockets fired from the north, people in the assembly began to grit their teeth in anticipation of the devastation that would be left behind by the northern army. All the same, they fell on their ruler's side and pledged allegiance. When the ruler saw so much support for him in his people's eyes, he asked his advisor to tell what the state expected from them.

With the book in one hand, the young man began to relate the story that had happened to an earlier generation. Many in the gathering could not follow the tale and looked confused. Advisor watched their faces and would repeat things every time he saw their expressions change, showing they were lost.

The story, which talked of kings, great armies and the destruction of entire creation, was no doubt philosophical, let alone shocking, for the audience listening. Advisor made sure to tell the part of the story intended for them slowly, using simple words, and he kept citing current parallels. At the end of his address, which lasted for well over two hours, the idea that

Advisor was a very brilliant young man was on everyone's lips. The work was to begin soon and it had to be done quickly, but perfectly.

# Chapter 14

Within three months Barbara had recovered, and Esther was living with her in the ruler's mansion. They led people in frequent prayer. Having known that Barbara was a fugitive – a term many did not understand until they were told she had been forced out of her state of origin – the people wanted to know why. When they learned it was because of her relationship with one of them, the people of Southern State developed great love for Barbara.

The near miss on her life, which she had experienced in the mansion, also made the public think she was one of them. It also made her a very good preacher, who converted many people from fearing God into loving Him.

The story told by Advisor had sunk into people's minds. Delay in Fox's attack saw them work hard on the project, and the planned bunkers were developing at lightning speed. Many loved it, working like bees, but some did not. Their misgivings were nevertheless understandable as the materials in use were hard, and had to be dragged from above and lowered down with ropes, which often broke. Loss of life was common. The underground work was often brought to a standstill as people had to clear the heaps of soil being excavated. The dug-out earth was dumped in a nearby valley until a group of God-loving people advised for it to be made into bricks. It is these well-baked bricks in a scorching sun that would be used later to reinforce the walls of the bunkers.

When the shape of the construction became clear, people became convinced that the bunkers would save their lives, and those who perished in the process were seen as true martyrs. It was emotionally touching to see them working under such circumstances. The sweat that came out of each person could tell a story. The tears that coursed down their checks when putting to rest a comrade could tell another. They developed a slogan – 'Bunker is work, and is life!'

It was at the end of a laborious season that the first bunker, below the ruler's mansion, was opened. As it was capable of accommodating many more times the number of people than the building above, the people in the neighborhood were invited to take cover inside it. With so many people from distant places becoming interested in learning the book of God from Esther and Barbara at the mansion, there would be no room in the bunker for those living in the locality in the event of an attack.

The mansion turned into a school, because lessons about loving God were thought to make people creative and add moral understanding to the task of building the bunkers. There was a misunderstanding, though, as they thought the crusaders equaled man with God, and the lesson would begin again from the start.

That was when Esther and all the other light-skinned preachers invited Barbara to clarify things. Talking in an accent slightly similar to theirs and giving examples with her mixed-race child by her side, Barbara always found this difficult. Not because she hated what she was doing, but everyone always turned their attention on her child.

Esther tried to keep the child away from the people, but they lured the girl back as soon as she took her. What should have been a lesson about God became about the daughter of the person giving the lecture. Some people even wanted to take the child with them. It disturbed Barbara greatly.

According to her, these women could easily be used to harm her daughter. She knew it was her duty to protect her child and not anyone else. When a woman who had been taking keen interest in her child approached, Barbara knew the woman wanted to ask about taking the child along with her. She pretended to be in the middle of something needing no disturbance, but such women would wait, and whenever Barbara lifted her face, there she was, still waiting to be heard. Nothing scared her more than their gomasi, seven by two meter-long dress. Local women wrapped themselves from waist to feet many times over, and yet they still wore other clothes beneath called bikoyi. Women in the south felt respectful in this type of dress. It was designed to make their shoulders shoot up, their hips to appear wide, and their stomachs to look large. The population regarded gomasi as the authentic outfit for women.

Light-skinned Barbara, who wore only tights, never stopped to imagine her daughter being smuggled into these wobbly local robes. Fear of the mansion woman, whose daughter had committed suicide, taking the opportunity to find someone in the gathering that would harm her child, overwhelmed Barbara. The mother thought of leaving her child behind with her father, but he was too busy supervising the bunker construction.

Though consciously aware that the baby girl was oblivious of her surroundings, intuition made Barbara warn her daughter about the familiarity of strangers. The girl promised her mother that she would obey by nodding her head, but this seemed merely to calm her mother's anger. The child realized doing what Mama had often warned against when Aunt Esther came to take her away from some stranger she was embracing. With her finger into her mouth the girl, looking sheepish, could observe her stern-looking mother. 'Come on, it's time to have something to eat, let's go, and say bye to everybody, darling,' Barbara would say while forcing the child's hand to wave.

# Chapter 15

The child had grown and was capable of speaking both her paternal and maternal languages. The issue of naming her was still a dilemma, although the mother had come up with a word that she called her when they were alone. Advisor knew of it and used it too. The growing girl became confused when her mother told her that her father did not have a name, but a title instead. She had known and thought that her father was Advisor by name, and that was all. Nevertheless, she continued to call him by his title and it worked amicably well.

Meanwhile, the opening of the mansion bunker was colorful. Work that had seen many people lose their lives would undoubtedly be reflected in emotional speeches. The leader was not a man who was good at talking, but, thanks to Advisor, his son was turning into a fine orator.

Ever since averting hatred and perhaps even his child's death, Advisor had viewed the heir son as a true friend. The son had presented Advisor and Barbara's case to the leader, who then warned the mother of his late daughter. Knowing her man and having borne no sons by him, the wife took the warning seriously, and she developed forced love for Barbara's child.

In return, Advisor and Barbara helped the heir son with his reading and the art of giving speeches. They also vowed never to let their friendship fade, but Barbara was most pleased with the ruler's son when he said they could name their child in the future.

Although that time had not come, Barbara hoped it would. After all, she had named her child in secret, and it was working. The girl knew her name to be Ingrid, and whenever one of her parents said it, she would turn. She was warned never to react if the word was said by any other person, and she was keeping the secret.

The heir son was the person who delivered the main speech at the opening ceremony. Many people were gathered and most had lost relatives during the project. There had been some absentees from many working sessions, people who found going to the occasion either insulting or unbecoming, if not mocking.

Women had not participated in the construction but had remained behind, looking after the homes and welcoming back their men, who went home feeling completely done in. The heir son was careful to remember the women who were mothers of the martyrs of the beautiful project. Although the number was negligible, those who lost limbs, fingers, feet or other parts of their bodies were to go down in history as gallant sons of the state.

Above all, the speech had to idolize leadership. Advisor had brought all of these points to the mind of the heir son. After watching him rehearsing the speech many times over, Advisor and Barbara told him it was brilliant. The beginning was rather difficult, but Advisor sat right behind the Speaker in case he was needed.

'In God we trust!' said the heir son. Seeing Advisor give him the thumbs-up, he knew he was on track, and vented forth, 'Our dear lord, respected men and women, both present and not present, allow me to ask you for a minute's silence in memory of those who perished for what we're cerebrating here today.'

People went down on their knees, but one minute became many. After a time that saw many feel pain in their legs, the son said, 'Amen!' The gathering then rose to take their seats, their faces full of longing.

'On behalf of my father, may I once again thank you, the people of this state, for what you have done to make this project a success. Let me assure you that we, the poor people of God, have somewhere to rest our skins now. But it is not enough, and may I say that it was perhaps wrong in the first place. I would have thought – and my father too – that a  safe haven for the children would be built first, before we thought of the leader. Otherwise, it is like God watching us perish while building a bunker for himself. He couldn't, could he?'

Although the speaker paused, probably in anticipation of an answer to his question, the people did not realize. They only knew that the young man appeared to know what he was talking about.

'May I therefore take this opportunity to say that this construction will be called the Child Bunker. The age of the children who will dwell in it when the aggressor begins his onslaught will be determined and sent to you for record. And with this, once again, on behalf of my father, the ruler of this child-loving state, may I thank you for coming, and may God bless us all.'

The speech by the heir son made him very famous. Many people of all ages talked about the wisdom of the young man reflecting what a great leader he would become after his father. The quality of the speech made those who had not attended, for reasons this or that, regret not going, and they vowed to work hand-in-hand for the sake of what was now being seen as statehood.

Bunkers were constructed, with the technology being copied from the Holy Book, which contained everything to predict nature. The people had come to accept that God loved them, although they continued to fear Him.

Barbara and her team had enough successes to feel proud. The people had accepted the course of nature and vowed to work hard to overcome Dunia's disappointments. The slogan 'Bunker is work, is death, and is life' was expanded to include 'God make us work even harder.'

# Chapter 16

After General Fox had prepared his force for a ground attack, an order came from the Millennium to halt the operation. The minister for religious affairs, Ingrid Savage, had appealed for all military activities to be halted, as the army was not complete. All deputies pulled their ears to hear the very first bill in opposition of Savage's new one-party government, being presented by his reunited wife.

She announced, 'As the House may well remember, the formation of Dunia Modern Army was only possible if priests, whom we chose to call chaplains, were a part. It was agreed therefore that every 300 men would be represented by one chaplain in peace time, and thirty men would be presented by one chaplain during wartime.

'To the disappointment of my ministry, charged with the responsibility of fulfilling our army's spiritual needs, I regret to announce the sending back of more than a hundred chaplains from the frontline on the orders of the commander of the Dunia Modern Army, General Fox.

'As you all know, this state, and indeed the whole of Dunia, believes and depends on God in all her deliberations. It shouldn't have been the commander, in whom all have confidence, who turned back believers attached to our army. I, for that matter, call upon the House to stop Operation ODOS from proceeding, for God and our creativity.'

Ingrid Savage then asked the chaplains in question to stand. More than 100 men and women dressed in green camouflage and wearing white bangles round their necks stood up. Each one was holding a Holy Book in their right hand, which they raised high above their heads in unison.

The Millennium, which had been thrown into a murmur, fell silent when the chaplains, who synchronized everything they did to rhyme, began to read a verse in the Holy Book: "When that which had never been thrown in battle before was thrown by so small a man, all knew the giant had been thrown by God rather than the small man. And then victory and humiliation fell on either faces like..."

After the loud reading, a unique silence engulfed the Millennium like never before.

The Speaker invited General Fox, who was dressed in green military camouflage with an insignia of the state emblem and a military cross. When he stood up, the House booed. Fox, in return, was militant, ordering and snapping at the deputies as if they were men under his command. The booing intensified. It took minutes for the Speaker to get the House in order, and a recess was called.

Deputies could be heard suggesting that the army be disbanded altogether.

Fox then had a private discussion with Savage. Whichever of them it was who left his microphone on, it enabled the press center in the Millennium to hear every word. The two men started to talk about recruitment, far and wide, the calling of which the media could not fully understand.

In rebound, Savage flinched and asked for his marriage to be spared. Fox barked him down by reminding his commander in chief that he was a man of clout and caliber, who many better women of his kind would vie to lay their hands on. At the end of a bitter, yet subtle exchange, the two men emerged and the Speaker called for the House to resume.

'Ladies and gentlemen of the House,' Savage began amid silence. 'It has taken our most decorated commander and me a time, not long, to find a solution to this stand-off.' He quieted, touched his nose, and started to speak again. 'Maybe I should draw you back to what skipped my mind all along when we were discussing the issue of the army and God, although I do not suggest that it escaped your minds as well, honorable members.'

Deputies whispered to each other, trying to remember what it was that they all appeared to have forgotten. Savage was not going to let them. 'So, ladies and gentlemen, just like me, you must have forgotten, just as humans do. Allow me then to remind you that when this army was being formed, no mention of the term God was made. And when one who is apparently no longer with us, Esther, did mention a God-loving army, we acted by throwing her out of the Millennium, although she was later seen to have conspired with another fugitive, Barbara, in letting our secrets out.'

The deputies held their heads in the air, appearing to remember, but only a few of them knew either of the two women mentioned. The majority of the deputies became spectators. Even then, those who knew and had served with the said former deputies were from the Northern Republican Party and very loyal to Savage.

Meanwhile, Savage to continued, 'It is along these lines that our army was formed. Building an army that could face our enemy gallantly, without a grain of fear, was the outstanding factor upon which this House agreed, and it was done.'

==

It would take months, if not years, to iron out what exactly had been leaked from the Millennium by Esther and Barbara. The two former deputies would have to testify in person by law. It was clear that Savage had set a precedent for the army to go and get the two women from the south.

The issue brought a new time boom for the first family. Ingrid Savage was considering leaving her husband once again if the issue of God in the military was not decided in her favor. When asked what would happen if Fox accepted her demands, she stated categorically that he was not a man to do business with.

The first lady and minister for religious affairs was firm on dropping Fox as commander of the army. That would result in the man entering retirement. Many deputies, especially women, joined the first lady, but they were not of sufficient number to pass a bill that would send the most decorated soldier into redundancy. In the meantime, however, the House agreed to suspend the ground attack.

—

Meanwhile, the relationship between the Savages had become a game of cat and mouse. The first lady could not remember the Millennium distancing the army from God, as her man suggested, and she began to behave oddly. The most powerful and perhaps most luxurious house of the state was now like a zoo, with Ingrid confined to her cage and Savage to his. Would the only other member of the family, the daughter, called Aan, stay in a cage of her own too? She didn't, perhaps because she was too young.

Aged ten, Aan couldn't stand the situation at home. The girl could not remember when her mother last spoke with her father. Then one day Aan asked her why she did not dine at the table with them.

'Have you been sent by your father?' asked Ingrid, who had resorted to a lonely, large room where she read Holy Scriptures and slept all day.

Aan grimaced. 'No, why?'

Recalling the recent separation of her parents, during which she had seen mother only occasionally, it was painful for the young girl to see the return of those sad days. Her mother seemed not to understand her concerns and tried to tell her about the problem at hand.

A steady stream of tears began to flow from Aan's eyes. 'God, why do you allow him do this to you, Mother? Mother, you have to come and dine with us at table,' she said.

Ingrid Savage was realizing that armies had been built on brutal lines since time immemorial and that it would require great caution to change the trend of things. She then recalled what her husband had told her while asking her to let things remain the way they were: My dear Fox is a man capable of anything if pushed too hard.

'I shall, my dear, I promise,' Ingrid told her daughter.

# Chapter 17

The period of political imbalance in Northern State was a further blessing to the people of the south.

The task of building bunkers progressed unhindered. Advisor had teamed up well with the heir son in spreading the importance of the constructions as household possessions. However, with public bunkers yet to be completed, private ones became a part-time task.

This process gave men no rest at all. They worked on the public bunkers during the day and on their private ones at night. Life in Southern State became a life of labor, which amazingly had been accepted by the people. Everyone felt duty-bound to participate in the agonizing labor scheme.

As for Barbara, her pain at being away from home appeared to be fading since bringing forth a lovely child, but many negative things had happened in between. The attack on the mansion was an incident that caused her and Advisor to be tense most of the time. Prejudice set in as he scoffed at the way Barbara's people had names that reflected peculiar things. The woman, in rebound, prided herself on the fact that at least her people had names.

=

Then one day after dinner, the couple appeared to have heard enough about their respective cultures. Barbara, who had put her daughter to sleep by reading her a story about two rival wild beasts that built a sanctuary for an endangered animal species in the middle of a forest, asked Adviser whether he had enjoyed the meal. He smiled and said he had never had such a fine dinner in his life. She was provoked into romantic talk and asked if he could recall how they met.

Advisor cleared his throat and said, 'Along the queue I couldn't imagine you would do all that you did for me really. But, to say...' He then fell silent and Barbara gave a smile, no doubt remembering her first job after college, he thought.

Barbara had worked for a bureau that specialized in finding jobs for academic dropouts. As time passed, the bureau became a hub employing immigrants from the south because they provided cheaper labor.

'What work do you intend to solicit for? That's what you asked me. Production work was what you said, isn't it?' asked Advisor.

Barbara did not say a word, but shook her head, although she seemed not to remember. She eagerly let the man carry on, least the good humor deteriorated into the tension she had endured for months now.

'Then you asked me to excuse you, as another man of your color, who was behind me in the queue, interrupted in a rather intimate manner,' Advisor continued. "You told him off and said he would have to wait until you were done with me. I thought surely this must be a different society from mine. Yet, when you turned back to me, you said your name for the second time, moreover with a handshake. Bar... ba... ra. I will never forget the humor with which you said it. Then I knew it was my turn.'

Their child turned in her sleep and Advisor fell silent for a moment. Then he went on, 'The handshake made me rather naïve and timid, but my sole focus was on whether this beautiful-looking, smiling lady was going to employ me. The feeling, will this one really qualify, overwhelmed me. It didn't take long. You started by asking what you could do for me. You said it in a typical accent and with emphasis. I saw myself as a failure after your intonation. But you again reminded me that there was a factory that employed people, regardless of what you called language fluency. I smiled, not because I was seeing a job in the bag, but because I could somehow manage the advanced man's language.

'You then lifted the phone and spoke to a colleague, who seemed some distance away. You grimaced after replacing the handset, but soon you smiled and asked whether I owned a car. No, I said. You thought for a while and then asked me whether I could work in Wenpenev. You observed my bewildered face and began to explain where it was. Not far from the airport, you said, while concluding your explanation. I was excited, as immigrant workers always said the airport area offered light work with good pay. You then handed me the telephone number of a person to contact in Wenpenev, where I would work in a food factory," Advisor added.

'Sure?' Barbara intoned.

'Yes, of course,' Advisor replied. 'Very exciting, I thought, when the man on the phone told me that he would pick me up at the train station and introduce me to my new job. To me, it was not only a new job, but also the first one since I'd left this poor, stricken land of mine. What an adventure! My mind lingered, wondering what it would be like to work in an advanced world. I couldn't sleep, imagining seeing the best technology, and perhaps manning it.'

'Oh, dear,' Barbara exclaimed.

Advisor continued as if her intervention meant nothing to him. 'The excitement in the shelter where I spent hard nights was overwhelming, and I wanted company in the middle of the night. No one came my way, of course. Anyway, there was another dark-skinned girl who was behind me in the line at the bureau, and it happened by coincidence that she, too, spent the night in the same place as me. Although she was from the south she had a name rather than a number. Believe me, she was called, "Barbara".'

'Is that so?' Barbara asked with a somewhat curious expression.

Advisor went on, 'She would also be working at the food factory. She had no name, but admired your gesture and so registered herself as Barbara at work. At first I couldn't understand her very well, especially when she told me what she did for a living. I had to shout too hard in her ears, and she burst back with a sniff that she would be working in a food factory in Wenpenev. What a coincidence! I grinned. I had found a friend. It was after we became rather intimate that she acknowledged having come from the south in search of work. I learned all about her story later.'

'Who was she exactly?' asked Barbara, exhibiting a lot of bodily expression.

Advisor could not ignore her. 'Barbara, you mean?' he asked, while venting what appeared to be corresponding body language, but he soon realized that he had to go on with his story.

'She was the only survivor on a boat full of people on its way to Directionland from where it was easy to get to the north in search of work. As she couldn't swim, she was tied to the boat. Because of that she remained on board after it fell to its side. Luckily, she was on the side out of the water. All around was blue, she said.

'The boat took its own course, finding its way to some cross-border guards, who took her to a reception center, from where she was taken to the bureau and met you. She told me of your kindness and willingness to help people in need. She had never met a woman like you before.'

'Our work schedules at the factory were different. I was to report the following day and she a day later. We nonetheless said goodbye to one another and hoped to meet at work.'

Barbara's irritation was beginning to show. She wanted to know what had really happened between them and inevitably cut into the story with some rather leading questions. However, her man concentrated on relating his work experience with the other Barbara.

He explained, 'It was not only our schedules that were separate, but our lines too. I was seen to be strong and made to work in the kitchen where it was hardest, while she joined the women's line for in-packaging. Women were seen to be more flexible and efficient than the ever-breaking-down factory machines. No one imagined what it would be like if the machines never stopped at all during the eight-hour shift.

'You have to use a catalyst if you're to get a first job at this factory, every worker said openly, with many making rolls of all kinds of combinations during recess.

Then work would go on with the workers enjoying every step, giggly. "Vak, Vak, Vak," the foremen would shout out to the rhythm of the machines as we labored like worker bees repairing a damaged hive.

'Although my introduction to Wenpenev Daily Foods was hopeful, it took me only days to regret the magnificent glass building with many flags flying at full mast in the front yard. "You came here to Vak, not stand," roared the foreman of the line in a deafening voice. At first my mind went blank and almost immediately I recalled my home, but then I became nervous, remembering the grinding poverty that engulfed my state. Then I considered why we should risk our lives helping another economy to flourish.

'I knew we earned something, but I kept asking myself whether the conditions under which we worked fulfilled our expectations. All along I had seen my going to the north for the better until this foreman barked at me. Maybe I wouldn't have taken it so seriously if he had been from the south, like me. I would then have regarded him as a bully boy. Turning, I looked through the great glass windows, feeling warm tears trickle down my cheeks. I tasted them, and they were salty and bitter, yet it made me firm. I developed courage.

'I went back to my work, thinking that perhaps the worst was over. But I was wrong and, if anything, what followed was worse. Luis asked me where I came from with a very ugly face and a steaming spade with which he'd been mixing boiling soap in a giant boiler. There was only an arm's length between us. His tone stunned me and made me gape. My hand went along with the conveyor belt and a piece of chicken I had been dispatching. It was all bloody by the time I pulled it out.

"I mean, do you come from North or South Dunia?" Luis asked when he saw my bleeding hand.

I grinned instead.

He sneered and ordered me to continue working. He didn't even spend a second looking at my hand. A colleague came and directed me to the first-aid box. Halfway there, I heard another command from Luis. "Over there!" he said. He wanted me to go to the cooler and set frozen fish fillets in tray carriages. Still bleeding, I defied the order. Luis looked at the clock. I was left with less than an hour to finish my day's work, and I thought he had found sympathy for me. Instead, he came after me and said, "No pay for you today; understand?"

'Tight-lipped, I just walked to the canteen. There, I found Barbara who had had a similar day, and the worst was yet to come: her name was not on the pay list. Not even her transport costs would be paid, and she was not to appear on the list for days to come. "Let's get out of here," I told her. "No," she replied. "I've got to wait for the foreman and talk to him privately, if I'm to work tomorrow."

'Her words made me paranoid and I pulled her arm, urging her to depart with me, and the action made me scratch my wound. The last train was due to leave, and we would have to move fast to get it. Despite our rigorous efforts, we missed it, and we had to walk ten miles to find transport to our ghetto home. Standing in the middle of the road asking one another whether we should actually start the dreaded walk, a car braked into us instantly. We dove for cover, cursing what a day it had been, only to hear voices call out, "Come on! Jump in at once!" They were colleagues from work, offering us a lift to the airport, from where our ghetto was easy to reach on foot,' Advisor concluded.

Barbara, while listening, had been overwhelmed with sympathy. All illusions about the other woman disappeared. 'There are some very bad people up there,' she said, and asked Advisor to pray before they retired to bed. In concluding her prayer with 'Almighty God,' she begged, 'although we know how much sugar we need for our cups, lead us to not put sugar in our cups before filling them... we ask.'

# Chapter 18

Advisor got no sleep that night. His mind was almost five years back, busy recalling his most memorable outing with the mother of his child in Northern State...

The train pulled to a halt just on time. Barbara got on, ahead of him. For reasons hard to understand, the whistle to set off the train went when some passengers were still getting on. Barbara grabbed his hand and dragged him inside. He was breathing fast and talking at double speed. They found a seat for two.

'By the way, I didn't book you a return. Does it offend you in any way?' Barbara asked.

'Offend me?' he asked back, looking utterly stupefied.

'I mean, are you to be back tonight?'

He laughed.

Barbara looked at him with a smile. 'Anyway, the way you answer questions, I do like it.'

'Are you sure?'

'Sure, man!' Barbara had answered, swinging her face back to him.

'Well, I must pinch my cheek then.'

'What's that supposed to mean?'

'A saying of my people that means lucky me,' he explained.

'Huh, sounds really nice. Can I say pinch your cheek?' asked Barbara, feeling her own.

'Of course! Then it'll mean lucky you.'

'Well, you're a very creative and brilliant man indeed.'

'What about my language skills?' he asked.

'Don't mind. You do better than I first thought, man.'

At a certain station, the couple alighted. She led him by the hand through the complex station.

'Now, where do you want us to go?' he asked.

'Have you ever been this far before?' she queried.

'Not at all,' he answered thoughtfully. For some time some strange person had been walking too close for comfort.

'Well, you're in safe hands,' said Barbara, pulling him towards her as they made a right turn.

'Oh, yes, certainly.'

They were now outside the station building. Barbara looked at him tenderly and asked him if he was in the mood for a disco. He hated dancing, but stopped short of saying so, wondering if it would be nice this time. Not allowing her to see his movements, he began to practice how he would dance. He was not really doing it, but think-dancing.

When he had still not answered her question, Barbara began to think that perhaps she should suggest something else. A colleague had advised her that suggesting taking a guy for an outing on a first date was not a wise thing. She remembered it too late, because she was the type of girl that did not meet guys. Actually, she had no desire for a romantic relationship, but out of curiosity she had been attracted to this guy because of his skin color. Before Barbara could volunteer another opinion, the man agreed to go to a disco.

The late answer had a lot of factors. He felt he was turning away from his culture by going out with a light-skinned woman. He had taken a vow not to turn away from it, yet he was curious and eager to learn about the people he was living amongst. Integration was what it was, and he had been told the word wherever he went. Nevertheless, he never stopped to imagine the enormity of understanding the light-skinned man's culture. He knew he needed a native close, because he couldn't dream of normal learning in a school. It was discriminative and expensive.

The couple took a walk that led them to a café. The entrance was silent. He thought Barbara had changed her opinion and opted for a cooler place. She disengaged herself from the entanglement and stepped forward to the entrance with her purse in her hand. She counted out some coins, and the first gate into the café swung open. A tumult of noise blared from inside and hit them hard.

Barbara shook her flat behind vigorously; praise to her great hips, she was dancing gracefully. She spread her hands out while singing along with the song that was playing.

He listened and recognized the number as being sung by a certain dark-skinned man whose great ancestors had immigrated to the north generations ago. Although he couldn't fully understand what the man was singing about, it was a very hot number indeed. He couldn't help it and started shaking his body.

She turned swiftly. 'Hu,' she said, grabbing his hand and drawing him close. 'From now on you are Jackson,' she told him when the song ended.

Though scared and unable to believe it, he accepted with a nod, and followed behind the her woman. The music turned into a cacophony when they got inside. A combination of tobacco and cannabis went straight up his nose. He sniffed and sneezed. Feeling dizzy, he longed for a place to sit, but the few chairs were occupied, so he leaned against a pillar in the center of the café.

The next number was by someone from the south, who was singing about how and why great Dunia had been split into two by a body of deep water. The singer poetically narrated how many lives had perished in the sea during this endless crisscrossing in search of work and better weather.

It was squeezed inside the café, yet the ticket seller at the gate seemed not to mind the situation, allowing more people in.

He asked Barbara if they could find another inn. She said the café was the nearest place to where they were to spend the night and that most of the others would be the same. She said the café would clear when people took seats. Barbara waded towards the counter to buy a drink. Ten minutes passed and she didn't return. Another round will not be possible, he thought.

The heat made people sweat like racing horses, yet no one seemed to mind. They were happy to squeeze together in this tiny inn as if it were the only place to hide from monsters outside. Barbara finally showed up, carefully negotiating her way while holding two glasses filled to the brim. He left the pillar and went to meet her, but before he could take one of the glasses, an incident happened. Someone dancing madly hit Barbara's hand. One glass dropped to the floor and smashed.

'Ja, ja, ja!' said the man to blame in excitement. Another man wanted to react, but Barbara asked him not to. While passing the glass over, she commented that drugs were good but not in excess. The dark-skinned guy looked at her confused, before she went back to the bar to get herself another drink.

Meanwhile, the man who had caused the accident continued to have fun. His T-shirt had some writing on it. Advisor was curious to read it, but the man didn't stay fixed in one place, not to mention that there were a lot of people jostling in between. The song ended and many people returned to their seats, but the man was so unstable that the writing on his T-shirt was still hard to read.

Then came a moment when the man settled down a bit and the T-shirt came into focus. There was a monster face smoking a rough wrap below the writing, its giant hands signaling victory and its mouth looking like a woman's vagina. The picture did not last as the man turned.

A map of Dunia, drawn like a plant, covered the entire back of the T-shirt, with the roots and stem representing the south and the leaves the north. The weeds were blooming, and there was writing across the leaves and branches. It read: 'NORTH HASN'T GOT IT, BUT USES IT!' The line below, across the roots and stem, said: 'SOUTH GOT IT, CANNOT USE IT!' The drawing was surrounded by the words 'DUNIA-LOVELY-LOUSY-LUCKY-LAND!!'

Barbara returned with another drink and a rag to clean the floor. He asked her why she had to clear it up.

'Well, man, it has to be done this way,' she said. 'Besides, it's dangerous left, so...'

'But it was...'

'Come again?'

'I mean it was stopping them from flowing this way,' he said.

Barbara pretended not to have heard and continued to clean up the floor.

'It was a buffer from the squeeze,' the man tried to explain, but a waiter, who was looking on, thanked Barbara.

It did not take long before the place was full of people once again. Then a song called 'Common People' moved the crowd into ecstasy. Barbara asked him to take to the floor. Although he wasn't managing well, either she didn't realize or had no cause to notice. They both loved dancing to the song.

'Perhaps we should move nearer to the wall,' Barbara suggested.

Terrific, he thought, nodding.

There were some vacant seats on a raised platform running around the arena, and the couple placed their glasses on a table near to where they were dancing. The air was conducive. He stopped feeling hot, and he thought Barbara appeared to be feeling better.

They held each other as they danced slowly to the tune. Her touch was gentle and tender. He felt her warmth tingle him like magic, and she felt it too. Curiosity about having the guy inspired Barbara into longing whenever she looked at his skin.

'Maybe we should leave soon to get some rest,' she suggested after a while. 'Do you know how to ride a bicycle?'

'Yes, of course I do.'

Barbara wanted to ask him more about his riding, but words failed her. She wasn't actually making logical sentences anymore, especially when their eyes met. When it was past three o'clock in the morning, she declared that they had to leave.

He hadn't realized they had been in the disco for so long. 'Time must have sped up.'

Barbara did not answer, but got up and asked if they could leave. The couple left holding hands and headed back the same way as they had walked earlier, right up to the station.

'I use this bike, especially after such evenings. It's forbidden to drive after midnight here. We like it anyway,' Barbara said.

She brought out her purse and appeared to be looking for the key to the bicycle. She found it after a long search, which saw the purse emptied twice. Then she unlocked an old-looking bike.

'You ride or I ride?' she asked with a tired voice.

'Well, I'll ride and you guide,' he joked, wiggling a finger.

'Of course. How terrific.'

They set out with him riding steadily and Barbara directing efficiently. They headed towards a canal and reached home immediately after crossing a tunnel bridge. She took the bicycle from him and chained it to a pole overlooking the house. He glanced around, thinking it was a rich-looking home. They sneaked inside, not wanting to be heard, and entered her bedroom. He noticed a nice carpet, many beautiful pictures hanging up, and a calendar on the wall showing a picture of the headquarters of her employer.

Barbara disappeared somehow and resurfaced wearing a see-through nightdress, and she welcomed him to her bed. From out of nowhere she sobered up and her urge for sex vanished. Barbara looked at the boy who felt likewise; his longing had died down like sudden rain. Then she developed a hiccup and he advised her to get a glass of water. Getting out of bed, she walked towards the fridge, but she collapsed before reaching it.

He rushed over to check on her, and their eyes met, their faces so close. She laughed, as did he. Barbara had never seen such evenly spaced white teeth, not to mention the dark skin that contrasted with them, and she kissed him. With desire rising inside her, she began to undress him by tearing off his shirt.

'Take it easy, baby,' he said, but Barbara just replied, 'Shoo.'

Thinking she was warning him to be silent, he embarked on the job at hand in silence. Yet the deeper he penetrated her, the more she made a noise that sounded like water in a pressure kettle that was about to boil.

The next day around noon, Barbara's uncle was knocking on her door.

'Who's that? Barbara asked.

'It's me,' said the uncle.

There was silence as Barbara was trying to work out where to hide her man. After a long fidgeting she knew she had to say something. 'Just a moment,' she said.

Her uncle could hear the hard threat with which she spoke. The man added one and two together, that is to say the time she had taken to open and the rumbling inside. 'I hope everything is all right with you? he demanded.

'Oh yes, Uncle, only that I hadn't fully got out of bed.'

'All right, I'll come back later.' The uncle then walked away, but halfway he stopped and looked behind him. Barbara was in her doorway directing a man of color towards the rear garden of her uncle's big house. It shocked the uncle because he believed Barbara was a girl without any interest in men. He actually thought she was still a virgin.

Thereon Barbara began to defy her uncle and eventually became interested in politics. She hoped to belong to a political party that would view the south as an equal state and southerners as natural humans, just like any other being living in Dunia.

Looking back, Advisor couldn't recount much of Barbara's political legacy, but what was clear to him was that her stay in the south would have been a dying ember if it were not for the birth of Ingrid. Both regarded their daughter as a bunch of dry twigs on a dying fire.

# Chapter 19

At six years old, Ingrid was already showing signs of having a brilliant future influenced by education, but Barbara could not find a suitable school to send her to. While Advisor had recommended many institutions, all the ones she checked looked rundown. On their way back home from each visit, Ingrid would be hopping and laughing, thinking that this time her mother had found her a suitable school.

Seeing how excited her daughter was, Barbara would cradle the girl and tell her, 'My dear, what is the point in a child having an education lower than her parent had?'

Ingrid would then realize that the search for a school was still on, and silence would accompany them all the way home. During this time, Barbara's past would hit her the hardest, making her think that it would have been better to stay at home and face the consequences rather than coming to live in a land where there was no future for her child. It was now that she needed her man's comfort, but Advisor was always busy helping the heir son, whose father was fighting a deadly disease.

Once a fat man, sickness had reduced the ruler to a human skeleton. Even a poor-sighted person would be able to count the remaining hairs on his head. It was worse when the man removed his shirt, which he often did now, complaining that it was too hot, for that was when his ribs made a pathetic show of rubbing against one another. Above them, his shoulders made pitiable movements up and down. Only an individual without any feeling at all could manage to watch him for long, which meant that the sick man was left alone most of the time.

Locals thought his ailment was a curse from God for producing a twenty-first child. Others, however, were generally sympathetic, because the kid was borne by the woman whose daughter had committed suicide. With almost everyone speculating on what might have caused the ruler's illness, the family decided to keep him indoors.

Medical doctors among the missionaries wished to find out what the disease actually was, but they also feared catching it. Surprisingly, however, their treatment did bring some pain relief to the ailing man and they became closer, as healers do, to their patient. The ruler was now spending most of his time in the company of God-loving people, to whom he enjoyed listening. But it was not so easy when they asked him to have a name.

The desire to not change the traditions of his people overwhelmed the man, but since he had not given a categorical refusal, the God-loving people did not want to push him. After all, their aim was to get him to reduce the number of his women to only one. With that they knew a shepherd had been won into the flock of God.

While the people of God wanted the ruler to retain his first woman, who was the mother of his heir, the man loved the youngest girl the most. However, the weak condition of the lord ruler was a hint to the son to prepare to inherit the throne. Accordingly, the ruler wanted his successor near him all the time, but the boy was uncomfortable seeing his father in such an ill state, so he tried evasive tricks such as asking to be excused to check on something.

Noticing this, the lord ruler decided to speak to the youth. 'My son,' he began, 'leadership is a very painful thing.'

'Why, Father?'

'Because you are exposed to painful decisions all the time,' he replied.

'What do you mean, Father?'

'Take parenting. Your child cries because it does not want to wash. You then look in your child's eyes and what do you see?'

'Tears, Father.'

'And how do they make you feel?' asked the ruler.

'Sad, I should think.'

'Exactly, but will you give in to that sadness and not wash the child?'

The boy shook his head. 'I don't think so, Father.'

The ruler smiled. 'Now, my son, I want you to view leadership in the same light; some things are painful to do, but they have to be done because it is how it should be.'

From that day forth the heir son remembered this lesson: the hardest thing in life was not life itself, but making decisions. He never abandoned his father ever again.

Noticing the chemistry between the two men, Barbara asked the heir son to speak to his father about recognizing his mother as his only woman.

The boy asked him, 'Father, I believe that by now you have come to understand the ways of the Holy Book?'

The ruler was pleased to acknowledge this, which he did.

The son continued, 'But don't you think there is yet one thing that you need to fulfill before you enter that wise world, as we all know it?'

'What is that, my dear son?' asked the ruler.

'You need to have one woman, Father.'

The man looked startled, but rebounded fast with the words, 'I hadn't thought of that, dear boy, but to give your heredity a blessing, I'll do what pleases you.'

Although bedridden by now, the ruler still spoke loud and clear, which confused a lot of people. This was because if you heard him talk and then saw how he looked, you would hardly believe it was the same person.

# Chapter 20

Weather in Northern State had changed significantly, and the general climatic conditions were now the worst on record. The soldiers could not stand the cold and began to desert their sentry posts. On hearing this, General Fox visited the posts to do a head count. Some fighters were absent, yet none of them were officially so. Fox declared the absent servicemen as being AWOL–absent without leave. Branding them enemies of the state, he called for them to be shot if found.

One senior commander could not stomach the order. 'Isn't shooting an overreaction, sir?' he asked. Fox was about to respond when the same man cut him short by adding, 'But, since it is what you have decided, so be it.' The commander saluted and kept quiet.

'Thank you very much,' Fox answered, before continuing, 'Shooting traitors is standard procedure in the military code of conduct, which we, as servicemen, must uphold.'

Many of the soldiers had wanted to resign all along, but it was impossible. The Millennium had made their careers compulsory until they reached retirement age, which was at sixty-five for commissioned officers and fifty-five for all other ranks. With life expectancy in the region having dropped to sixty, the soldiers had condemned themselves to life service.

Many deputies had close relatives in the army, and the legislators argued that the bill was not only harsh, but inhumane. Savage defended Fox. 'My fellow countrymen, the servicemen know a lot of state secrets, and if left on the loose, enemies of the state could exploit them,' he reasoned.

With the earth in the northern territory frozen over completely, the Millennium sat to evaluate the bizarre climactic changes. It ordered more scientific research to find out why Dunia's weather was behaving in such a queer manner.

One scientist put the House on alert when he mentioned that it was all blue skies in Southern State. Savage's response was to advise the resumption of medium-range shelling on their foe. The scientist then stunned the House by saying that such launches had contributed to the poor weather, and he advised for them to be scrapped. When pressed to explain, he said, 'The south is a haven for trees, yet the rocket shells, while temporarily clearing the blanket in the atmosphere, end up polluting the air, which poisons plants and kills the trees.'

Savage asked the House to invite Fox to give his opinion on what he called the man on the ground. As expected, the general defiantly told the members to give his plan of firing rockets another chance. The issue came to a stalemate, leaving Savage as the only person who would break it, according to the constitution. He gave Fox the go-ahead, but the rockets did not fall far from the coastal city of Hollyfield, where they were launched.

Soon after, pregnant women around the launch zone began to bear children with abnormalities. The babies had more limbs than normal, and the majority had two heads; resembling twins, and they shared a number of vital organs. With rumor rife that these children carried a deadly bug, people began to strangle the newborns and incinerate their bodies in containers filled with highly corrosive substances.

'God abandoned the state for abandoning him,' the God-loving people said after hearing what had happened.

People, especially the young, had turned their backs on the houses of God. 'We are tired of living on a bloody island' had become the motto of the youth, for whom intoxication had become the norm. Efforts by parents and church leaders to make them change their ways were fruitless, as alcohol was cheap, and in some places drinks were even given away free.

Then appeared something in powder form, which, when sniffed, gave an effect far more sophisticated than that of alcohol. The houses of God were quick to condemn it through graphic expression in church sermons and by embarking on public crusades. Perhaps they should not have bothered, because the young people only became more eager to try the stuff, and some ended up addicted to it.

Meanwhile, the ailment of the southern leader was unrelenting, and it soon became clear that the man was losing the fight. One God-loving person with knowledge of medicine diagnosed an incurable illness, but not wanting to cause widespread alarm, he assured the sick man's relatives that he could be cured with treatment in the north. Nevertheless, the patient objected to being taken across the boundary, even when the Millennium granted him what it called amnesty treatment.

The heir son had been considering his father's promise to remain with one woman. He told no one, knowing the potential commotion that the issue could bring. Barbara, however, thought she had waited long enough for an answer and decided to approach him.

The son replied hesitantly, 'Yes, he agreed, but...'

'But what, brother?' asked Barbara, who had recently started calling him by that term, but she failed to formalize the whole phrase by adding the words 'in spirit' to it.

'I mean, what woman should get the holy matrimony?' asked the son.

'I thought the oldest one, shouldn't she?'

There was a smile on the son's face when they parted.

The ceremony to unite the ruler with his oldest woman in holy matrimony was not as colorful as it should have been for a leader. Meanwhile, the other ladies were busy protesting and asking for their share of the property before the marriage was conducted. The heir son promised to be generous and caring to all the women with whom his father had formed a relationship, but some people were pessimistic, particularly the wife-to-be.

The people of God, who had acquired the common name of missionaries, vowed to assist if the heir son did not fulfill his pledge. Missionaries were known to be wealthy and kind, so the women allowed the ceremony to take place.

# Chapter 21

Although the ruler turned down the offer of treatment in the north, the missionary doctor monitored his sickness carefully. He took samples of blood, stools and saliva, and sent them to a bigger laboratory in Northern State. No one was sure whether the results would return while the patient was still alive.

Preparations to bury the man, who was now viewed as a believer, were underway. There would be what the God-loving people called a service, during which readings and singing would be central. The people of Southern State only sung while cerebrating jubilant occasions, such as a girl being taken into marriage or a birth.

Occasions such as a burial were viewed as times to grieve, during which singing did not apply. Months later, however, the family would gather to perform a kind of ritual to send the deceased's spirit to a wiser world. It was during this ceremony that friends of the family offered music and drinks.

The God-loving people began to prepare for the ruler's burial, which they called a send-off. Special songs called hymns, which were in the light-skinned man's language, brought tension because the bereaved would be singing them. The elders said that only the young people should sing and openly rejected this 'archaic alien heritage.'

To avoid downgrading the host's heritage, the God-loving people told the locals that their leader had chosen what was best for mankind. When the natives asked to know the best heritage that their leader had chosen without telling them, the missionaries replied, 'That of God.'

The natives responded that the light-skinned people wanted to dominate their culture, and the argument went on throughout the night. Barbara asked Advisor and the heir son to intervene, because most of her colleagues appeared to have had enough, although the sick man was expected to 'kick the bucket' at any moment.

The next day a group of young singers, who had been given the name of choir, began to practice the words to be sung. It remained a linguistic paradox, however, for although the words were spelled out to them correctly, the choir said them colloquially, presenting different meanings, which was often funny, immoral, and at times abusive. The God-loving people were not pleased to be sending off a man who had repented in such a way.

Thus the words were gradually dropped until the choir had to sing the hymn with only one short word. Many were tried until 'la' won, because both the southerners and northerners pronounced it in a similar way. The choir practiced for hours and the rhythm came to life, yet after a lot of 'la, la, la, la' there was just an assonance rhythm of 'laaaaaaaalaaaaa.'

Esther, who was a church choir mistress back home, introduced 'd' and 't' into the stanza, because they maintained the same sound between the southerners and northerners. The choir then practiced them and the sound came out as 'dot,' which was exciting, so the practice went on unhindered. This was followed by 'la,' together with the two consonants, 's' and 'm.' The vowels 'o' and 'i' were then brought back into the chorus. By the end of the first day, more letters had been discovered that agreed well with the rhythm of the hymns.

When the ruler stopped talking, the God-loving people who were dressed in white robes came and prayed for him. In the middle of the prayer, Barbara was asked to uncover a pot. The doctor touched the water inside and murmured some words, while nimbly feeling the face of the seemingly dead man. The rest of the audience kept meditatively silent until they said 'Amen' in unison.

Then everyone began to sing, acting as if they had forgotten the dangers of the motionless body they were standing so near.

By now the patient's eyes had stopped blinking and his mouth had fallen open. The doctor walked over and closed his eyes, but when he tried to do the same with his mouth; it did not budge, so he covered the ruler's face with a white cloth.

It was now clear that the leader had passed on, and the family's sorrow and grief began to devastate the home. Just as it often happened in the south when someone important in a house died, weeping relatives began to destroy property within the mansion. The people of God tried all what they could to calm the tempers in vain, and instead called upon the choir to sing at the top of their voices. In the end, family members were worn-out after a long cry, and it was only the singing to be heard as the body of the ruler was laid in its coffin.

Throughout the burial, the name of Solomon was used, instead of ruler or leader. Many southerners looked at each other in complete ignorance. Advisor, for one, knew the late man had been baptized. Esther informed the gathering that their leader had been sent off as a repented man, and that it was only King Solomon in the Holy Scriptures that he could be likened to.

With the dictator dead, the Millennium passed an amendment bill to cease hostilities against the south. But the north had a lot to consider; although there was a new leader, he was a son of the dictator. All the same, many deputies asked for the new ruler to be given time, claiming that the expense of maintaining an army for war had been very high, after all. With all of the military equipment at the frontline damaged by bad weather, the Millennium needed a negotiated settlement with the young leader.

# Chapter 22

After only months on the throne, the young ruler of Southern State was busy assembling a working committee comprised of people with influence among the masses. It was not clear to the public how he came up with such an idea. The reality of the matter was that Barbara and Advisor were the people behind it.

Barbara was said to have told her man that people must share power if the hostilities were to cease. Based on what she had heard, the Millennium had altered a lot, and the change in policy in the south could pave way for southern children to gain scholarships to study in the north. Her daughter would be one to enter such a scheme, she thought.

But Ingrid was growing up very fast, and the reform program would take some time to be accepted, let alone be considered by the Millennium. Barbara therefore began to trace her relatives back home in the hope that her daughter could begin her future in a more promising world.

In the meantime, Barbara taught her child what she felt was the order of learning in Northern State. It was not possible to send her to stay with a friend or family member there, as censuring people to ensure a steady population growth was the norm in the north. Ingrid would have to be sent to a very close relative. That way, if the state was in any doubt about her, as often happened, a DNA test would exonerate her.

Sadly, Barbara was a woman without any traceable relatives, her parents having been killed in unexplainable circumstances at the peak of their political careers. Family members had warned her not to join politics, but Barbara went ahead. The only close relative in her life was her uncle, but bringing a dark-skinned man into his house had divided them.

Mr. Simple Satan, for that was the name of her uncle, threw her out of the house. SS, as the family referred to him, was one of those light-skinned men who regarded darker people as inferior, ungodly and cursed. As a prominent, rich inhabitant of Lostsummer, SS was often called upon to lead people in prayer, in appreciation of the donations he extended to his local church. They thought the man would take up politics as a candidate for PP in the area.

However, citing how his only brother had been killed, together with his wife, in what looked like a political vendetta, SS turned down the request. His church responded by keeping its distance, and never again was he called upon to attend any event it organized.

The church council did not search for anyone to fill the gap left by Barbara's mother, whose passing allowed the constituency to be taken over by seculars. Therefore, when they approached the daughter, after she had completed her college study, it was like sending a caged lizard to fend for itself in the grass.

People always told Barbara that she had a similar charisma to her mother, but in her eyes that brought her back to the realization that she was cheated of the opportunity to know her parents. She came to hate the comment, even avoiding those who said it to her.

Upon finishing college, however, Barbara began to view such similarities as something to be proud of. The girl began to ask whether it was true that she looked like her mother, a person she had never known, as she had died when Barbara was still a toddler. She then decided to follow in her parents' footsteps, which nearly all her relatives were bitterly against. After winning a seat in the Millennium for Lostsummer, she never saw her close family again.

Thus it was difficult to trace a relative to whom Barbara could send her daughter. All the same, she wrote Uncle SS a letter about the matter. She received no reply, but kept writing to him anyway, along with other members of his family.

Esther, who had been sympathetic to her friend's frantic efforts to find a suitable school for her daughter, decided to break her silence. 'Sister,' she said to Barbara, 'what if the houses of God sent a request to the north, suggesting their children come and holiday in our good weather, in exchange for our children going there for a better education.'

Although the two sisters in spirit decided to inform the God-loving people in Northern State of their idea, Barbara did not want to divulge her whereabouts. Esther accepted to be the originator and contact person, and letters were sent out. Some God-loving people were interested in the idea and contacted their colleagues in the Millennium about it. Mrs. Savage proposed for it to be discussed in the House, and the Speaker put it on the agenda.

==

At the same time Advisor approached heir son with the idea. Heir son thought about the exchange for several weeks before agreeing to the exchange. The idea was shared with the elders, then the media.

Reports of a change in policy in Southern State made the Millennium approve the child-exchange program with a comfortable vote. The Ministry for Religious Affairs was given the task of organizing it, and the minister was placed in charge. The ministry thought very few students would want the adventure and considered sending secondary school students on a holiday to the south while waiting for their results.

The Millennium called the project 'School Trial Excursion into the Unknown.' On implementation, the Ministry for Education chose to write it in the acronym of STEITU to guard against scaring parents. Very remote schools with almost no significance were to begin the exercise, and their chaplains would head the trip.

Since the journey was long and the roads impassable in places, the students would fly, and the date for their departure was fixed. Southern State had no facilities for large aircrafts to land, which sparked another discussion in the Millennium. While some deputies called for the exercise to be aborted, others insisted on it being a long-awaited opportunity to bring the people of Dunia together. The argument lasted for a couple of weeks without anyone agreeing on the matter.

Seeing the project fail, after all the time and effort she had invested, was unimaginable for the religious affairs minister, so she tried to steer the matter in a completely different direction. 'What if we sent a technical team to construct a place where these planes could land and take off from, ladies and gentlemen?' she asked. Her suggestion was greeted with overwhelming support and a technical team was dispatched for the task. In reality, many hoped this would lead to an opportunity for them and their family to experience the Southern State's agreeable weather in the future.

After one month the airfield was ready, but testing was required before airplanes could land on it. There was some haggling in the Millennium regarding who should perform this; some deputies insisted on civilian engineers, while others pushed for military men. Those towing the civilian line began to accuse their colleagues of fronting acts of aggression against a regime that was doing its best to reform. Meanwhile, the supporters of military personnel called it a chance to send security forward without necessarily negotiating.

Savage responded by inviting General Fox. The army commander spent almost an hour explaining what he called Dunia-force; knowing the terrain for future operations. No deputy wanted another argument with a man whom they regarded as mentally derailed, and so the general received a muted response. Fox had gotten what he wanted. The soldiers would not return home after finishing constructing the runway.

The God-loving people, who included Barbara and Esther as project pioneers, were there to welcome the flight from Northern State carrying the first batch of students. The plane was to return with the same number of children from the south. Unlike the northern students who had merely come on a visit tour, those from the south would be found schools.

The weather in the north changed not long after the arrival of the children from the south. A meter of ice was reported in many parts, and many houses lost power. Meanwhile, the students from Northern State were struck with amazement the moment they set foot in the south, where the temperature required them to remove some of their clothing for comfort. Many had arrived with small, portable telephones, and they called their friends and relatives immediately to tell them how life was in the south. The team of journalists who accompanied the students was busy sending live pictures back to the north. Although the first batch of students wanted to extend their stay, the waiting list back home had grown.

Unfortunately, the next group of students was far fewer in number, because living space was limited. When they arrived, a place for them to sleep was still under construction because the initial building, located in the soldiers' quarters, had been abandoned following a hand grenade blast which went off, tearing one of the soldiers to pieces. The visiting students fainted as a result. Missionaries treated many of them for shock in a clinic located close to the mansion house. The students ran amok when they were told to return to their dormitory. The commander agreed with the missionaries' idea to keep the children out of the barracks, and an alternative place was sought, which turned out to be a tent inside the ruler's palace wall. Constructing a new sleeping shelter for the hundreds of students would take quite some time.

However, the blast did not affect students alone. Locals living near the soldiers' quarters abandoned their homes. Even those earning a living at the airfield did not return. The only locals who remained were children, anxious to know what had made such a booming sound. Their curiosity weaned when they saw the soldiers tie their colleague who threw the fatal grenade to a tree and shoot him.

The people had been asking their leader when soldiers, in green camouflage driving huge, earthmoving vehicles close to his residence and the urban center, would leave. He called upon the commander of the soldiers and asked when they would leave. The soldier replied with something about obeying orders, which the leader did not understand. The commander then asked him to contact his superiors in the north. As this meeting was going on, a plane landed at the airport. It left behind two soldiers and took off immediately with the two dead ones.

# Chapter 23

The order to halt launches after the Hollyfield incident had brought calm in the Millennium. Fox was not 'bubbling,' as most deputies were now calling his way of talking, and they felt relieved. However, after a while the general did say something, but unlike his usual self, he was humble, so the House fell silent.

'I have been thinking a lot, and I have something of great importance to tell you, honorable members,' Fox began. 'Inasmuch as we have made all kinds of military arsenal that can best be called military might, we are yet faced with a task. My people, we have to develop equipment to counter what we have created. Most of you may wonder why we need to do such a thing, but let me assure you that if my dream comes true, we will be in gloom and doom.'

The House, which had begun to murmur, fell silent until even a pin drop could be heard.

'For I dreamed, gentlemen, that...oh, sorry, and ladies...that authorities in the south captured all our military equipment, together with the men trained to operate them, and the rest of our army was in disarray. I remained behind, wanting to face the enemy alone, and that was when I woke up.'

Savage, without obtaining permission to speak from the Speaker, as the House rule demanded, stood up and said that General Fox's dream had to be taken seriously. The deputies looked at one another. The minister for religious affairs asked what the cost of the project would be. The Speaker, having resumed her authority, called upon General Fox to answer.

Standing erect in a manner never seen before, he replied. 'The cost may be the same as that spent to create the arsenal, if not even higher, Madam Speaker.'

The deputies could not control themselves. The Speaker sounded her bell once, and when calm returned she suggested the House vote on the matter.

Before the vote was taken, Fox asked to speak. 'I feel duty bound to let you know what it might be, as if our entire military arsenal were set against us,' he said. 'We have the most deadly weapons ever made, so just imagine that moment, ladies and gentlemen.'

The House was thrown into utter silence.

The minister for religious affairs asked to say something. 'Ladies and gentlemen,' she began amid silence, 'should a democracy like ours listen to wild imaginations simply because they are being said by highly placed individuals?'

There was a lot of foot stamping and murmuring, but when the results were announced, Fox's dream project was passed, with only one vote against and very few abstentions.

The national reserve fund was reported to be unable to fund the project, which had been given the name of Antis. When the deputies tried to craft a presentation to their constituencies, the people could not hide their disgust, thinking there was always something costly to be discussed. Many asked their representatives whether they had elected them to create institutions that would make their children anti-human while bringing unnecessary costs for them to bear.

—

Although no member of the family had shown any interest in knowing what had killed the ruler, when the results of the biopsy eventually arrived, the doctor felt it right to inform them. The tests proved that the southern leader had died of a disease never heard of in Dunia, and there was also no known cure for it. The family calmly accepted whatever the doctor told them.

The story was different in Northern State, where similar news had leaked to the public through the media. Doctors tried to explain, but people became wary and restless of any new disease that did not have a known cure. Many called their personal doctors seeking an immediate check-up.

Some locals ran out into the streets, lamenting, and blaming the creator for sending death on his people. But the God-loving people calmed them by blaming Satan instead. The believers cited a man with a similar illness in the Holy Book, who, after many years of agony, was said to have recovered. The charm used by the people of God when reciting the allegory soothed everyone.

# Chapter 24

The children from the south had a difficult start in Northern State, and the weather made them curse all the time. Their schools became concerned and changed the rules by allowing warming devices to be run at full throttle. Outdoor activities also made the children sick with colds; their limbs could not function well.

Conditions were so unbearable that the students boycotted all outdoor subjects, which the schools called physical education; but since it was compulsory, they were forced to do it. As a result, they developed high temperatures and other abnormalities. The Ministry for Education was consulted, and a rule was passed for all schools to conduct physical education in warm gymnasiums.

Ingrid had spent a few months at school when she received a letter from her mother, directing her as to where she could trace her maternal parentage. At the age of ten, the girl could not make the journey alone and asked a friend to accompany her. They opted to use underground transport.

The two girls were curious and sat at the front. Since the vehicle could only stop if a passenger pressed the bell to disembark, the driver suspected them to be strangers, and he asked where they wanted to alight. They presented him with a piece of paper on which the name of their destination was written.

The girls got out at the right place, but the people around were not friendly, and the complex roads were too much for them. The amount of traffic puzzled them, and a number of body-to-body collisions with cars were narrowly avoided. A near miss with a tram made them abandon the search.

On their way back to school, the two girls thought about this new complex world in different ways. As her friend's mind admired the wonders of the north, Ingrid was busy comparing it to the south. She could not imagine her home state becoming like this one any time soon, but she did hope for it.

'God didn't create it like this here, after all,' she said, hating the feeling that her own land might not look like this one during her lifetime. Meanwhile, her friend was considering not going back home at all if she had an opportunity to stay.

Back at school, Ingrid wrote a letter to her mother, expressing her failure to trace her relatives. Although Barbara was sorry, she eventually thought well of it. In her reply, the mother told her daughter that it was education she had sought and that she should seek it ambitiously. 'Relatives will look for you once you make your mark on Dunia, my dear,' she concluded.

The letter made Ingrid think. All along, the girl had been told that schooling was the key to everything. With all the wonders she now saw as being the result of education, her ambition began to rise. While fearing that her state might not acquire what the north had during her own lifetime, Ingrid felt duty bound to make it happen. In her reply to Barbara, the girl wrote of her overwhelming determination.

After posting the letter, hard work and prayer became Ingrid's daily routine, and she developed a motto: I have to learn and learn it all. She became a solitary girl, always in the library reading, and she asked for help when she did not understand something.

＝

The weather changed in Northern State after a period of what everyone was calling too long to bear. Places of luxury were open day and night, with new types of street drugs being introduced on a daily basis. More people deserted the houses of prayer.

The words of the believers seemed to fall on deaf ears in the houses of God, and they resorted to open-air crusades to push the message 'love God and trust Him.' They did not harvest much because the largest percentage of the population, the youths, called them a bunch of frustrated people who should go and do their deceiving overseas. The body of water bisecting Dunia was by now called a sea, and many northerners had heard about the abject poverty prevalent on the other side. It was because of this that the word God became an acronym to them for 'Go Overseas, Deceive.'

The change in weather had given General Fox something else to do. He was going through the records of the soldiers and planned to make most of them take refresher courses. According to him, the awful cold had caused them to be lazy and lacking in enthusiasm, making them ill-prepared to carry out surprise attacks.

No one knew whether the Millennium would give the go-ahead to attack the south, but, whatever the case, the military had to be on maximum alert, according to General Fox. And, if the House did not budge, the general's tricks would never run out. Of late he had acquired a new strategy. Whenever the Millennium came upon him with questions intended to make him deviate, the general would pepper his answers with military jargon.

In one particular incident, Fox overstated himself. 'Yes, I mean maneuvers, combat readiness, military secrecy, military strategy, insubordination, reprimand, execution, ambush, attack, withdraw, pursuit, harbor, shelling, overheads, SOS...' He then asked whether there were any other questions.

The fact that the deputies did not understand him brought a sense of high alert in the House. Most, if not all, were far more educated than Fox, yet they did not comprehend what he said. The general's speech was followed by the longest silence ever in the Millennium.

=

In Southern State, the situation was equally preparatory. The new leader heard of the malevolence on the other side of Dunia and summoned his chief of security. It was the first time he had called the man, who had been appointed by his late father, not because he had no task for him, but due to the two men regarding one another with misgiving.

The chief had always made cynical remarks such as 'gang-of-three,' implying the leader, Advisor and Barbara, and he won over a number of people to sideline the trio. However, when the young leader called people into collective leadership, almost everyone began to oppose the chief of security.

Barbara saw the danger of leaving out a man who was entrusted with state security. At the time it was heard that General Fox was refreshing his northern army, so she encouraged Advisor for the chief to be brought back into the fold. This was timely, because the young leader was having sleepless nights. Hopeless thoughts of what his security guards might have to do to stop Fox's army had affected his attention and body weight.

All along, Barbara had taken center stage in making the young leader aware of his obligations. She had come up with a new term for when he needed to tackle issues that placed his ability under scrutiny. 'Diplomacy is what a leader has to adopt,' she told him. The young man was hearing the term for the first time. When he turned to Advisor for help, it seemed he did not know the word either.

It took a lot of deliberation for Barbara to make the leadership understand the term, and even as they seemed to comprehend it, she unavoidably used it in adjective form. Whatever the difference between diplomatic and diplomacy, the leader began to use both words interchangeably.

It was at the committee to discuss the imminent invasion that the leader used diplomacy and diplomatic to mean security and preparation, respectively. He then clarified himself by ordering the chief of security to strengthen not only his men, but his defenses as well. The leader then called upon Advisor to close the meeting.

Advisor, who had spent many nights listening to his woman explain how diplomacy and democracy could straighten things out, ended by condoning the ignorance expressed by the leader.

'That is diplomatic diplomacy combined with democratic democracy, my dear statesmen,' he said.

All the committee members vowed to double their efforts to work like bees on the bunkers.

# Chapter 25

Barbara spent some time blaming herself for something, and then one night it blossomed into a loud dream. Unaware that his woman was talking in her sleep, Advisor asked her what the matter was. Barbara tried to answer, but she was actually dreaming, so what she said was something like this, 'Ingrid, Ingrid, Ingrid... No, no, no... can't be... I mean it, yes, it's indeed my fault. Yes... yes, sorry... wrong... yes, I mean... me.'

Advisor was so frightened that he turned to his woman and shook her. Barbara did not wake; instead, she continued talking. He barely understood anything until she said it was too late. 'Late for what?' he was quick to ask, feeling relieved to finally hear an understandable sentence.

'She shouldn't have been given that name to use over there. The first lady is Ingrid; moreover, she is a member of the Millennium. We're both due at the same time. She knows me. I remember telling her that I like the name Ingrid. It may raise some suspicion, I'm afraid,' added Barbara, uttering the short sentences very fast.

'What do we do?' asked Advisor.

'I was just thinking that maybe she should change her name.'

'Don't you think it's too late now?'

'Do you think so?'

=

Ingrid had been asked for two names and registered herself as Ingrid Advisor. A year later, the name made many people raise their eyebrows. Ingrid had become a very sharp girl indeed. Although she came from a non-academic background, as the north viewed those from the south, the native pupils were finding it hard to match her performance. Out of a class of forty,

Ingrid came third in the first year and second the year after. She was now preparing for her final year, and the name with which she had been registered, Ingrid Advisor, could only be changed in court.

The girl received a letter from her mother late that evening, as the establishment gave letters to its pupils only after school activities. As a rule, however, the schools opened the letters that were sent from outside the state and read them before handing them over. It did not happen so with Ingrid, because Southern State children were expected to have numbers and letters instead of names.

The Ministry of Education sent official letters detailing the respective numbers and letters of southern children to their parents back home. The missions, which received the letters on behalf of the parents, only sent verbal messages such as 'your child is doing fine' to the parents concerned.

'I would like you to change your name from Ingrid to Decent,' Barbara stated in her letter.

The girl considered it for a moment, but ended up laughing. It isn't bad, though, she thought to herself, and settled down to reply to the letter. Ingrid wanted to tell her mother about the academic progress she had made, but there was a snag – she wasn't sure how best to start the letter.

'Dear' and 'hello' sounded equally pleasing openings, but Ingrid had not compiled many lines before abandoning the letter. The following day she approached her language teacher and asked, 'Can you please tell me how to address a letter to my mother, sir?'

The teacher looked anxious. 'Who is your mother?'

'Barbara...' the girl began, but stopped short after remembering her mother's cautionary words that she should first gauge any person to whom she told her mother's name. She would not have suspected the teacher, but the man's body language became excited, and he even asked the girl to ask her question again. Then the man's ears grew longer and the veins on his foreface stood out, which made his face look darker than its natural light color. He fidgeted with his nose and sniffed as if it were running.

Ingrid remembered the same characteristics in her mother whenever she acted suspicious. 'Barbara is a woman who adopted me and I regard her as my real mother, sir,' she told the man.

'Oh, thank you, then "Dear parent" will do. Anything else?'

'Nothing sir, and thank you very much.'

Ingrid could not wait for the school day to break before answering her mother's letter. In it she rejected the idea of changing her name. She told her mother that while she understood her concern, nothing of the kind would ever happen. She ended the letter with...Your lovely daughter, I A.

On receiving the reply, Barbara was very pleased with the way the girl wrote her sentences. It was a very different story from the last letter she had written, telling of her arrival and her experience in the air. In that letter, Ingrid had written what Barbara called uncoordinated words. Although she understood what the girl meant, it would be very difficult for someone not of the south to understand.

There was, however, something that almost skipped Barbara's eye due to her excitement. It was the beginning. In her first letter, Ingrid's opening phrase was 'Dear Mamah,' written and said in the typical southern way, but this one began with 'Dear parent.'

Barbara compared the two phrases. After a moment, she felt that 'Dear Mamah' was natural and humorous, but the new opening was expected of her daughter. She was filled with joy over the rate at which her girl was progressing, and she threw both hands into the air.

&equals;

If she passed her final exams, Ingrid would join the college as a student and learn only career subjects. The school arranged a trip around the state to visit places of varying interest beforehand. Pupils had to pay for the journey, but the Ministry for Education covered all the expenses for pupils from families with a low income. Those from Southern State benefitted automatically.

The trip, which was officially known as an excursion by the school, began one week before the exams and lasted until the day before sitting the first paper. Research had discovered that pupils tended to read a lot immediately before a test, and many became stressed. Therefore, if the students came back from the journey exhausted, both mentally and physically, they would read nothing until they set eyes on the examination paper.

The trip took off in a convoy of four buses, each one carrying an estimated sixty people, less the driver and teacher in charge. It was a journey that all of the pupils had been longing for, irrespective of their state of origin. With the list of places to be visited called the Great Wonders of Dunia, the high curiosity among the pupils was understandable.

Pupils from the south were anxious to see the main airport, while those from the north looked forward to viewing animals from the warm part of Dunia. The students had been told of human-eating animals being kept in a place called a zoo, and that made tensions rise until they were told that the animals lived in strong metal cages and were not aggressive.

When the pupils asked why, they were informed that the creatures were no longer wild because they had grown up among humans. The northern pupils still did not understand and asked whether there were no people where these animals come from. The answer had heightened their eagerness and anxiety.

With the zoo the last place on the visiting list, the students from the north turned to their friends from the south with some very intriguing questions. Since many of the southerners could not express themselves well in the northern language, Ingrid attracted a sizeable crowd. Yet, as a girl born and bred in the urban confines of a state mansion, life in the jungle wasn't something she knew much about. Arguments and counter-arguments became commonplace, such that the teachers were forced to rule out any zoo discussions along the way.

# Chapter 26

The excursion reached its mid-point at Eden, the capital city of Northern State. As there were many places to visit, it was planned to spend a number of days there. Most intriguing was a trip to the Millennium when the House would still be discussing the defense budget. Among the top speakers to be heard was the minister for religious affairs, Mrs. Ingrid Savage, and the commander of the armed forces, General Shroud Rough Fox. The leader of the state, Mr. Humane Savage, would also say a word or two to welcome the pupils.

Numbering 240, the excursion team occupied nearly a quarter of the House. They were placed on one side, far from the Speaker, who sat at the highest spot in the wide hall. In front of every seat were speakers and earphones. Teaching the visitors the rules of the House and how to use the various gadgets took thirty minutes. The pupils were told to ask questions only after the debate, which they should do by stating their full names first. It was also important to let the students know that whispers were communicated in the same way as proper talking.

'Let me take this opportunity to welcome our young trees...'

The Speaker beckoned Savage, but as this was not the usual way to interrupt a person who held the floor, the leader carried on until the Speaker did the inevitable. She sounded a bell and all the visitors screamed.

'Yes, this is what I wanted to warn you about," she told the students. 'This means order; well, actually silence, but it has a culture far beyond that in this House. The laws we pass here are called bills, and this bell is sounded three times to imply that a bill has been passed. When I raise the gong in my right hand, it means I'm going to sound the bell, so in the right-hand corner of your table you'll see a green button that you should press to minimize the bang. The red button, however, as I believe you've been told, is for questions and the black one is for your vote, which will appear automatically on the screen over there. So, eyes on me most of the time, please.'

The Speaker then asked Savage to continue, this time with a gesture of the hand that was retiring from showing the giant board.

Savage did not say much, except, 'You must be very lucky indeed, because you are going to hear from the best of our speakers.' The leader extended his talking with a few words of praise to the Speaker for allowing the 'young trees' into the House on short notice. While summing up, he added, 'Please be attentive, because the burden of managing Dunia is being passed over to you. Thank you very much, and enjoy the debate.' Savage then took his seat.

Speaking first, General Fox talked about the amount of money required for the defense of the state, which the Millennium preferred to call figures. It was not clear why it had to be called so, but defense required quite substantial sums of money, which, whenever mentioned, made the members in the House shriek.

Even then, 'military figures,' a term meaning defense budget in the House, had been rebranded 'staggering figures' by the media. The state fired the journalist who introduced the term, for what it called 'letting out government secrets recklessly.' The move only made the term famous within media circles, and the day's newspapers were certain to have 'Millennium Debates Staggering Figures' as their main headlines. Journalists attending the debate had indicated so on their writing pads.

General Fox talked about his strategy for the future. He did not forget the Antis project, which, according to him, was to cover fifty percent of the whole defense budget.

The Speaker initiated the argument by calling upon the first lady in her capacity as minister for religious affairs. Although Ingrid Savage's words sprung forth with much euphemism, General Fox understood her to mean that 'enough is enough with defense budgets, and the House has been pushed too far for too long.'

Ingrid wanted to assault the soldier head on, but she had not forgotten her daughter's concerns or the words that her husband had repeated to her that morning: Remember, this man can throw us out and replace us with the military. We have to handle him with care.

Fox rebounded rather harshly. 'Let me remind the first lady minister that the Millennium is spending a lot of money to make houses of prayer glitter with marble, yet they see no people at all. Some of them are even too costly to be called churches, acquiring names like cathedral and basilica.'

The man quieted down and glanced around before continuing, 'Fellow countrymen, isn't God something we should regard as past now that man has to strive, and strive alone?' He paused again as he noticed the audience becoming inattentive. 'I wonder whether God can send his army to defend the state in the event of enemy attack.'

The first lady was a God-loving person who had called herself a believer ever since her political party, the PP, had been banned. Fox's words stung and she made an aside, 'What? How dare he?' She then raised her voice and retorted, 'You made us draw almost all the cash from the Treasury when you called ODOS foolproof, and you said the first drop would see the dictator sliced to pieces, didn't you?' She pointed a finger at the general.

Fox did not answer, and neither would the first lady let him. She burst forth instead, 'It is known that two innocent children died, among other casualties. The innocent! Who the hell do you benefit, anyway? You couldn't even report back until we had to contact other sources to get feedback. Aren't you ashamed of your wickedness, you evil being in the shape of a man?'

Pressmen roamed the House, wanting to coordinate the story, but not a single person would give them audience. Tempers were running high, and to many it was the hottest debate ever.

A terrible flashback hit young Ingrid. How she had been injured, together with her mother, was a mere story, yet here she was confronting what had really happened. She recalled what her mother had told her: It is education that can pay back those evil people! But the poor girl had not prepared herself for coming face-to-face with such evil.

Ingrid lifted her head and saw a dreamland filled with harmful people. As tears coursed down her cheeks, she decided to bury her face in her hands on the table. Reaching for her hanky to blow her congested nose, what should the girl see but the large scar on her arm left behind by the incident.

Something settled in her throat. Ingrid tried to swallow it down, but the thing was too big and sat still in her chest, wanting to tear her head off. Unable to stand it, the girl burst out crying.

# Chapter 27

The following morning, the eye-catching front headline of all the newspapers read the same: Mixed-race Alien Bursts into Tears at Hottest Millennium Debate Ever.

Although none of the papers included any particulars of the alien girl who had cried, the people were reading an article they had not expected. Ingrid had made herself an icon on the political stage of Northern State. Everyone was confused as to why a girl of thirteen had burst into tears during a discussion about an attack on a dead dictator, whose presence would have denied her the opportunities she was currently enjoying.

The next day some men traced Ingrid's whereabouts and asked her to accompany them. When her teacher objected, they threatened him with obstructing state duty. The man became so scared that he demanded he go along, too. It took some time for the men to accept his request.

A team of deputies, appointed to look into the girl's unique behavior, was waiting for them at the Millennium. They began by asking Ingrid who her parents were. She told them that she had been abandoned as a toddler and grew up with missionaries. The deputies then demanded to know which mission she grew up in, and the girl answered that she did not know, because she was moved between various places.

When asked the origin of her name, she replied that Ingrid was her first missionary keeper. Then the deputies wanted to know what she looked like, but the girl said she didn't get the chance to know the spiritual woman.

The interview, which lasted for four hours, ended when Ingrid began to cry after every question. When the team recommended that she  be seen by a  psychiatrist,  her teacher objected that such authorization had to be granted by the school. As it was not possible to reach anyone there, the team leader ordered the investigation to be closed.

The next destination for the excursion was a collection of what mankind had gone through since Dunia first began making records about its existence. Called Gallery, the building contained different types of art by the most famous names the great island had known. Nearly everything was so beautiful to look at that Ingrid even began to forget the Millennium saga.

With her concerned teacher constantly by her side, the girl felt quite consoled and began to feel like her old self. She became highly interested in whatever she saw and loved every moment of the trip, probably because nearly all of the paintings were similar to those in the mansion back home.

The light-skinned men came from very far, Ingrid thought, but why should they keep such things, and even ask people to pay to see them? People never forget their past, whatever it is.

The girl was still pondering the journey travelled by those in the north when she saw something bearing a human image and the writing of the south. Ingrid was about to yell out, but her hand was fast to cover her mouth. Pulling out a notebook, she wrote down what was written instead.

With no income apart from handouts, Barbara had believed this particular ancient piece of art would earn her enough money to pay for the upbringing of her child, so she had taken it from the mansion and given it to someone to sell. The brother to whom she gave the item was paid a substantial amount of cash, but she received far less of it. Even then, what she was given was still enough to keep her daughter at the level of a middle-class family in Northern State. With the help of missionaries going to and from the north, she maintained a steady acquisition of modern learning gadgets for her child. It made Ingrid able to compete with the northern-born children at school.

After the Gallery, the excursion went to visit Eden People's Illegal Centre. Commonly known as EPIC, everyone at the center did whatever they liked, even what the laws of the state forbade. Young people looking weak and sick, with distorted postures, wandered around the compound aimlessly. Everyone appeared to be in a hurry, yet no sooner had they reached one point then they would rush off in the opposite direction.

The students were amazed at how oblivious the ill-looking people were to the weather. Temperatures had dropped, yet nearly everyone at EPIC was dressed casually. 'Could it be that they did not have warm clothes to wear?' asked the students. 'No,' they were told. What was it then, they wondered.

The pupils were informed that the people were drug addicts who had been brought here and given drugs for free. 'Why not keep them off the drugs?' the students asked. They were then told that the users were at the stage of being junkies and could not live without them. Whether the teachers had said enough to prevent the pupils from adopting the habit, the children learned that drug abuse was part of the culture in the north.

Beyond EPIC, men and women of all skin colors appeared to be almost naked, only wearing underpants and bras, and some were completely nude. However, a special type of shoe, which made them look taller by pulling their shoulders back and pushing their chests forward, seemed a must-have for every one of them. Looking like they were in some kind of show, they stood in glass cages, calling upon passersby while signaling how much they charged for sex.

Engaged in what was known to be the first money-earning career in Dunia, the prostitutes, as they were called, had mastered the skill of the business. They related the various services on offer by using signals, which they were capable of doing in the blink of an eye.

Even men called upon men who wanted sex with their fellows. Called GG, meaning going-gay, the issue caused heated debates in the Millennium. Gay couples wanted a bill passed that would legalize them to get married in houses of prayer. The believers spoke out loudly against it, saying that legalizing gay marriage would be the cruelest offence against God.

In return, the gay men accused the believers of misunderstanding the writings of God, and asked to be shown which verse in the Holy Book actually forbade same-sex couples. To this, the believers asked whether same-sex couples could actually produce a child, because matrimony meant the making of a mother.

It seemed that gay people had lost the battle because the argument died down, but after some time it remerged when they called upon the authorities to allow them to adopt children. The matter caused a storm in the Millennium, but such a bill was passed. Many gay couples made trips to the south in search of children to adopt, and dark-skinned youngsters were brought over the boundary under the new policy and given names.

Ten years later, however, the decision proved to be counterproductive, as most of the teenagers brought over under the adoption bill were now living rough in the EPIC area. The Millennium revoked the bill.

In response, lesbian and gay deputies called upon their counterparts and staged a peaceful demonstration on the streets of the capital. Their slogan accused the state's considered decision of being harsh and unbecoming for a democracy. While answering questions from scribes they accepted that some of the same-sex couples had failed in their duty as parents, but they blamed the state for generalizing the matter.

Not wanting to argue with its citizens who were making their voices heard in a non-violent way, the state responded by issuing a statement in which it said it would try to give whatever the parties needed, apart from recalling the bill. The lesbians accused the state of wanting them to do something that went against their beliefs. In their view the state wanted them to produce children, rather than adopting them.

The race among scientists to give gay men something similar was on, and a state-funded project launched an ambitious scheme of implanting female reproductive organs into them. Believers rallied the masses and asked why the state should be spending money on something that nature had to offer in abundance. The gay deputies had an immediate answer. 'The scheme is not about nature, but science,' they said, which killed the believers' zest.

Same-sex couples returned and their numbers mushroomed all over Northern State. Shops filled with sex gadgets became the fanciest business once again. Pictures of people having sex with animals, especially pets, became a common feature in magazines where men and women could be seen happily sucking their genitals. In some cases penetration was also visible.

Inasmuch as men had been able to grow breasts due to reasons only known to science, now some women decided to change their natural appearance and carried breasts the size of their heads. Many people boasted rings all over their bodies, and some even made media confessions of piercing their genitals as well. Others showed off drawings on their skins that depicted bloodsuckers and monsters. Such people were viewed as stars.

Deep inside this human exhibition, known locally as Erotic Village, were cabins in which shows of people having live sex were common. Some rooms had been designed for private-screen watchers, who only had to toss a coin in the door. Many curious by-passers ended up inside.

Right in the center of the village was a cathedral of magnificent design where the pupils stopped for a rest and a cup of tea. Many of them, especially those from Southern State, would have declined the beverage, but the reception they were given was typical of a house of God, and the students were amazed.

Ingrid, who had forgotten her Millennium experience, could not let the vicar of the cathedral go unchallenged. 'How come a house of God is in such a place?' she asked.

'We're here to prepare the way for Him,' intoned the vicar.

'For who?' asked Ingrid and the southern pupils in unison.

'The Lord,' said the vicar, grinning.

The vicar's explanation was accompanied by self-correction, because the pupils' expressions looked confused. The teachers sensed it and asked them to leave. The visit to the village had caused the students from the south to gather in coteries to whisper in wonder.

One of them had experienced a far more personal encounter and identified a woman from her village behind one of the glass doors. Although the woman was disguised in artificial, long blonde hair, false eyelashes, blue lipstick and very long, red fingernails, the pupil had identified her as a prostitute.

The student said the woman used to tell her people back home that she worked in a big hotel, and often visited with a lot of money and modern things. She was even building a big block house in the south.

The excursion was to enter its final phase at the zoo located near the airport. Many animals had died from the cold, and the pupils, especially those from the north, were unhappy to hear that the snakes, crocodiles and hippopotamus were no longer there. Their mood, however, lifted when they learned that they would be able to see the jungle giants: elephants, rhinos, giraffes, zebras, and the four biggest wild cats – the lions, tigers, cheetahs and leopards.

On the way to the airport, the students were excited to see giant planes landing and taking off in endless streams. Then something even more thrilling showed up in front of them, creating pandemonium on the buses. The teachers appealed for calm. Nervousness turned into curiosity as a gigantic bridge rose towards the sky. It used to open every hour, but when the weather took a complete turnaround, the great structure was unable to rise anymore.

Operated by solar, the idea of having sufficiently bright sun to lift the giant creature became a dream. However, on this sunny afternoon, an exciting moment in history unfolded when Ridge Creature Bridge woke up after years of lying dormant. Everyone left their vehicles to take snaps as Dunia's widest and longest drawbridge ascended and descended again.

# Chapter 28

Ingrid had made a lot of notes, which she wrote stealthily, not wanting anyone to know what she was doing. As a result, some words were unclear, and she was worried about losing the right meaning. She was about to begin rewriting when 'lights out' was called. The pupils needed a long rest before their exams the following morning, prompting the lights to be switched off earlier than usual. After all, most of them had been snoring in the recreation hall after dinner, which coincided with their arrival.

The next day, immediately after her first exam paper, Ingrid settled down to write her mother a letter. There was a lot to tell, beginning with the antique, which she knew had been collected from her state. Then, as the letter progressed, the Millennium saga became the subject matter. Emotion overwhelmed her as the whole episode came flooding back.

Ingrid tried to cut the long story short, but the feeling of missing some important point grew as she wrote. Eventually, realizing that the letter might make her mother upset, she decided to begin a new one.

There was a teacher in the room who approached her, perhaps wanting to guide her in her revision for the next paper. Admitting that she was writing letters instead of revising would not be good, so Ingrid abandoned the idea.

It was after the exams that she finally settled down properly to write to Barbara. The subject matter of her letter had changed by then. She related how she'd found the exams very simple and that she was sure of passing. Relaying the prospects of taking on the toughest study in her educational scheme became the main theme.

Ingrid told her mother that she was willing to take Analogy between Man and God (AMAG), a study that revealed how man lived on Dunia. It could lead a person into becoming a priest or politician, although many other careers were in reach, especially in a society such as Southern State, where technology was a future dream. Remembering her mother's words, 'You need to take up a study that will benefit your people,' Ingrid knew she would be pleased.

Lastly, the letter progressed on to the excursion. Besides the Ridge Creature Bridge, EPIC was the main subject, and Ingrid mentioned her shock at seeing dark-skinned people in the glass cages selling their bodies. At the end she mentioned the Millennium, and the stolen antique became her bottom line.

Ingrid posted the letter and then set about waiting for her exam results, which would take some time to be known or returned, as the school saying went.

=

When General Fox told the House that the number of back-up troops to escort STEITU would quadruple, everyone expected the first lady to bounce back aggressively, but, oddly, Ingrid Savage said nothing. There was a long murmur, which was silenced by the Speaker's bell. Then the minister for education was called upon to read out the list of students who were going to take part in the next trip to the south.

Since the names had been written in alphabetical order, Aan, the daughter of the Savages, topped the list. The mention of her name was followed by booing in the House, which took the Speaker some time to silence. Yet, even when quiet fell, a few stubborn people continued to whisper and even stamp their feet.

The first lady could not leave the situation unanswered. 'May I inform the House that I will be going to the south too when my daughter returns, and I ask all of you to pray for her in delivering God's message for us, which will doubtless open doors for a political settlement with the south.

One deputy asked the first lady to inform the House of the sort of message a girl of about fourteen could possibly deliver on behalf of Northern State. This turned into a bitter argument between the first family and the rest of the House.

'I wish to ask the honorable member to tell the House if he could allow his child to make the same journey if he was in our position,' said Aan Savage's father.

The House roared in sympathy. The deputy who had raised doubts over Aan was a gay man whose partner was fighting for his life after an operation to make him productive had gone horribly wrong.

$=$

Back in the leader's mansion in Southern State, the mother of the late ruler's youngest child died, shortly after the latter's own death. The young ruler was worried because rumor was rife of the ruler's 'disease' having infected his entire family.

Barbara was quick to calm the situation by telling him not to think about dying. Whether it was some kind of personal consolation, since she was also part of the family, the woman knew that the state would fail if its leader was worried for his life. In her view the new ideology of inclusiveness would have no one to guide it, and, thinking ahead, youngsters like her daughter would end up being the biggest losers.

Meanwhile scientists in the north were ready with their findings, in which they proclaimed the disease to be an abnormal one and quite infectious, and a team of them were asked to present their findings to the Millennium. The director of medical services, who was a veteran scientist himself, intended to inform the deputies of the dangers posed by the sickness on Dunia.

Doctor Uglyman began his report in the humblest way: 'Madam, Speaker, honorable deputies, ladies and gentlemen, I'll try to be as simple as possible.' He was a man of technical words, but, thanks to his wife, a deputy had written the speech for him. 'The disease that killed the most recent dictator in Dunia, and later a number of his household, has come under our scrutiny, and I'm glad to say we have its life in extreme detail.

'Fellow statesmen, it should have been professor Anusman, the physician who concluded our findings, that presented this to you, but he asked me to do it on his behalf. Thank you very much, Professor Anusman.'

The professor, a physicist believed to be the best in Dunia, bowed to the House.

'I feel terribly sorry to report that the disease has no cure and can be passed through the atmosphere,' Doctor Uglyman continued. 'The origin of this disease is rather confusing. There are two proven theories, I'm afraid: one being a wild primate, native to the warm part of Dunia.' The director paused and made a searching look around his audience. 'And, ladies and gentlemen, the fusion of gasses as rockets are fired.'

There was booing in the House and the Speaker sounded her bell.

Doctor Uglyman went on, 'We wanted to conduct posthumous research on the first known victim of this disease, the late leader of Southern State, but we found no trace of his remains in the grave. This led us to believe that the disease is caused by a very resistant virus that consumes the bones of its host after he or she succumbs. It is not clear how many people are infected as we speak, but research based on the speed and flow of currents puts the number at one in every ten people.

'When this virus makes the body weak, we call it disease onset. It is chronically aggressive and we have no cure. The period of onset varies from person to person, but we believe someone would show symptoms within ten years. Having known this disease to be aggressive, chronic and immune, we gave it the name ACID.

'May I take this opportunity to tell the government that we need a substantial amount of money to carry out further research if we are to alter the stride of this dreaded virus," he concluded. 'Thank you very much, Madam Speaker and the House.'

It was then resolved that there would be no news coverage of ACID. The blame on missile launches was dismissed as misguided by Savage, who appealed to the House not to let a project that cost taxpayers so much money to be victimized, which he said using the phrase, 'put to the cross.' Nevertheless, the imminent STEITU was suspended.

# Chapter 29

The center of Eden woke up to a very tense morning, following the death of a famous journalist and writer. Wolf, aka Pressman, had instructed his family not to take him to hospital when his doctor made him aware that he was immune to treatment. Soon after his demise, the family posted his last moments online.

Wailing people made endless streams on the streets of Eden where traffic was brought to a standstill. Those affected included deputies heading to the Millennium to conclude a report on how the government should make ACID known to the public. The drafting of it had led the House into many debates, all blaming the military. Most of the deputies wanted the army disbanded and the missile launches stopped.

However, Savage was still firmly behind his most decorated soldier. 'Let people be told of the epidemic being a result of polygamy,' he said.

After that statement, nearly every deputy agreed their leader was not the magic bullet they had always believed him to be. Those who had to fight their way through the streets thronged with people arrived late for the session and, as a rule, were not able to enter until the Speaker allowed it.

General Fox was speaking. 'As you were, ladies and gentlemen,' he began. As the listeners started to feel edgy, the general began to use literal language. It did not take him long to get to the point: 'Launches are things without which the situation would be far worse.'

During his speech, a person who enforced discipline in the Millennium, called a sergeant at arms, came rushing in to talk to the Speaker, who had to sound her bell, requesting interruption. The Speaker then asked Fox to take his seat while the National

Television screen in the House was switched on. The announcement of the death of Pressman had just been made, and the streets were heaving with people from all walks of life, many of whom were wailing bitterly.

The announcer came on screen and silence engulfed the House. 'The death of the most celebrated journalist and classic writer, who earned himself the name of Pressman, is as yet a mystery. The family couldn't say a word until now, but with me in the studio is the family doctor of the late Pressman. You're welcome to the studio, doctor.'

'I'm grateful, thanks,' he answered.

'Now doctor...?'

'Pimphouse.'

'Yes, sorry, Doctor Pimphouse, I understand you're the family doctor of Pressman. Is that right?'

'Yes, indeed.'

'Let me begin by expressing my condolences. But, doctor, what makes this particular death so remarkable?'

'Well, may I say it's the nature of the disease; sadly, science couldn't save this very famous son of the state.'

'Life takes its course to death, all right. But since this was a result of a disease, as you've just said, and you're known to be among the best physicians ever, tell me, why couldn't you save his life?'

'Well, we all know death is a natural thing, but maybe the time has come when death is taking its place above science and research.'

'What do you mean by that, doctor?'

'Well, I shouldn't be saying this, but we have a disease called ACID, which has managed to fight off the latest cocktail that we hoped would solve the mystery.'

'How does this sickness come to dwell among us?'

'The disease is believed to have been brought to us by our technological advancement. It is contagious, and my appeal to people is to keep their distance from the body of Pressman before the entire city perishes!'

'Could you say more about that technological advancement, doctor?'

'I'm sure the Millennium will be doing that. We presented everything to them. My question and the question of every physician is what on earth is the Millennium doing to tell the people about our findings, in which we stated the necessary precautions. My appeal is that time is fundamental in a matter like this one!'

'Thank you very much, Doctor Pimphouse.'

As the television was switched off, the deputies looked at one another, bewildered. The Speaker waived in the late arrivals who had been watching the developments from the door. All members of the House were now present. The Speaker then called upon one deputy, from among those who had just entered, to give his side of the story on the town scram.

However, Mr. Savage gave the deputy no opportunity to speak. 'Ladies and gentlemen, Madam Speaker,' he said, 'we should agree that the situation is pathetic, and may I ask the House to immediately pass a bill placing the home of Pressman and its surroundings under quarantine.'

The situation in the Millennium, which was not paying any attention to the bell any longer, saw General Fox gain a chance to contribute as his voice rose above the rest. With many parts of the city slipping out of control, the deputies fell silent, wanting to listen to the man who was used to such situations.

Fox spoke with a clenched fist and said that all of the affected areas should have tanks, armored personnel carriers, water cannons and marksmen placed around them. One deputy asked why. 'Because what's happening is hooliganism,' Fox replied.

This time, Savage looked unconvinced with his general's approach, and he asked the House to hear the opinion of the paramilitary commander, Mr. Black Wolf. Many deputies considered that all men in uniform shared the same thinking and saw no point in calling upon Wolf. One even cited him as being a relative of Pressman, a development that was beginning to cast a shadow over the commander's partiality.

Savage would not let his idea be swept under the carpet just like that. 'Wolf is coming as a technical man, rather than a relation to the deceased.'

Wolf, who was on his way to the Millennium to brief Savage, showed up in less time than expected. When he started to give his proposals for combating the situation, the deputies began to hear things that brought smiles to their faces. The whole House lit up, as if the matter at hand was a laughing one. Wolf called the situation 'unrest' and referred to people as 'protesters' who needed minimum force to deal with.

'I suggest people should be asked to gather at one place, where a top politician can give them a word of consolation,' Wolf concluded.

The House, which had been listening attentively to the paramilitary commander, was by now calm, and votes were conducted as to which approach was best.

The Speaker, in announcing the decision, said, 'The vote in front of me overwhelmingly gives the paramilitary a chance this time around.'

—

The paramilitary had been undergoing secret intensive training for handling unrest. When starting their operation, leaflets were dropped from helicopters all over the city.

People collect at Adam Square
Let us give the state time
To handle the funeral of
Our celebrity, the dearly missed
Mr. Pressman.

Printed in the state colors of the rainbow, the leaflets made a spectacular fall, which inspired people to chase after them. Upon reading the message, the protestors gave in and collected at the city center. The paramilitaries, who were on standby, resorted to working as guides and scouts, organizing people into orderly groupings.

It was there, at Adam Square, that the first lady, who had been chosen by the Millennium, gave a state farewell speech to Mr. Pressman. Using some well-selected words from the Holy Book and speaking with feeling, Mrs. Savage won over the hearts of the people. They believed the state was sorry and had nothing to do with Pressman's death, but that God liked things to happen the way they did.

Mrs. Savage gave her closing remarks after warning people against polygamy: 'It is, however, the moment to ask God to replace what has been taken away, if we are worthy of another person of your charisma, Mr. Pressman; may your soul rest in peace!'

'Amen' roared up from the mammoth crowd and carried through the city center and beyond. Masked men then carried Mr. Pressman away to be cremated.

# Chapter 30

Ingrid Advisor passed her exams with what the education system called 'Super A Grade.' She was invited to join a college for bright students on the outskirts of Eden. Although her heart had begun to wander over what to study, which was to be called faculty, she was the kind of girl who was conscious of her word, and so she decided on AMAG.

Ninety-nine percent of the students at the place of learning were light colored, a concept that mirrored its name of White Academy College. WAC, as it was commonly known, was based on a geographical theory that argued that cold conditions made youths at school understand better and more quickly.

Although the scholars that thought up the idea called it 'Phenomenon of assimilation,' the scientists who did the research renamed it 'Theory of Understanding.' This implied that children from the north were brighter than those from the south, where it was warm. This idea, however, needed to be argued further when Ingrid proved otherwise to her lecturers at WAC.

The girl passed the first phase very well, even though it was known to be the most difficult part of the faculty. Ingrid had understood the difficulty of her studies to the extent of calling it a misunderstanding. It all began with the opening lesson: why man resembled God, yet God was a spirit and everywhere.

Many students had found the analogy ironic, confusing and ambiguous, and the answer from most lecturers was to take it the way it was. So, the students took it for a dogma. However, during one heated debate, Ingrid had had enough of the dogmatic analysis and decided to break her humble silence.

'I have spent a lot of time alone, revising and going through the Holy Book, with the  intention of understanding the theory that relates God to man,' she began. 'I find this issue more than challenging, and I'm bringing it to the attention of the class with due possibility of discussion and thorough understanding. To me, the relation is not God to man, but God and man. I say this because God is a spirit and man is flesh, but it is flesh with spirit that governs and runs our entire human body through our senses. This makes our study more scientific than maybe any of us thought.

'Unlike all other living things, particularly animals, man has more developed senses... senses that allow us to question our every move. Other animals lack this ability; what they have, which God gave them for their survival, is the ability to connect their bodies with their spirit – something they happen to do far better than us. This helps them in their immediate rather than long-term survival.

'So, I came to conclude that we have very similar senses to God, our creator, although ours are in the mediocre stage. But, I also believe that "human life" is the final examination of the very complex cycle of our spiritual life. When someone dies, our senses are more developed, probably to suit the environment that is associated with God.'

Ingrid's explanation left the lecturer and the entire class filled with wonder, and thereon the college nicknamed her Reference.

Ingrid had often admired the way in which the people of the north lived, yet she never praised it. To her, the northerners were a people living in denial because they had neither fear nor faith in their creator. She then realized that her own society might adopt a similar way of life if it acquired earthly possessions. Fear overwhelmed her.

However, a common philosophy in Ingrid's course – that man's creative instinct was a human weakness rather than a means to a better life – often made her see the brighter side of things. The way God loved the northerners by giving them knowledge and wisdom on a daily basis continued to baffle the girl. Why did he refuse to give these things to my people, who know him and praise him, but gave to  those who have turned away from him, if they ever knew him at all? Maybe he will punish them and take away all that he gave them?

As if waking from a dream, Ingrid realized that wishing evil on someone was in itself evil. It was during such times that she could pray and meditate for hours. Planning for her society became the modus operandi after such moments. She needed to stop her people going in a direction that she considered unacceptably wicked, and the idea stalked her like an old, toothless wild cat.

A shower always relieved Ingrid when she was in such a mood. After that she would intend to write her mother a letter, but usually the pressure of college work, which involved guiding other students, caused Barbara to write first. Their ideas were similar. Her mother's opening phrase was always, 'My dear, please know that education is the only weapon to improve your people.'

# Chapter 31

Savage asked the House to extend his powers because every decision had to go through so much discussion before being made into a bill. The deputies, according to the constitution, could not do a thing about his request, as the people had to be consulted in a presidential poll. If Savage achieved over fifty percent, he would be eligible to pass bills, and his title would change from state leader to His Excellency, the President. The state would then revert to being a republic.

The deputies were refusing to be persuaded by Savage. By accepting his idea they would have done what most were calling a career mishap: They knew their land was a republic before, but this was generations ago. History was not clear about why it had to covert from the type of governance their leader was asking them to revert to. Interest for this political change to be part of the education curriculum had vanished with time. The deputies tried to trace the truth in the national achieve, but no mention of it could be found there either, so a date to hold elections was set.

Elections were held, but the people appeared unconcerned, and the registered voters could not make the required percentage. A new round was called at a future date. Savage, however, used the time in between to lobby those colleges and schools where he thought his influence would be decisive. He promised a wide range of subsidies. By the end of his campaign low-income families did not have to pay for school requirements, and college students would pay zero fees in the last semester of their courses.

Savage won the election with more than the required percentage. Unifying clauses in the constitution opposing a republic, hence presidency, were found soon afterwards. He reacted this way to the discovery: 'I don't think a modern democracy like us can place a paper written many years ago above the mandate of the people. Besides, we all agreed recently that the constitution is legal only when it reflects the needs of the day.'

None of the deputies were in a mood to argue. After all, Savage's new title of president would not be preceded by His Excellency, according to the agreement that gave the election the go-ahead.

The first decision by the president was to pass the Antis Bill. This saw General Fox embark on the new task of recruiting young technicians for the military department that would manufacture missiles, to counter what had been created earlier. In his speech to the Millennium, the general had said that small weapons were capable of destroying very large ones. He emphasized, yet again, that Antis would be very expensive to manufacture and warned against what he called bouncing back for more funds.

While tired of asking the same question over and over, one deputy would not let General Fox sit down for long. 'Why should the military spend so much on an invisible enemy?' he asked.

The general rose immediately and replied, 'Preparation is the most important phase of war and, as such, the most expensive. Let me remind the House that the military, unlike all other institutions, has to plan well in advance for even small operations.'

The deputies looked at each other in awe.

⸺

Southern State had acquired a professional army. Unlike that of the north, which was highly technical with a variety of military arsenal, this one had rifles and grenades. Barbara had worked tirelessly to get in touch with deserters from Dunia Modern Army, which was locally known as Fox's Army.

Many parents in the north were having trouble keeping their sons who had deserted. Barbara headed the committee that regrouped former servicemen into camps. With the help of the church, the veterans, as they wished to be called, received aid. It was there that Advisor asked them to assist in training the army of Southern State. They would not have to pay taxes, which was something they could only dream of in the north. The men accepted and even surrendered their names to be called MC+number, which stood for Mercenary, followed by a numeral.

To begin with, the deserters taught close-combat drills and small-arms skills. The leader passed out the soldiers after nine months of intensive training. In his speech, written for him by Advisor and Barbara, he thanked the mercenaries, whom he referred to as instructors. In conclusion, he emphasized the need for the army to develop the bunkers of 'a better standard.'

The construction of barracks similar to those of Dunia Modern Army began immediately after the last batch of soldiers finished their course. The project would house up to 10,000 officers and men. Half of the homes would accommodate married couples, not to mention that those for officers would be far larger and better equipped. Each barrack would accommodate up to 1,000 soldiers. Inside there would be administration blocks, quartermaster stores, catering halls and a school for children.

The entire project was running concurrently in ten areas across the state, and yet the state coffers had no money to pay for it. In contrast to the plan for the bunkers, the leadership asked people to pay for the project, rather than getting physically involved.

Selling the idea to the masses was hard for the leadership, which had not discussed transforming its guards into an army. Explaining what the word army meant was in itself sufficient to cause dismay and fear. There was no way of saying it without triggering people's memories of the soldier who was tied to a tree in broad daylight by his colleagues and shot. The incident had left the children who saw it scarred for life.

The leadership thought they would collect enough money from the people by raising taxes, but this backfired. People started to cry foul, and the chief of security's talk of gang-of-three came back – it was clear to them that the leader son, Advisor and his woman were all out to enrich themselves at the expense of the public.

Upon being made aware of the people's grievances, the leadership resorted to the philosophy of inclusiveness. The trio made many addresses to soldiers, asking them to tell their parents how good the institution of The People's Army would be when assisted by the people. Even then, only a few responded, and the barracks project was in danger of failing.

Through Barbara, the leadership sought help from the richest institution in the land – the God-loving people. They agreed, but had one demand: We shall assist in building the army if it puts God first.

The army was living in conditions prone to disaster. Locally made sewage systems flooded areas of the camps, into which many drunken soldiers and their children fell. The grass-thatched mud huts in which they lived often caught fire, leaving casualties.

The situation left the state with no option but to accept the missionaries' demand. The orphans in mission schools had bricklaying and mason work as compulsory lessons, and it was time to put them to the test.

After one year, the entire army, which had been renamed God's Own Army (GOA), was living in block houses with proper sanitation systems.

# Chapter 32

Scientists and journalist came to meet Ingrid in the closing phase of her college study. She was busy arranging a crusade, due to take place at the college campus, in commemoration of the late Pressman who had been a part-time lecturer there.

The people of God had taken this as the moment to tell Dunia how the creator made decisions, perhaps in response to the overwhelming public outcry of, "Why did God take such a man, of all people?"

Such moments of limbo made believers spring forth with good witticisms during their crusades, which won them converts.

Ingrid Advisor had become a strong member of the God-loving people and a good crusader, according to those who heard her in action. Like her mother, she left listeners wanting more. She was even better, perhaps, because the combination of her paternal and maternal abilities placed the girl in a class superior to that of her parents. She would adopt her mother or father's individual styles, where applicable; something that came naturally to her.

Ingrid's ability to pull in the crowds, coupled with excellent academic performance, provoked the team of scientists to come and interview her. As the girl was southern-born, they believed she would make a harmless guinea pig. The scientists intended to ask questions and use surgical techniques to find answers with the aim of improving their understanding, irrespective of the effect on Ingrid. They had even deemed surgical operations necessary if the girl answered the oral questionnaire with what they called a degree of excellence.

The interview, as they chose to call it, began with questions regarding Ingrid's life history; they wanted to know her birth and all details relating to her origin. Not forgetting her mother's words, the girl chose not to cooperate. The questioning should have stopped there, but the scientists chose to continue.

The interviewee gave answers that the interviewers were not expecting, and questions that were not on the agenda arose, but she answered those too, just as smartly. Quizzes on people's ability to understand, based on diet and environment, particularly the weather, were employed.

Ingrid asked if any of the scientists had ever lived in the warm part of Dunia long enough to be able to cross-examine what she said. There was a moment of silence and hard breathing as they stared at one another. The interviewers then recommended that Ingrid have surgery, which she turned down on the condition that she wasn't sick.

The following morning a photograph of Ingrid Advisor headlined all of the newspapers with a fascinating introduction: The girl of mixed race from Southern State that shed tears in a Millennium debate four years ago is back in the spotlight. The teenager is breaking record levels of human intelligence in WAC academy and, moreover, taking on a tough faculty – AMAG.

Ingrid was called before the Millennium, but she turned down the invitation until they threatened her college with closure. At the House, the girl was made many offers, which included her appointment as minister of state for religious affairs in the government of President Savage. She would have been the person responsible for exporting religious values across Dunia.

The girl did not budge, so the first lady tried a joke: 'How nice would it be for the Ingrids to be running the most innocent ministry on Dunia?'

The girl just answered with a grin, bringing the meeting to a close.

==

Ingrid wrote her mother a letter. She called what had happened in the Millennium a moment of miscalculated temptation. On receiving it, Barbara called Esther to tell her what she called pride.

Esther saw the other side of it. 'She should have accepted. Then the ministry here would have grown like a bushfire, sister,' she said.

Barbara spent some time considering what Esther had told her, and once she felt that she had digested it fully, she wrote back to her daughter and asked her to give in. It was just before sending the letter that she decided to have a word with Advisor, whom she now treasured for giving her a very brilliant girl. The conversation was not what Barbara had expected.

'Why didn't you tell me about it all along?' was Advisor's response.

'I'm sorry, but you were busy,' she replied, humbly.

Both parents later agreed not to send their daughter the letter.

＝

Ingrid was strong enough to overcome the pressure of the media and sat for her final exams in a calm environment. The college closed down before the results were out. Being the only student from another state, Ingrid had to wait for her results, and she didn't know who from. In the past she had posted newspapers from house to house as a job, and although it had been a nasty experience, she was wondering whether to do the same thing again.

Although her father had man to blame for his suffering in the north, it was the weather in her case. Ingrid had done well during her first week of delivering newspapers, but the order of the game changed when ice made the roads slippery. Her limited experience of cycling became a recipe for falling frequently. In the process, the newspapers she carried were soaked in ice and the print became patches of unrecognizable figures. Unable to read their papers, the recipients complained to the agency, which reacted by terminating her employment, without pay.

Ingrid was not only unable to earn anything from her first job, but it also left her with bruises all over. Her mother's birthday was due and she had hoped to buy her a present. Not being able to do it made the girl feel sad. Her colleagues advised her to sue the agency, but she declined and instead swore never again to do vacancy jobs.

Ingrid needed to pay for her accommodation while waiting for her exam results, which would only be known in six months' time, so she needed a job. A fellow student with whom Ingrid had done some crusades at college approached her and asked if she might like to accompany her home for the long holiday.

Ingrid enjoyed the atmosphere while staying with the religious family on the outskirts of Hollyfield, and she asked to know more about the area. Perhaps she should not have, because she was then told something that hit a raw nerve: babies being strangled and thrown into drums full of concentrated acid. That night Ingrid could not sleep. In the morning her friend's mother told her that the incident had made the area very religious, and the girl's nerves settled.

During her stay in Hollyfield, Ingrid soon noticed something that bemused her. Special houses, designed to grow plants, dominated the landscape wherever she had travelled in Northern State. Called greenhouses, they offered similar climatic conditions to Southern State, but Hollyfield didn't have them. She asked why.

'My dear, Hollyfield is a place with a climate far different from the rest of the state. It's very sad that our beautiful climate is changing. Every year the graph grows steeper,' replied her friend's mother. Then she paused and looked sorrier than she had done before. 'Yes, the launches intended to bring about good have brought the very opposite to us. Anyway, we still have hope that God will answer our prayers. But when that'll be, only He knows.

'Unfortunately, more people are getting fed up,' she added, 'especially the young, who keep seeing worsening weather conditions and hearing empty promises from the state. It's quite sad, because our lovely saying of "best of times" does not apply to us anymore.'

The icy weather had completely frozen Hollyfield. Incarcerated indoors, Ingrid's dream of writing a book, which had begun after deciphering the college dogma about man and God, resurrected itself. She had carried out good research and developed a title for her book: Writing to Ease God's Expressions.

Ingrid chose to write it in anagram form (Twege), which meant 'let us learn' in her father's dialect. Writing it in a simpler style to that of the Holy Book, Twege progressed well, and the girl was sure the task would be easy. Yet, as the text grew, she found herself locked away in a room for days, writing and rewriting.

Her host became concerned and asked her to stop, but Ingrid was the type of girl who never turned away from her decisions. Her aim was to create a simplified version of the Holy Book. But what was confronting her was the phrase, 'writing and reporting is a talent,' which had made the late Pressman a famous lecturer at college.

Ingrid was almost finished with the first draft of her book when the newsman made the long-awaited announcement: College results for WAC bachelor students are out.

Although other institutions of higher learning awarded degrees to successful students, WAC awarded merits, and Honors First Class was written in green ink at the top of Ingrid's merits.

The academy had organized a party, which began soon after the merits were handed out to the successful students by the chancellor of the college. It was during this function that the best student was always asked to say a few words. Amid cheers of 'Reference, show them' from her fellow students, Ingrid began her address. 'People of God gathered here,' she said as people glanced around in silence.

Though taken to be a mere gesture of protocol, the Speaker was expected to address the guest of honor first. The head of the college approached Ingrid, probably to rectify her wrong beginning, and she paused. He handed her a small piece of paper.

Thinking it would be irreligious not to accept it, Ingrid took the paper, glanced at it, and then continued, '...allow me to take this opportunity to ask the good leaders of this land, whose titles I might not be obliged to mention, to take the issue of recognizing Southern State and help it to upgrade its infrastructure. I am going home, but taking with me a message that we shall work as sisters with equal shares of Dunia, as it is the wish of our creator. I should end by thanking everybody, especially those I had the opportunity to work with. May God bless us all.'

# Chapter 33

Ingrid's return home after eight years was a big moment. Accompanying her parents to receive her at the airport was the leader of the state. The occasion attracted a lot of people from all walks of life. Esther had organized the choir, which was made up of familiar faces, who had seen off the ruler when he went to his grave. The singers had improved with age and were now very good. Today, they planned to welcome Ingrid with a special song that they would start singing the moment she stepped off the plane and on to the waiting red carpet.

Things were hectic, but everyone felt happy, apart from Barbara, who looked worried, although she did not say why. Observers assumed it had something to do with not seeing her child for many years. Advisor, whom she had married, was well placed to understand his wife's concerns; the ceremony had taken place while their daughter was away.

The decision to marry was forced on them by the church after learning that the two were cohabiting. It described their relationship as sinful, evil and ungodly. They were even stopped from having Holy Communion. Advisor and Barbara promised they would live separately, and reunite after their wedding, to be performed when their daughter returned home. However, the house of God responded by barring them from entering the church altogether.

Advisor took the decision lightly, but Barbara could not. The church had become part of her soul, such that she was determined to fight  the decision.  She made another appeal, this time in writing, to the senior clergy in the region. After weeks of waiting, she received an answer in the form of an open letter.

"After carefully considering your appeal, the church has resolved to stick to its laws and shall make no changes to its earlier decision. The church shall, however, conduct the ceremony at no cost at a time of your choosing."

Barbara was devastated by the reply, yet in the end she had no option but to remain part of the organization that defined her soul. Two weeks later, she replied to the letter, asking for the ceremony to go forward. The church, in response, expressed its delight, and Barbara and Advisor exchanged vows of matrimony.

The brothers and sisters of faith organized a party for the newlyweds, but they did not attend. Barbara, who had always dreamed of her daughter being present to see her parents wed, could not come to terms with what her church had done. The woman spent days crying, unable to set foot outside, and those sad memories were now being rekindled by her daughter's return.

Ingrid's plane would be landing at General Fox Airbase (GFA), the only airport in Southern State, which maintained its name against all odds. Individuals such as Barbara, who should have opposed it, given what the general had done to them, preferred not to. Instead, they hoped it would make people have a rethink about introducing naming as part of their culture, and hopefully accept personal names.

The last time any airplane, let alone one carrying hundreds of passengers, had landed was to return the students, of whom Ingrid had been one, after completing their short courses. That was five years ago, and the authorities in the north had to ascertain whether it was still possible for aircrafts to land at the airfield.

A special plane fitted with geological cameras capable of spotting objects as small as building nails was dispatched to fly over GFA. Its data revealed that the runway was broken at regular intervals and overgrown with shrubs. The aviation authority in the north made it clear that Southern State should improve its facilities before any aircraft was cleared to land.

The southern leadership was searching for a company to renovate GFA when some army deserters from Dunia Modern Army, who worked in the Department of Field Engineering, volunteered to do it.

Thus Ingrid had to wait a long time to return home. She was even beginning to think it was payback time from the Millennium for turning down their offer to stay. Newspapers in Northern State had run many articles about Ingrid, every one of them emphasizing her return being a matter for the Millennium to decide.

Whenever the issue came up in the House, the answer was always the same: The only landing place in the south is not ready. Ingrid's request to take a small plane was dismissed; not even her passage across the stretch of water was granted. Incidents of marine vessels capsizing dominated the press at the time, and all cruises had been suspended.

The sea between the two lands was said to have strong underwater currents, and specialists of this particular study relayed disturbing theories about this evolution. One renowned environmentalist, who correctly predicted many things in the recent past, was keen on the idea of the sea hosting many isolated islands and mountains as a result of molten lava breaking through the seabed. He noted that the incident would be catastrophic, with large stretches of land along the coast being permanently flooded.

What surprised the people was that the Millennium was quick to warn against what it termed 'wolokoso.' Which they had to do because most industries were situated along the coast where it was warmer, and relocating inland would require more energy to run them, necessitating the construction of more power stations. Yet it was not even clear whether the heavy industries, on which the economy of the state depended, would be able to cope with the harsher weather conditions inland. Therefore it was imperative that the Millennium pass a law barring any newspaper from mentioning environmental issues without permission from the House.

It was decided that the plane transporting Ingrid would also take researchers who would carry out a visibility study for moving heavy industry to Southern State. Many factories had registered people for the trip, and a small plane was not big enough for all of those interested in the trip. But there was yet another secret behind Ingrid's return: Aan Savage would be on board.

While waiting at the airport to welcome Ingrid, Barbara recognized some people who knew her, and she wondered whether to receive her daughter as planned, even though they had been apart for eight years. So then why did I spend all that time knitting a flower to present to her on her arrival, which is almost the day of her eighteenth birthday? Come what may, she eventually decided.

When her daughter started to walk the stretch of red carpet, Barbara sprang from where she had been quietly seated. The two women met halfway, where they embraced and shed many tears. After presenting her with the flower she knitted, Barbara opened a piece of paper that she had been holding in her left hand. It was a letter that Ingrid had written to her.

Observers looked on confused as a wall of silence swept around the airport. Ingrid read through the parts of the letter that her mother had highlighted with a yellow marker. It regarded the antique that had been taken from the ruler's mansion, which she had found in the gallery in Eden.

Ingrid smiled and observed her mother, who was sobbing. People approached them in sympathy, but Advisor called it an intimate family matter and asked them to step back.

Barbara whispered to her daughter, 'I did it. I had to do it for your sake. I had no other way, and your father and I...'

Ingrid, who was becoming frightened by her mother's behavior, embraced her. After pulling away, mother and daughter observed one another with the motive of learning what the eight years had done to each of them. They had both changed, but the breasts on Ingrid's chest shocked Barbara the most, who covered her gaping mouth with one hand.

In contrast, Ingrid did not notice many changes and didn't wait to comment, 'You look pretty, Mother.'

'So do you, my dear,' Barbara replied with a sigh.

The two women then walked hand-in-hand towards the pavilion to take the seats reserved for them.

Ingrid was told she should say a few words, but the function would begin with a prayer, led by Esther. With the antique now quashed from her mind, Ingrid considered what to say. Many topics came to mind, but not one to fit the occasion. She thought about the Millennium saga, but, glancing around at the many northern delegates wearing smiles on their faces, she felt it was not the time to open old wounds.

Ingrid then considered the excursion, but felt it was also inappropriate. Since the time to talk was quite limited, with a cloud of rain threatening to pour, she had carefully worked out what to say by the time her turn came to speak.

'May I thank God for bringing me home alive and well,' she began as the word 'Amen' engulfed the entire crowd. 'I bring to you greetings from the people who have kept me, and gave me the knowledge and wisdom I now possess. Since this is not a moment to demonstrate what I have acquired these past eight years, I have something for you. I am in the closing stages of my book, Words to Ease God's Expressions, which I call Twege.'

Ingrid paused as the crowd cheered, before continuing, 'I believe Twege will explain, in the simplest way possible, the relation between us and our creator. It's true we are backward in knowledge, but this is actually only in structural knowledge, for we are quite forward in spiritual things. My sole message to you in this book is for every one of us to realize how precious we are, as individuals, before our creator, which I believe will make us understand Him more than we currently do.

'Our cousins on the other side of the water do not practice this much. God gave to them, yet they seem to have forgotten him. I am not their judge, but in my book I do urge you never to forsake God, however much you happen to possess. In God we must trust.'

While the delegates from the sister state took her words to be insulting, Ingrid's closing remarks made Aan Savage understand them differently. The phrase 'for God and our creativity,' which the northern politicians once took up as a slogan, was barely heard nowadays. Instead, speeches in the Millennium were debates that often abused the creator. It seemed worse when Aan thought of the common man who had turned the houses of God into structures of historical beauty. After that recollection, the president's daughter clapped, only it was late, and she did it alone.

As rain began to drizzle, the leader asked the people to forgive him, as he would not be making a speech then and there. Instead, he invited everyone to his mansion to celebrate what he called 're-acknowledging the pillar of knowledge.'

On the way from the airport, Ingrid was delighted to see some positive changes to her land during the eight years of her absence. Barbara, who was explaining everything, told her that the God-loving people had made a lot of developments. People had been introduced to the ways of farming with better tools, and Ingrid noticed how the gardens looked larger and better. When she asked how it had been achieved, Barbara said the God-loving people's missions had agreed to help finance the projects when her father approached them.

# Chapter 34

At the mansion, the men whom Ingrid had once known as guards were now soldiers, dressed in colorful uniforms, looking smart and alert. Somewhere in the compound was a brass band, led by a veteran of mixed race called Knots, who had been officially retired from Dunia Modern Army. He chose to cross over to Southern State with his wife, Decent, who was a violinist.

The local people gathered near the loudspeakers dotted around the compound. Following a prayer at the banquet, the leader intended to address the gathering. Everyone was impatient to hear what he would say. Some thought the leader should denounce the ongoing misgivings with the land from which the guest of honor had gained her education. Others thought he should talk about the girl only, and make no mention of the bullying state.

The wait was long, and gossip mounted as the people were kept on tenterhooks. Sadly for those wanting to gauge their leader's body language, the earlier drizzle had forced the organizers to move the podium and high table indoors.

Although the tables running across the guest room of the mansion were full of food and drink, in her prayer, Esther thanked God for providing what she called the 'little before us, which isn't what we need, although it is what we appear to want now.'

She continued, 'God, at a moment as remarkable as this, we ask that you provide us with food for our minds, rather than to fill our stomachs. ' The Amen that followed her prayer was a mere murmur.

Meanwhile, the bond between Aan Savage and Ingrid was developing like a chemical reaction. The visiting first daughter was an invited guest to the banquet with a reserved seat at the high table. Although she declined to say anything there, perhaps on advisement from the Millennium, Aan found herself feeling at home the moment she set foot in the leader's mansion.

At the high table, the leader sat in the middle with Advisor and Barbara on his left, and Ingrid and Aan Savage to his right. The conversation in the room went well, but when everyone began to eat, some faces became shy. Those watching the high table keenly could not believe what they were seeing – the leader acting timid.

The leader constantly ran his eyes romantically in the direction of the females. Noticing this, Ingrid and Aan just looked at one another. They had both just turned eighteen and had never had a relationship with someone of the opposite sex. To them, a man old enough to be their father was simply mocking them.

It was after the main meal that the leader got up to say something. While holding his glass of wine at chest level, he asked for a toast and everyone stood up. He then turned to face Ingrid, who was on his immediate right, and clicked his glass of wine against hers, which contained water. Unlike his usual speeches, this one was full of gestures. The man said almost nothing.

During this impromptu short speech, which his audience followed with their eyes wide open and their lips and hands making anxious gestures, the people knew their leader was about to demonstrate his wit; but instead, he gave a dry cough, thanked everyone for coming, and sank into his chair.

Although Advisor assumed the leader was attracted to the light-skinned girl, his wife thought otherwise. Barbara asked her husband if the leader had ever discussed any personal matters with him or whether he'd ever overheard him talk on such a subject. Advisor did not recall, but after running his mind back, he remembered the leader saying he might marry at the age of forty. When Barbara asked how old he was now, Advisor realized he must be about that age.

Although the couple did not talk much more about it, Advisor recalled the leader saying the girl he married would have to be young, well learned and a native of his land. He also remembered the leader saying that she should come from a home known to him and have parents highly placed in the state.

Advisor's heartbeat quickened. 'It's funny,' he told Barbara.

They exchanged suspicious glances when they recalled how this very man had saved Ingrid, against the wrath of the woman whose daughter committed suicide. After the hanging, they were planning to leave the mansion and find a place to live nearby, but it was also a time when the natives viewed light-skinned people living in similar conditions to them as a curse. However, Barbara had reconciled herself to being called that for the sake of removing her child from danger. That was until the leader, the heir apparent at the time, stopped it all by encouraging his father to warn the nervy wife against hating Ingrid.

Since that incident, they had known the leader as a dear friend and even promised to give him whatever he wished. Little did they know that later on they would possess something far greater to offer him. Before the party ended, the leader asked Ingrid to dance.

When the party ended the leader decided to approach Ingrid's parents, who were in their chamber alone, the girl having just left. 'As I mentioned before,' he began, speaking frankly, 'I'll be forty in a month and I should be marrying.'

Barbara asked whether he had found a woman to marry.

'I've been waiting for her. I told him,' the leader replied, pointing at Advisor.

Back in her room, a strong sudden hiccup attacked Ingrid which made her remember an old saying about overhearing someone talking about you. As a person who had spent most of her life being indoctrinated against superstition, it was simple for Ingrid to ignore the thoughts entering her head. But, after wondering what the leader could be talking to her parents about so soon after her departure, it was tempting to accept the saying.

The room was too warm, so Ingrid did not cover herself with her blanket. It was not enough, so she slid off her clothing as well. Sleep will probably come now, she thought, but, no, there was a ritual to come first – mosquitoes swarmed the room, welcoming her back home.

Ingrid's room had seen no one sleep in it for months, and the night-marauding insects appreciated the evening's guest. They attacked in squadrons. For eight years, Ingrid had never heard a mosquito sing by her ear, let alone been bitten by one.

As uncomfortable as the girl felt, she was finally at home, but sleep would not come. Sighing, she got up, lit the room and resorted to writing her book. As if understanding her feelings, the mosquitoes mainly kept their distance, but continued to sing one at a time in her ear.

Ingrid became so irritated that she began to hunt the insects. Yet, after she traced one on the wall, she recalled her school studies about the poor creature: it would risk its life to ensure its survival as a species.

In the morning, Ingrid woke up feeling too tired to write, so she decided to do some outside activity. She gathered some bread, went out into the courtyard and began to call the birds. While the people in the north fed wild birds, here it was domestic foul that came to eat the bread. Ingrid liked it because one mother hen and about two dozen chicks were among those eating.

The scene reminded Advisor of her mother when she first arrived. Barbara often gave bread to the birds back then and her husband was all the time bitter, because she frequently mistook new bread for old and gave it away.

Barbara was neither pessimistic nor optimistic about her daughter marrying the leader. But one morning she woke with her mind made up. She felt it was a good idea, because her daughter would be able to spread her bright ideas to the people with ease.

Ingrid tried to use her naivety as a reason to turn down the leader's request, but Barbara pushed her into accepting. Her

149

father had not been so forceful, however. Whenever his daughter approached him about the matter, Advisor always referred her to her mother.

One day, Ingrid told her father that she would not marry the leader after all. Advisor told her somberly that it might result in her mother being sent back to Northern State. The girl sat and observed him for a moment, but after a while she could not stand it anymore and left.

Ingrid went straight to her room and lay down on her bed. She began to see the bitter side of life. All this time she had wanted to make her people understand what personal decisions meant, and how to implement them, yet she was unable to choose her own destiny. The thought of her mother being deported pained her, and she buried her head into the covers and cried.

===

Meanwhile, news that soldiers were deserting the Northern State army began to make headlines. Rumors had been circulating of light-skinned soldiers viewing themselves as superior and the true natives of the north. Many soldiers of color had brought up the issue in a number of barrack meetings, but their superiors accused them of inciting racism.

News came over the radio one Wednesday morning about a mutiny, organized by Sergeant Brown, one of those having the highest rank among the dark skinned. It worked well since it was only men of color doing night duty at the mechanized depot.

One report said the mutineers were in control of the main barracks near the capital, and another mentioned the newly commissioned Antis being used for the first time. The reporter eventually spoke of General Fox being in control of the situation.

Ingrid turned off the radio to seek her mother.

It was hard to verify what was going on in Northern State, but the truth of the matter was that the situation in Eden was tense. Mutineers were rolling all over the city in military vehicles, and power had fallen into the hands of servicemen who were non-commissioned officers. All high-ranking officers, apparently light-skinned, had been confined to their barracks, and rumors regarding executing them were rife. The government had gone into hiding and there were talks of a military coup.

Things began to change later in the day. Fox spoke to the people over the radio: 'I am General Fox, calling upon the state not to panic. The army is winning the fight, and I advise the rebels to surrender before the harsh hand of the army crashes them.'

The mutineers responded by shelling the radio station from which the general made the call. It left a huge crater and claimed the lives of one journalist and two studio employees. General Fox, who was not there, was reported to be well and advancing with his counter attack. The streets were deserted, with people obeying the newly announced curfew.

Later on Wednesday, almost twenty hours since the news of a military coup was first heard, General Fox went on air, saying that the mutiny had been overrun. In his words the rebels had been dealt a devastating blow, and death by firing squad awaited them.

Statistics later described the cost of the one-day civil war as staggering, and commentators said it would take years for the state to recover—too much damage had been done to people and property. Taxpayers feared having to pay higher taxes for many more years to come, and they anticipated more scary-looking military hardware claiming right-of-way on the public streets.

# Chapter 35

Marriage arrangements for the leader and Ingrid not only ended a period of speculation, but also captured people's interest. The population would witness a state wedding for the first time, which made the wait so feverish.

Although quite aware that there was no known cure for ACID, as expressed in the report by the doctor following the death of the southern leader, Barbara tried to convince her daughter otherwise. She told Ingrid that the report was biased and wanted to turn away tourists from the north. Ingrid tried to listen to her mother, but something more evident was on her mind. She had read a lot of articles by scientists about this particular sickness when she was at college in Northern State.

Newspapers recording Pressman's death made it clear that the renowned writer had died of the same sickness as that which killed the southern leader. The findings about the similarity of these two cases had been kept in a special place in the college library. Ingrid had read through them many times. Everything the scientists said about the origins of the virus had been well documented. Ingrid then told her mother that it was true the family of the late ruler carried the virus. Barbara replied that she couldn't say that because no one had undergone a proper test to prove it.

Ingrid wanted to be tested before her wedding, but her mother reminded her that a meaningful test could only be carried out in Northern State, where it was currently unsafe to venture following a failed coup by people of her skin color.

In one family sitting while Ingrid was still at college, Barbara and Advisor had spoken at length with the rest of the family about the deadly ACID. Barbara and Advisor, after seeing how edgy the family had become, told the rest of the family to guard against stigma by not accepting that they carried the deadly virus. They appealed to the family by calling stigma the springboard for stress and early death, but their words seemed to fall on deaf ears.

In an earlier discussion Barbara tried to address the ACID issue from another angle. She asked the family to accept their bodies carried the virus, but seeing fear on the faces of her audience made her speak spiritually. 'Something beyond the means of man could stop God's plan,' she said.

Still seeing fear on the faces of those listening, Advisor felt it incumbent upon him to say something also: 'Strength is what life needs during times of fear, yet it is hard to find. Perhaps we should try to find it by considering how lucky we are. Many have perished, some far younger than us, while others live far more impoverished.'

Two days before her marriage Ingrid talked about ACID before the family. She told them that the disease was real. Nearly every family member, looking sad but determined, asked Ingrid how she knew that the disease truly existed. At first it was hard for her to answer, so she tried dodging it by changing the topic to her marriage, but everyone asked the same question. She quieted for a while, recollecting the articles she came across in the college library. 'The death of Pressman,' she began, 'a very famous man; it was unavoidable for scientists in the north going to extreme lengths putting ACID under intensive study...'

Ingrid explained how the disease came about. She said the virus that caused it was invented as a war machine, and that the mansion family must have acquired it when Fox's army fired a missile on the building when she was a baby. It was after this lengthy talk that was both scientific and spiritual that she advised being tested in order to know whether one carried the virus, which she claimed could lie dormant in the body for years.

The group had become somber. Barbara approached her daughter, whispered something, and the bride-to-be stopped talking.

Although it was regarded as unusual and impossible by others, Ingrid was thinking of making a public speech on her wedding day, only moments after answering 'I do' to the minister.

But what a bride should say to the crowd after tying the knot was something Ingrid needed advice from her mother about. At first she thought of talking about the age gap between herself and the leader, but Barbara called that a poor description. When Ingrid asked why, she told her she was lucky.

Ingrid thought her mother meant lucky to be married to the leader of the land, yet Barbara meant something else. Ingrid had not known that her mother was far older than her father. The short woman with beautiful legs and a young face kept herself fit by doing physical exercise, and eating fruit and vegetables. The result was as she wanted it to be; Barbara, who never revealed her age to anyone, looked years younger than she actually was.

What concerned Barbara was Ingrid's future life as a wife. Even if the girl looked cheerful in the days before the wedding, her mother felt that she needed advice about the task ahead. On many occasions she tried to talk to Ingrid about the ministry of marriage, but the girl behaved as if she knew it all. Yet, whenever she told of the Erotic Village experience in Eden, Ingrid's facial expression was nothing short of disgust.

Even Esther approached the girl, but the answer she got was, 'Aunt Esther, I will, of course, cooperate. After all, marriage is one of the issues I emphasize a lot in my book.'

The wedding day was on a Sunday and held in a newly completed house of prayer on the outskirts of the mansion village. Given the name 'Grand Cathedral,' it was packed full when the couple arrived. Women's piercing voices sounded above those of the men, but the military band was louder than everything. It was clear that the state was beginning a new page in its history as the different sounds mingled beneath the sun.

The atmosphere was ecstatic and the scribes were unsure how best to report on it. One would have thought this was due to the royal occasion, which, of course, was true, but the sight of light brown skin in a transparent, long dress made the people cheerful.

Many had removed their upper clothing while others, mostly women dressed in bright new gomasi with dry banana leaves tied around their waist, danced in organized groups. The people cheered, many with tears coursing down their cheeks. With the high table covered in all the skin colors of Dunia, shiny brown stood out fantastically. This would be the woman to marry their leader, and it was because of this reality that the atmosphere was so ecstatic.

It was after an hour of jubilation that the bridal couple finally found their way inside the Grand Cathedral. Praise was due to the army, who had been called upon at the last moment; otherwise, unarmed policemen were supposed to guide the spectators. Everyone, including the police, battled for a view of the couple. People who had been sitting at the top of trees descended when the bride and groom arrived. That was when the fight  began in earnest to enter the house of God and find a vantage point.

The occasion had to be rushed and many speeches were dropped. Then the orthodox allegory was asked, 'Anyone with a reason to stop these two people from taking holy marriage should say it now.'

The minister's request was met with loud laughter. Once it had died down, he continued, 'Let him or her not say it at any future time.'

There followed much heckling from the audience, which lasted for quite a while, rendering the famous 'I do' statement by the couple inaudible.

After the joining of the two people, the speeches began. Before retiring to his seat, the minister announced how the function would proceed: someone from the husband's side would say a few words and then someone from the bride's, followed by any other business. There were many whispers amongst the brothers of the leader, but no one volunteered to speak.

After a speech from Advisor, as a contribution from the bride's side, Ingrid asked if she could say something. The organizers were still considering her request when she rose and began, 'I thank you all for being here today, to accompany me on this momentous occasion of matrimony.'

People cheered.

Ingrid continued, 'I know, just as you do, that functions where people accept to live together aren't done this way here. Many of you might think it's the way of the people from the other side of Dunia, but let me assure you that this is the holy way of doing things, and it is also the way of God. And those questions the minister asked are in line and quite relevant.

'I don't wish to undo the custom of throwing a handkerchief on the man who will be the lucky groom, which brides happen to do in the middle of the night, but I feel that people should accept one another before coming to a life decision. Perhaps I should now turn to why I have used this unusual moment to speak to you. All along, you've heard my name, but none of you have heard the name of my man. Luckily, however, I've taken someone with a title, and the word leader has been said all along to mean my husband.

'Now I want you to imagine we are two people without title or name – how would this ceremony have progressed? This is my message to you: we must have names and have them soon if we are to be rightful creatures in the eyes of our creator. May God bless us all.'

# Chapter 36

Although Ingrid assumed the people she had invited from the north did not show up at her wedding because of her refusal to serve in the Millennium, Northern State was actually having a state function on that day. General Fox, who had called back the government from hiding after crushing the mutiny, was being rewarded for what the state called an act of gallantry. The occasion was a national day, and all government officials were obliged to attend.

With the rank of general being the highest in Dunia Modern Army, Fox's reward of promotion took the Millennium through a lot of haggling. Many deputies thought it unnecessary since there were no other generals, but others argued that Fox's actions warranted some kind of military reward.

Some suggested a medal of honor, which was rejected outright by Savage, because it would take months to formulate. 'Fox not only silenced the rebellion, but his project, viewed by many as wild, helped to avert disaster,' reasoned the president.

The entire discussion ended nowhere and the matter was referred to the cabinet, but even those members disagreed. Some ministers said Fox had climbed all the ladders, so what more did he want?

Savage felt more than a badge of honor should be granted to Fox and asked the military establishment to be revised. When skeptical ministers asked how, the president's answer was 'upwards,' which did not make sense because general was the top rank, so the matter dragged on even further.

After the cabinet failed to reach an agreement, the president came up with yet another term, which he called 'motion.' After quoting the constitution, he said, 'I propose a motion calling upon a senior serviceman who is a technical man, knowledgeable when it comes to military matters, to help us find a way forward.'

Not wanting to attend, the cabinet ministers claimed to have busy schedules and advised that the 'Fox issue' should wait. Savage hit back by asking them what their schedules would have been if the coup had succeeded. The ministers succumbed and the military man was invited.

Wolf, the man second to Fox in seniority within the army, said, 'The military does not count beyond three, but general, being the highest rank, is given the opportunity to have four stars. It will therefore be unexplainable in military science if another star is added.'

Whatever Wolf said just passed through the ears of those listening, because military things did not interest them. The ministers could be heard complaining that the coup would not have happened if the army had not been there in the first place.

With the motion defeated, Savage forced a veto, which introduced one rank above that of general. 'It remains to the technical men to make it fit well in their tradition,' he concluded.

=

After laboriously consulting the historical military establishment, it was learned that a four-star general who won over a rival army and deposed its commander in chief became a marshal. The establishment, however, found there were three types of marshal; namely, field marshal, air marshal and marine marshal. The president simply promoted Fox to the rank of marshal regardless, and also made him minister of defense.

In his acceptance speech, Marshal Shroud Rough Fox promised to speed up the trials of the mutineers in a military court, which would be formed by his ministry.

The very next day the president announced that Wolf was to take over Fox's old role. He would, however, not be commander of the army, but joint chief of army staff (JCAS) instead. Under Wolf's immediate command would be three chiefs to command the military forces of air, marine and land with their titles of air chief of staff (ACoS), marine chief of staff (MCoS) and land chief of staff (LCoS), respectively.

As the function progressed live on TV, the audience saw something new – the soldiers were displaying perfect orderliness and smartness. The officer who was standing alone in front of the smart, orderly men was interviewed after the function was over. The first question he was asked was how human beings in their thousands could perfectly take command from one man without a loudspeaker.

'It is called a parade,' began the officer. 'And I was the parade commander,' he added after a pause.

'How long did it take you to arrange all this, officer?' the interviewer asked.

'Well, not that long, but to answer your question, a couple of weeks.'

'Sounds little time to me,' replied the interviewer.

'Well, the soldiers do this right from the first day of their career. Perhaps it's important for you to know that discipline, on which the army is built, is what makes the drill easy.'

# Chapter 37

Life in Southern State had become better as people went to the north regularly and returned with goods. Although the phrase 'cross-border trade' was not commonly used to describe what was happening, these visitors always returned with essential commodities for the day-to-day survival of the population.

With time, the practice transformed many parts of Southern State, and many huge buildings were constructed. The locals called them towns, but the cross-border operatives who built them preferred to call them shopping malls.

However, the body of water separating north from south, known as Dunia Sea in the north and Middle Sea in the south, had widened and deepened. Those traders who had made the route a magnet while crossing on canoes became victims when their vessels could no longer cope. Many traders perished, sparking the first political task for the first couple.

Ingrid could not stand by and watch her community degenerate. In a meeting with her mother, sister Esther and father, who was now more of an elder than a mere advisor to the leader, Ingrid described what the trading sector was going through as 'facing forward, but moving backwards.' It was agreed that Esther would coordinate the traders and the state pay for the passage of vessels carrying goods, and then impose a tax on what was delivered to warehouses and stores.

In the recent past, Northern State had imposed a tax upon goods crossing into the south. A team was sent to find out how much this was, only to learn that the figure was more than the product and profit put together.

The southern leadership resolved to dispatch what it called a 'high-powered delegation' to the Millennium to discuss the matter. The team included Ingrid, a few natives of elderly age and some members of the mission. The authorities then contacted the Millennium and asked it to allow the visit to be a high-level state one. The House reacted with optimism and sent a special plane to GFA to collect the team.

Although the family wanted Ingrid to lead the delegation, she turned down the offer. Brother Moses the Shepherd, a light-skinned priest from the mission, was appointed instead. He was delighted and asked for the journey to be blessed.

In her prayers Barbara had a lot to ask for, including the unity of what she called the two peoples. When Advisor asked his wife to go to the Millennium in his place, she shook her head, but Ingrid said she had to go. Barbara asked to talk to her daughter in private, and when the two women reappeared, they had smiles on their faces.

The delegation that boarded the waiting plane included two light-, one brown- and three dark-skinned people.

Pressmen waited anxiously at Eden airport for the high-powered delegation from the south, which was dominating newspaper headlines. The first lady, Mrs. Ingrid Savage, headed the host delegation that was waiting at the airport with bags of warm clothes to give to the visitors on their arrival.

A brass band began to play at the very moment when the delegates stepped onto the red carpet, laid from the plane to the VIP lounge. The temperature was below zero and the guests were handed warm jackets. Even then, the host spoke of the day's good weather, simply because snow was not falling and visibility was clear.

Everything went well until a moment that made most people regret their presence at the airport. Some, especially those passengers en route to somewhere else, panicked, and children began to cry uncontrollably.

'Oh dear, very noisy indeed,' Mrs. Savage commented after the echo of the twenty-first blast died away.

'What was that, anyway?' one of the delegates asked.

'Gun salute,' she replied.

'What for?'

'Diplomatic custom for welcoming powerful delegations,' Mrs. Savage explained.

'What about the discharge?' another delegate asked her.

She shrugged. 'Nothing really.'

'What do you mean?'

'Only gun powder, no discharge, so we are told,' replied Mrs. Savage with a smile.

The delegates looked at one another in what looked like a synchronized fashion. They were then led into the VIP lounge, and while there the topic of conversation changed.

Pressmen interviewed the delegates and the cameramen covered it all. Ingrid felt that Moses the Shepherd was only scratching the surface of matters, because he turned out to be a man of few words, forcing her to take over the role of spokesperson. However, the fact that a light-skinned man was heading a delegation from a land known to be native to dark-skinned people had already made news.

There was more to report beyond the purpose of the visit. Another light-skinned woman, Barbara, was wearing shades and a large hat, despite there being no sun. Most intriguing of all, the brown-skinned female, who had made headlines in the Millennium and later at WAC as a student, was among the delegation.

If Barbara thought that she had disguised herself adequately, then she lied to herself. She only escalated curiosity, and the head of the home delegation was beginning to remember her.

Ingrid noticed her mother behaving in a way that made her vulnerable. She was about to panic and call her aside, but on second thought she realized it had been her idea to include Barbara in the team, so she was duty bound to help her conquer her fears.

Ingrid announced how they were looking forward to their stay in Northern State. Mrs. Savage turned to face her, nodded, and then said she looked forward to them having prayers together.

The two first ladies began to make jokes while Barbara, who was developing a sweat around her nose, wiped it off with a smile.

The journey from the airport was classic. Limousines escorted them, with paramilitaries on motorcycles, to the Millennium, where the deputies were waiting inside.

Upon their arrival, a brass band played the national anthem, along with a song from the hymn book that was meant to represent Southern State's song.

It was something the spokesperson had to correct before tackling the agenda.

'Thank you very much, honorable members,' Ingrid began, 'however, allow me to go off topic in saying that we also have a state song, which we call, "The People's Anthem."

Deputies whispered to one another, wondering how a state that did not seem to consider its people in its day-to-day running could reflect them in its protocol.

Their reaction only made Ingrid prolong her correction. 'I am also happy to inform you, honorable members, that you'll see more changes in Southern State, which should liken it more to Northern State.'

Her statement provoked some deputies to call for more details, but the Speaker rang her bell for order as the House became chaotic.

The opening meeting was not what the visiting delegation expected. The Millennium wished to understand every detail of how Southern State was run. When Ingrid tried to evade the questions, the president cut her short. 'Our state cannot commit itself if cases are not fully presented,' he said.

Feeling that the Millennium might take an opportunity to settle old scores, Ingrid asked Moses the Shepherd to speak. Seated between her and Barbara, the returning spokesman spelled out the aims of their visit. Halfway through, Ingrid nudged him. 'Excuse me,' he said, and turned to listen to what she had to say.

'Talk about transport in general, in case the water issue fails,' she advised, forgetting that whispers were audible in the room.

The Speaker said the visitors' position was now clear and called upon them to continue.

Moses the Shepherd was overwhelmed by the curiosity of the House and asked for help from his party. Ingrid wanted to give her mother a chance to speak, but Barbara, who kept her head down and had not removed her dark glasses, shook her head slowly. Ingrid spoke of the need for a water trade between the two states, which would benefit both. The Speaker announced that the sea route to which the honorable guest referred was closed and currently under study. Ingrid then tried asking for a waiver of taxes on goods entering the south via any route possible. The Speaker called upon the minister for trade to speak.

'Madam, Speaker,' said the minister, 'revenue collection is the bedrock of our state, and changing the way it works might be catastrophic to the economy. I don't mean that it cannot be changed, but it would need to be done in stages, which could take a very long time.'

'How long?' asked the Speaker.

'Months or even years,' the minister replied.

According to the president, the visiting delegation had failed to spell out its route to democracy.

—

On their way home on the plane, the delegation from the south was silent as their failure to achieve their aims stared them in the face. The situation was so somber that Ingrid even had to turn down her meeting with Aan Savage, which she had arranged earlier. She was so outraged, regretting every moment of taking over the role of spokesperson.

On the one hand, Ingrid thought the Millennium had refused to listen to their request because of her, but after carefully looking at how she performed, she cursed herself for concentrating on asking for taxes to be lifted. She felt that clarifying her role in the running of Southern State, which, according to her, had made Savage conclude the team had underperformed, was what made the north reject their demands.

She hated the comment so much because it made her feel what she hated most – that she had failed to deliver what was good for her people.

On the other hand, the young lady was beginning to understand how things worked. Democratization meant empowerment, revenue collection and accountability, but there had to be something to show for it at every stage.

# Chapter 38

The trial of the mutineers was fast, as Fox had promised, and the court martial handed down a death sentence to all two hundred servicemen. The men, all apparently brown-skinned, were summarily executed by firing squad.

The incident provoked more desertions of brown-skinned soldiers to Southern State, where almost all of them were conscripted into the army upon arrival. According to the southern leader, this was a good thing, but Ingrid saw it as bringing an egg that might not hatch.

When asked why, her answer was that the army had to be scrapped. Ingrid thought that merely enlarging the force was meaningless; she wanted the soldiers to trust in God, because the enemy they faced was far superior. The first lady felt that faith was the only way to victory for the southern army.

In response, the former head of the southern defense force, commonly known as chief of security, was heard saying openly that the gang had been increased from three to four.

Ingrid knew how verbal explanations could lead to misunderstandings and aimed to complete her book sooner. She would have finished it by now, but writing wasn't her priority. She was occupied by incidents to better the livelihood of her people, yet she wanted to cover everything she could in the book; of course, not forgetting that she was to make a subtle writing, the Holy Scripture, understandable to a population that was semi-illiterate.

Demand on Ingrid increased. Rhetoric from the chief of security making her number four in the 'leadership gang' was causing daily damage. She had to find a way to counter it, which she did by abandoning doing things from the mansion and moving closer to the people.

The first lady soon identified two major players in the society – the young and the old. After learning that the latter were against change and the former were moving with the times, she made a shocking announcement: 'A child by me will not necessarily be the future leader of the state.'

Hearing this, the leader pondered, 'Could that be the reason why she hasn't conceived?' But he could not imagine losing a woman who combined brilliance, determination, courage and beauty simply because she was not pregnant.

Meanwhile, Ingrid went around asking the people what they saw wrong in the running of the state. The leader, feeling that his wife was going too far, cautioned her, but she reacted by asking for a divorce. Having never expected Ingrid to react in such a way, he asked her parents to quell what he called 'a nightmare.'

Advisor spoke to his daughter about the 'dangers' the state would face if its people were called into collective leadership. He told her the current committee was enough for now, and warned her to take things easy.

As her father spoke, Ingrid recalled her promise to redeem her people. Refusing to remain and work in the luxurious north was not a decision that she had taken lightly, nor her marriage to a man of her father's age. Ingrid wondered whether her book, in which she had to explain the leadership role alongside togetherness, was a farce.

'Father,' she began, 'the only committee you are talking of is a group of puppets put together. Can't you see that? At this rate not even your grandchildren will see a democratic, developed and progressive state.'

Advisor told his son-in-law that Ingrid was intoxicated with the knowledge she had gained and was determined to use it, come what may. Ingrid's husband was now well aware that his wife would listen to no one, so when she said the township closest to the mansion needed a council to run it, no one dared to object. The issue at stake, however, was where the taxes would go.

The mansion had collected taxes in the past and handed them over to the leader, who was the cashier and accounting clerk. Ingrid proposed that the first family retain forty-nine percent of the collected funds, with the rest going to the township's treasury. With a gloomy face, the leader asked why. Ingrid was so irritated that she did not know what to say.

'I suppose it'll be up to the financial committee that's elected,' Barbara said.

An election day was decided, with the missions as observers. While Northern State wanted to field observers as well, either there was not enough time to organize it or they saw it as an expensive venture. Either way, it did not happen. The Savage regime was in its closing year, after all, and there were more demanding issues than a town council election in a so-called sister state.

Many candidates stood for mayor, but the real competition was between the chief of security and Advisor, who had to face each other in the final round. Family members were not allowed to vote for them, a ruling endorsed by the leader and his wife before what had come to be known as the election committee. Even so, Ingrid, while promoting her book, which was due to appear, thanked her parents for bringing her up the way they had.

The final result saw Advisor win with a resounding victory. People chanted slogans of 'Long live Advisor and the great daughter you brought among us.'

The project to construct a suitable council office, which Advisor had spoken of eloquently during his campaign, allowed him to beat his opponent with ease. The winner had explained to people about the importance of housing the council and how it could be achieved. He told them it was high time they stopped depending on other institutions, such as the missionaries, but instead, the town had markets from which a substantial amount of money could be collected.

Meanwhile, the chief of security, who had lost miserably, had a lot to worry about as he also lost his job. Drum Sergeant Knots was nominated to replace him, but the title had been changed to that of army commander. Refusing to accede to his successor, the defeated chief of security told people he would never hand over to gang staff.

The leader made an announcement as soon as he was told what was going on: 'The retiring security chief has to hand over immediately or risk spending the rest of his life in prison.'

The old security chief, who was thinking of dividing the army with the intention of staging a coup, was unable. Knots, as army commander, had announced new appointments, whereby deserters from the north would take up high office. Nonetheless, the news of mass executions of mutineers in the north was very humbling in the south, and any support among the soldiers for the foul-crying native security chief would be only empathy, not action.

The people, let alone the mayor, had seen how poisonous illiteracy was. If the security chief had been a man with some level of education, he would not have used his poor performance as a weapon to incite a mutiny. The populace had seen it all, and they were determined to have intelligent council members.

For people like the mayor, the youth would be better to work with because of their modern skills of bookkeeping and the like. But it was not a foregone conclusion that these young men and women, who had benefited in the education exchange program, would be appointed. Many elders who had been committee members in the mansion lobbied for positions.

Ingrid approached her father and told him, 'Father, I want you to understand that the youths I toiled with are seeking survival behind market stalls, and the few lucky ones are teaching in mission schools where they are given food, medicine and clothing as salaries.'

Advisor understood his daughter, but the job applicants had to pass an interview by the electoral committee, which would then give him a list of those viewed as competent for his final choice. Ingrid knew that the higher the number, the bigger the chance, so she began to lobby the youngsters with the message, 'Come now, let's build the state together.'

# Chapter 39

The Millennium came to regret how it had handled the issue presented by the delegation from the south. People were approaching their local councils, complaining of having to pay high fees to cross the border. After a while the ministry for tourism started to receive similar calls. In contrast to the northern coastline, where the sea normally ended at a level with the land, almost the entire southern shore ended at a sharp cliff. Landing sites were located in isolated places, making it hard to enter the summer state unnoticed.

With a steady cash flow across the southern border, the construction of the council building was progressing fast. Waiting anxiously to use it were the twelve councilors who had been nominated. Just as Ingrid had wished, all except one were youths who had benefited from the education scheme in the north. She now wished for the inauguration of the council to coincide with the launch of her book.

The mission under Moses the Shepherd would be printing Twege. However, although the book was ready, reports of there being insufficient copies to satisfy demand were commonplace. Those missionaries who had read the manuscript commissioned it as a true testament, suitable for a forward-thinking man and woman. Even then some verses were viewed as far reaching.

Some missionaries, Moses the Shepherd being one of them, said the custom of naming, which had turned out to be the central theme, was abusive when it described the naming culture employed by people of Northern State. After calling their way immoral, Ingrid stressed that names had to reflect decency and morals, and she called upon her people not to choose ones that exhibited creatures of terror, as had happened in the north. She urged them to take names from the Holy Book instead, but warned of there being too few to go around. She asked people to supplement them with things that meant decency in their language, such as love, peace and neighbor.

One mission priest challenged Ingrid by saying it was inappropriate to baptize someone whose name was not in the Holy Book. The debate dragged on until the matter was referred to the Synod, which was a gathering of senior theologians in the region.

After days of discussion, the Synod concluded that people could have many names, but one of them should come from the Holy Book. It, however, did acknowledge Twege for explaining appropriately the many 'dogma verses' in the Holy Book. And even went as far as praising the writer, Ingrid, for bringing scientists and believers closer together.

Thus, Barbara and Esther were joined by other missionaries in their support of the book, which shocked Moses the Shepherd, who had been thinking that Esther was on his side. In conclusion, the Synod did not ask for any changes to the original manuscript and ordered more copies to be printed.

Left alone, Moses would not accept defeat so easily and responded by bringing up another issue - the title of the book was not spiritually moral. One of the members asked the sitting to view the content and not the title.

'Why not use its true title?' Moses asked.

'We should understand that the book was written for a particular audience,' the other member answered.

Before the argument could become nasty, the chair to the Synod ruled that the author should be interviewed.

The next day Ingrid was invited to the Synod for the interview.

Dr. Whitely began by introducing himself. 'You are welcome, my dear, my name is Dr. Whitely,' he said, paused, and continued, 'I am the senior advisor of the church on spiritual writing and have invited you for a short interview about your book. Before we begin, let me congratulate you on this project.'

'Thank you very much. You are very kind, doctor,' Ingrid acknowledged.

'I can see how daunting the task was. Can you tell us how you came up with this idea?' Whitely asked.

'Just an awakening,' said Ingrid.

'Of course, my dear, such writing should be, but as we all know, Scriptures are hard to translate literally, and yet you seem to have done just that,' Dr. Whitely spoke.

'It's exactly that very statement that gave me the zeal.'

'Can you tell us why and how?'

'I have always been inspired by the Holy Book. But in my view, no version of it explicitly tells the needs of my people. Most of the verses are difficult for them to understand, such that even at college some of our lecturers used to ask us to understand them the way they are written. So, when I thought about it, it came to my understanding that the style of writing in the Holy Book was not for today's generation.' Ingrid spoke her last words louder, after she mentioned Holy Book, for the second time.

'Well, that is interesting, but why did you not write it in your people's language?' Whitely asked.

'At first I thought of it that way, but then I saw that a wider society beyond my people did not understand the Holy Book.'

'Can you quote what exactly they could not understand?'

Ingrid thought for a while, 'take, for instance, the verse and God created man in his own image; to many people, image is outlook, and yet the very writing goes on to say that God is a spirit that is everywhere all the time. To me this only inspires people to create spirits and eventually take up witchcraft.

'Yes, and that is why Scriptures should not be translated literally.'

'That may be right, but is it intended for mankind or not?' Ingrid asked.

'That is why we are there to give the meaning, my dear.'

'In my view that is why society is degenerating and shunning away from the houses of God, where preachers just want to show their talent rather than saying the Word in simpler forms. It is because of this that societies are condemned to hope, and it is because of this that believing has wilted and sin is on the rise.'

Whitely ended the interview and thanked Ingrid for her time. That evening the Synod allowed Twege to be printed and published without further delay.

=

The council building was completed, and a date was fixed for the councilors to be sworn in. Arrangements for the occasion were made, and a number of God-loving people from Northern State were invited. A military brass band, together with Esther and her choir, plus Mrs. Knots with her violin, entertained the guests.

The first family and the mission had jointly worked out a plan for launching Twege. Even though Moses the Shepherd had been pessimistic since losing the Synod argument, he still sent out invitations to all the missions in Dunia. Nearly all of the guests turned up and spent the evening at the mission, where the book had been printed. The assembly saw the largest number of people who worked for the ministry of God gather in one place for the first time, and they also agreed to ordain Ingrid, making her the first female priest in Southern State.

The council building was named Covenant, and a pulpit for its inauguration was built at the front of it. All of the guests had been consulted on the name and asked to choose between Testament House, Covenant House, or Believer of God. After a night's discussion, the people of God decided on Covenant.

The function began with a prayer, which lasted slightly longer than an hour. Then, what would make the book launch iconic followed when the leader stood up and asked to be baptized. When the priest asked for the name to be given, Ingrid, who was standing beside him, replied 'David Ngobi Waguma.'

The gathering was overjoyed when she mentioned the last name, which in the local language meant 'you endured the suffering.' Cheers went on for a long time until the priest could not wait any longer, because, for the second time, the holy water in his hand was dripping out.

The first lady, who already had a name, but had not gone through the ritual, also stepped forward to be baptized. When the priest asked what the new lamb should be called, David said Ingrid Ngobi Waguma.

The function then returned to its original schedule and all eyes fixed on the mayor, who, instead of getting up to give a speech, remained seated and conversed with his wife. After a few minutes he rose from his chair.

'Fellow countrymen, I feel it incumbent upon me,' he said, before giving a wide smile and a glance at his wife, who was also beaming, 'and also upon my family, that there cannot be a better moment for me to accept the ways of our creator than this one. I, for that matter, ask that I please be given a name on this momentous occasion?'

All of the people of God began to sing hymns. Barbara rose to join her husband at the pulpit, from where she asked for him to take the name Abraham Isabirye, after Moses the Shepherd faintly said, 'Let us give this servant a name.'

Barbara was forced to explain her husband's last name. 'Isabirye, just like Abraham, means father,' she said, and there was loud laughter from the crowd, because she pronounced Isabirye in a funny way.

All twelve councilors followed in a line towards the pulpit to be baptized. Ingrid announced their names to the priest, and when they were done, the local people took to the queue as well. When the priest eventually announced that the holy water was finished, everyone returned to their seats.

Abraham Isabirye stood up and presented the twelve councilors to the audience. In an order that looked to be upholding equality, every councilor said a short speech, which began with their name and function, and ended with a long prayer.

# Chapter 40

What had happened outside the Covenant spread across Dunia like a wildfire. Locals were calling everything that had taken place Twege, including the building, because most of them could not pronounce northern words. Things like mayor, violin, choir and brass band were Twege, as was the baptism. Waguma and Isabirye were names that made the people applaud Ingrid's book as a true writing of their culture.

Individuals jammed the houses of prayer, wanting to be baptized. The church could not cope with the numbers, so the missions discussed other options. It was agreed that people could stand in shallow streams where priests would conduct prayers and confirm their chosen names.

However, there had been no rain for some time. Stream beds were muddy, paying homage to deadly amphibians, insects and reptiles. The only places containing fresh water were deep, and not all of the people could swim. In the end the priests agreed that people should be baptized in Dunia's longest river.

Known as Kiira in the south and Line in the north, the river which started its 4,000-mile journey from the highlands of the south, ended up in the sea, and the journey to reach it would take some people weeks. Unfortunately, the priests were located in isolated places.

A synchronized form of baptism was announced. 'Starting from sunrise until sunset on every Sunday, people will stand along River Kiira in twos, collect water with their hands, and make crosses on each other's faces while saying the other's chosen name,' Moses the Shepherd said.

The missions made sure those people who were unable to leave their homes for various reasons were not left out by sending groups of volunteer priests from home to home. A few months later, the state declared that the entire population had been baptized.

Those invited from Northern State by the mission to attend the launch of Twege called for it to be introduced in their own churches as a prayer book. The Millennium rejected the idea right away. Those pushing for the book to be introduced were flabbergasted, because the constitution was clear on the separation of politics from religion. The northern politicians agreed with the campaigners, but told them that introducing something with the capacity to change or influence the established code of conduct needed approval from the Millennium.

With time, the politicians employed a different tactic. 'They lift taxes on our people seeking to go for holiday over there; we launch the book here,' demanded a statement from the Millennium.

Priests saw this as surrender and launched Ingrid's book in the biggest basilica, but it was not to be. Paramilitaries sealed off the place and told everyone to turn back.

In the meantime the Millennium was reviewing Twege, word by word. As expected, Southern State's non-naming culture shocked them. The House summoned those who were trying to launch the book in the north. Those invited would not listen. 'God's message to his people cannot be silenced,' was their only answer. The Millennium called their utterance a statement of resignation and promised to challenge them in a court of law.

All churches in Northern State began to preach from Twege, such that Ingrid was predicted to be God's future messenger, and churchgoers were eager to get a copy. They were met with, 'Sorry, we cannot help you, but it's on the open market across the border in the south,' broke the hearts of many believers.

Demand for Twege rose so high that churches arranged with their counterparts in the south for deliveries. The first consignment was impounded by custom officials, which brought the matter into the hands of the politicians.

Thinking that change at the top would calm the storm, the Millennium called for a re-election of Dunia's religious head, acting as arbitrator. However, the politicians were oblivious to the fact that all of the senior priests with the potential of heading the church were in favor of Twege being introduced. All of them had agreed to rename it The Third Testament.

The new religious head of Dunia, whose title had been changed from His Worship the Bishop to His Eminence the Archbishop, received similar requests from his church regarding The Third Testament.

In its examination of the book, the Millennium stumbled upon a verse that it could not stand: Man marrying man or woman marrying woman is the worst sin that mankind can knowingly commit... and man changing his status for woman or woman for man is a total farce. How do you expect to harvest apples from a mango tree? As for adoption, blessed be those who improve the lives of others from their natural habitats rather than take them away. For that is human captivity.

The Bill 'Homosexual Marriages Legalized' had just been passed, and more than half of the deputies were homosexual. The Millennium accused Twege of being antagonistic and contrary to the law of the land. Yet the church, under its new head, wanted the book to be introduced, and were preaching against an evil world evolving wildly.

The heated scuffle with the Millennium changed when some deputies received invitations to attend the ordination of the author. Mrs. Savage, as minister for religious affairs, was specifically invited to go, along with her daughter. The first lady wanted to keep quiet about it, however. A campaign to replace President Savage, whose last term was nearing its end, was making her schedule difficult.

Mrs. Savage was to battle it out at the elections with the most decorated soldier in the north, Marshal Fox. The other aspirants were not much of a threat, according to the first lady, but her journey to officially witness the crowing of a book that outraged some of her supporters was a thing to think twice about. But then again, her non-attendance could be equally damaging, if not worse, especially if the God-loving people and churchgoers turned their backs on her.

Mrs. Savage was on the horns of a dilemma and asked her family for advice. Her man appeared lukewarm, but was in accord with his wife regarding attending the ceremony, and they all agreed to keep it secret. The issue then was how to keep it from the paparazzi, which was following Mrs. Savage's every move. Savage advised his wife to announce that Aan was attending the ceremony, which she did, in a church after the service.

═

The function to ordain Ingrid into priesthood began as scheduled in the Covenant, and His Eminence, the Archbishop, was the preacher of the day. During his sermon, he praised the relationship between what he referred to as the two peoples of God. The Archbishop had said what he felt was enough about the two states, which he kept calling islands, when he saw the first lady and minister for religious affairs being led to a seat at the front.

The prelate found it vital to say more about the north and south. 'Allow me to thank the first lady of Northern State and the minister for religious affairs for having offered to be present in person on this spiritual occasion,' he said. 'One may think the similarities between these two ladies – name, position and beliefs – have forced Mrs. Savage to attend, but no, she has come just like any one of us. I hope she will have some words for us,' he concluded.

Meanwhile, Mrs. Savage, holding some flowers she had brought for Ingrid, wished to disappear beneath the earth, especially when she saw some reporters from the Pool, a press unit affiliated with the Millennium.

Guests were invited to have food and drink after the ordination. Ingrid Savage, who declined the invitation to say anything during the ceremony, mingled in the crowd while seeking the newly ordained female priest.

Ingrid was excited to see the first lady of the superior state, accompanied by her daughter. She started to engage Aan in casual talk when Mrs. Savage put her finger to her mouth and hushed her. The first ladies then began to whisper to one another. The daughter was standing close, but she could barely hear what was said.

When they had walked far enough away from the crowd, Mrs. Savage told Ingrid, 'Let me congratulate you first,' and she handed over the bunch of flowers, carefully wrapped in silver paper with golden embroidery on it.

'My pleasure,' Ingrid replied, smelling the flowers and smiling.

'Now, I don't know whether I could find a better moment to have a word...?'

Mrs. Savage was cut short by her host, who invited her to go to a more private place, deep inside the Covenant. 'There isn't a better place, my dear,' added Ingrid, showing her to her father's official chair.

Mrs. Savage had not answered when the handle on the door turned and it swung open. Abraham, Barbara and Aan entered. Mrs. Savage gave a sigh of relief and warm handshakes went around the group.

'Good, we shall have to talk some other time,' said Mrs. Savage, only to be asked to go ahead by the host first lady. 'We need your help. Actually, I need your help!'

There was silence before Mrs. Savage continued, 'We are faced with a stiff campaign that may see a soldier lead Northern State. I shouldn't have to tell you how Marshal Fox will treat you, as you must know. It's because of this that we need to help each other. I'll be standing against him, but opinion polls put him ahead of me. He's using the slogan "Unifying Dunia for One State" and claims the population will spend their leave here. He has already convinced people that your state is a summer province of the north.'

'How do we help?' Ingrid asked.

'Before the election, may you see to it that enough people who favor me will have immigrated to Northern State?'

Ingrid had been sarcastic in her question, but after recollecting what happened to her in the Millennium when this lady introduced the ODOS failure, and the manner in which Fox had reacted, tears sprung to her eyes. There was no alternative but to prevent the monster of a man from coming to power in such a strong nation.

'We shall see what we can do,' Ingrid said, raising her head.

# Chapter 41

Unlike the rest of the newspapers, the most vocal one called Daily Snow showed images of the two first ladies chatting together for over an hour. As the article was not specific on what was said, it caused readers to speculate and triggered different interpretations, which resulted in all sorts of arguments in all walks of life.

With ordinary people asking why Mrs. Savage had left without informing the state, the believers asked why she did not mention it in church, either. The homosexual deputies simply called her a treacherous woman.

On hearing what was being said, the president felt his legacy was under attack. Savage was quick to tell the state that as an ordained priest had written the book which the politicians were questioning, so the ministry for religious affairs was best suited to address the matter.

The retiring president also told the nation that his daughter had to accompany her mother because of the peer intimacy the young ladies had developed when she accompanied the writer back home. 'Dialogue has to have something to kick start it,' he concluded.

In response, Marshal Fox warned that Ingrid Savage was an enemy of the state and that the president's utterance was unfortunate.

As the two presidential candidates exchanged bitter arguments, it become clear that one was for the good of a friendly sovereign state and the other was intent on a 'Dunia State' that would draw its allegiance from Eden.

In the south, Ingrid was busy spreading the gospel of her book. She chose to begin by asking people to decide who their leaders should be. There was friction in her family, and once again the first lady threatened her husband with divorce.

Abraham also argued with his daughter, but he conceded when she threatened to take her life in a family meeting. Taking Ingrid's threat seriously, her relatives promised to respect her demands, of which they wanted to know more details.

'Grant, grant, grant,' Ingrid said as tears coursed down her cheeks.

Barbara got up to hug her daughter, before turning to the men and asking them to say something. The men looked at one another. The room was silent for a while until Ingrid burst out crying.

'Okay, let it be done your way,' yelled David.

There was total silence until all of a sudden, Ingrid said, 'We must work to ensure all is achieved.'

The meeting was closed.

=

In schools throughout the Southern State, Twege had made children understand that they were a true reflection of God. It made them realize that he was an everlasting spirit on which human life thrived, and that failure in human life meant hardship in the spiritual one thereafter. This made children understand that good behavior was essential if they were to excel in life. The basic principles laid down by the book were love, unity, respect for one's parents and elders, and good neighborliness.

In order to sensitize the children, the schools required them to tell their dreams to their elders each morning. Every day their teachers reminded them it was their responsibility to bring fortune to the state, which they had to do by following the teachings of Twege.

=

It had been awhile since Ingrid broke down in tears in front of her family, asking for more say to be granted to the public. The first step was to choose people to represent the view of the masses in an assembly called the House of Commons, which originated from Ingrid's catchphrase, 'We're common in the eyes of our creator and in our own eyes,' which she had used during her campaign.

This confused people, so Ingrid had to explain, 'We are not common in body, but in our goals.' She also told her listeners that the common goal was 'a common place that will bring together individuals elected by the masses.'

People appeared to understand, but whenever Ingrid asked questions, she barely received any meaningful answers. Realizing they only wanted her to believe they understood what she meant, Ingrid turned to those who had never opposed her ideas for advice.

One fine morning, after greeting both her parents, Ingrid asked to have a word with her mother in private. 'I am a bit stuck, Mother,' she began. When Barbara asked her why, she answered, 'Things aren't going to schedule.'

'You shouldn't expect miracles, my dear,' Barbara replied, running her palm tenderly over her daughter's head.

'Not necessarily, but I am overstretching to get my message across. I'm worried the election may find a vacuum!'

Barbara observed her daughter. 'Well, I can see you've lost weight. You need a rest. How about your husband, can't he help?'

Ingrid was about to answer when her mother continued, 'Wait, I was thinking that maybe we could circulate your ideas in the dialect of the people on a regular basis. What about that?'

Ingrid, looking convinced, nodded her head.

The lady priest began to call upon those who could write well to work at a special office at the Covenant, which would be called the Press-center. Individuals who had benefited from the education scheme came in great numbers to write articles for distribution in schools and village centers.

Although the message was similar to that of Twege, the articles were written in the local language, and anyone who knew how to read could understand them. By polling day, Ingrid's ideas were clear to the masses.

# Chapter 42

Presidential elections in the north and people to represent the view of the masses in an assembly in the south were conducted concurrently, which made it difficult for Ingrid to honor Mrs. Savage's request for help. Eager to learn how she had fared, the first family switched on the TV to find a newsman rounding up the results.

'Although the promise to break up the army boosted his chances, analysts believe Fox's last campaign slogan, "To make the Southern State a Summer Province," earned him the presidency,' the newsreader said. 'Many people cannot understand why they have to pay to get into a state where their spending will better its economy.'

In the south, the House of Commons was a finished structure opposite the Covenant, which housed the office of the mayor and council officials. Leading personalities had assembled in its gardens to swear in the people's representative. Beyond it, in full view, was Adam, the capital city, whose name had been passed by councilors after a long meeting. After narrowing the choice to New Eden or Adam, some felt that by choosing the former, Northern State would think the south was imitating it.

Yet that was not the reason. Some councilors did not have the chance to visit Eden, and they did not know what went on inside that city. But during recess, their colleagues told them about the Erotic Village and drug addicts. Thus it took a matter of seconds to decide on Adam.

But it was still a breakthrough. Aside from the state headquarters and the village mansion, which drew its name from the luxurious house standing on it, all places nationwide lacked a name. Villages were identified according to the number of hills they were from the nearest valley. Only settlements were located on high ground.

People had to count the number of valleys between given points in order to locate a particular village. Directions north, south, west and east were called up, down, sunset and sunrise, respectively. Village names were phrases such as Hill-one-up, Hill-one-down, Hill-one-sunset and Hill-one-sunrise. However, people preferred finger pointing while showing a particular direction, and it was because of this that identifying individuals with fingers was viewed as an act of contempt.

Those being sworn in as people's representatives were hoping to use the day's opportunity to give names to villages, but it was not to be. 'Some traditions are deep-rooted in the day-to-day livelihood of our society,' a group of elders who had gathered to witness the event told their representatives.

There was no time to argue the matter, because the function had to be performed in haste before Marshal Fox was sworn in across the sea in the north. It was feared that the history of missiles being fired might repeat itself, and David was ready to show the southern people they had a strong leader in times of crisis. After being sworn in as head of the House of Commons, he planned to address the nation on his achievements since coming to power.

The leader's public appearance brought into question the rumor circulated by the retired chief of security that the sickness that killed his father had struck the son, too. With David looking healthy, those people who had been considering the gossip were confused.

In a wild twist of the tongue, the retired old guard said David's appearance was a cover-up by a sick man being kept in shape by expensive medications, paid for by taxpayers' money. The disgruntled, retired man was the only individual known to have rejected taking a name. Wanting to recapture people's attention, he said that Ingrid, who had not been seen in public for some time, had caught the disease. He had also been telling people there were no state developments; a gang was personalizing the state assets instead. A small number of people believed the old man. David wanted to react robustly by throwing him behind bars, but his closest associates advised him that the facts would speak for themselves.

Ingrid's disappearance from public view was because she was due to give birth, and her pregnancy had been difficult. The doctors from the mission clinic who checked her spoke of the possibility of twins. Giving birth to twins was celebrated by an archaic custom, according to her book, yet Ingrid had not discussed what she would do if it happened to her. Barbara and Esther were always praising her for being a woman with all the characteristics of a great mother, so Ingrid became firm and looked forward to giving birth to twins.

Abraham and a few other councilors flanked David, who looked strong as he walked briskly towards the high table. The day was very bright and the army had performed its military parade formations, commanded by a deserter from the northern army.

The Southern national army, GOA, had changed in shape, color and relevance. Ranks had been introduced, and the parade commander was a major whose name was Duncan Dumcree; a tall, well-built man with a voice that made people straighten their backs and raise their chins whenever he gave a command.

As soon as David arrived, the people's anthem was sung. Then the commander shouted and the parade of hundreds of men responded in unison. Duncan marched majestically towards David, who was accompanied by Brigadier Knots, the GOA commander. On arrival, after a halt that sounded like the earth had broken, Duncan swung his sword up and down twice before kissing it. Knots took the salute as David looked on.

After inspecting the parade, David, who looked healthier than ever, walked to the podium to give his speech.

'Greetings from my wife, who, for reasons of nature, couldn't be with us on this great occasion taking place on such a brilliant day,' he began.

People in the audience cheered, although some supporters of the retired security chief booed.

'I ask you to pray for her,' David continued before clearing his throat. 'As you might have been told, this occasion will let us name our places, which have hitherto been referred to by counting valleys and pointing fingers. May I take this opportunity to declare that we are now standing in the village of Adam, which is also our state headquarters.'

There were cheers from the crowd, which lasted for some time.

'This occasion will also see the name confirmed of the place that will house our political elite. My beloved people, may you please join me in applauding the House of Commons for our political headquarters.' This time David did not wait for the clapping to end, before adding, 'And may I finally call upon the representatives of the people to take the oath.'

As the ninety-nine representatives stood up, Moses the Shepherd waited in a corner in front of a table, on which Twege was the most noticeable object. He led the congregation in prayer before people were sworn in. The priest began by asking God to give Ingrid an easy and safe delivery, and he ended by asking for the soul of a servant who took his life during the polls to be allowed to rest in peace.

David, who was to head the House of Commons, took the oath ahead of the others, which increased the number of members to one hundred. After the last candidate had taken his turn, people in the audience chanted, 'Long live Twege, Waguma and Isabirye.'

President-elect Fox appointed Aan Savage to head the ministry for religious affairs in his government-in-waiting. The population was stunned and wondered what might have caused the marshal's action. As if to divert attention, Fox unveiled his plan to establish another force, called marines, which would be the most sophisticated and battle-hardened wing of the army.

A recruitment date was set, and graduates from institutes of higher learning were offered top-priority spots in the marines.

With the training said to be unbearably tough, the recruits would start earning money from the first day of conscription. On passing out, they would receive pay equivalent to that of a medical doctor with ten years in active practice.

This outraged the taxpayers, who called for a protest match to coincide with the date of recruitment. The president-elect called the protestors bandits and warned of dire consequences for them. The outgoing president summoned the Millennium, and the two political leaders spent some time talking behind closed doors.

When they emerged, Fox promised to address the grievances caused by the creation of the marines. However, he also said the sea was the source of people's suffering and that it needed closer monitoring. In his view, the marines would make it their home, and act as an early warning device against hurricanes and storms that had recently become part of the weather pattern along the northern coastline.

The recruitment process went ahead as arranged and many medical doctors took part. At the end of the exercise the recruits numbered thousands, and the cost of training would require the highest tax increase in living memory.

# Chapter 43

The newborns in the mansion brought the first family together like never before. Ingrid, who had given birth to a boy and a girl, was doing well. It was a moment for the late ruler's family to put to rest the medical reports that had claimed their babies would not last one month.

All of David's brothers had dismissed the idea of getting married due to fear of carrying a deadly virus. It was worse for the girls, who could not come to terms with the loss of their sister, who had hanged herself. So, when David had tied the knot with Ingrid some four years ago, all of them had kept their fingers crossed.

The fact that Ingrid failed to conceive all that time only served to scare the women more, thinking the couple had decided not to have children due to rumors that symptoms of the disease showed when one conceived. Also, when their sister-in-law announced that a child borne by her might not necessarily become leader, they had considered it a consolation, as giving birth meant signing a death warrant.

People thronged the mansion on the day the twins were baptized, even though the family had restricted the function to family members only. For some time all of the churches had made the lady priest a theme, and the baptism of her babies was announced a week to the day. However, as much as the sentries at the gate tried to keep them back, the enthusiastic crowd overpowered them, and the party was moved outside.

While the two babysitters, who were employed as soon as Ingrid gave birth, were walking the twins in the compound for everyone to see, a woman in a red gomasi approached them. She reached for her waist and removed a bottle containing a milky-looking substance, but when she drew it towards the baby girl's face, Barbara, who had been observing every step her grandchildren took, screamed.

The bottle slipped from the woman's hand and fell to the ground. As the contents poured out, a dry, choking smell filled the air. People among those gathered in the compound to celebrate the twin's baptism pounced on the woman and asked who had sent her.

Upon hearing the commotion outside, Ingrid, who was inside the mansion talking to the organizing team, rushed to the scene. A certain woman was being stoned and scorned. The first lady battled through the crowd towards her, pleading that she be set free.

David, who was standing right behind his wife, had come with two guards who approached the woman to see whether she was all right. She began to cry and one of them slapped her, but Ingrid told him not to. The other guard asked her to say who sent her.

'I was sent by the retired security chief,' the woman said and burst out crying.

The priest, after naming the twins Barbara and Stephan, denounced the woman's act and called upon those responsible to repent. 'Babies aren't a thing to punish, however immoral you might be!' he said, calling it an unforgivable sin in the eyes of God.

The woman who claimed to have been sent by the retired security chief to harm Ingrid's children came forward and knelt before the preacher to ask for forgiveness. Her dress was torn and she was almost naked. The preacher, after momentarily taking a sympathetic look, prayed for her until people in the crowd shivered and sobbed. Finally, the preacher asked God to forgive the woman, whose name was later known to be Magda Kayaga.

At the end of the party, David ordered the arrest of the retired security chief, but his wife responded differently. 'It is high time the retired hero understood his mistake and loneliness, and came to live the way the people of this land have chosen,' Ingrid said.

The retired chief had a lot to reflect upon in his quest to undermine the ruling family. At first he had come into contact with someone who claimed to possess the power to send lightening to kill people, so he hired him to kill David. The man asked for many things, including cows, goats, sheep and a lot of money. The retired chief paid promptly, but the wait dragged on without anything happening to David.

Impatient, the retired chief could not wait any longer. He was told of a voodoo priestess claiming to be able to send deadly diseases into people, and he was convinced it was true when he met her.

The woman had supernatural looks, and when she explained how the late ruler had suffered in a way that only someone who had been by his bedside would know, the retired chief knew he had finally met the person he had been seeking. The cost of the job, however, left the retired chief landless because he had to sell his farm.

His last fight was that chemical attack executed by Magda Kayaga, of which he was watching every move from a nearby treetop. When the crowd apprehended his agent before she could execute her mission, the retired security chief, who had disguised his looks, climbed down from the tree and left the scene unnoticed.

A few days later, he was found dead in his bedroom. His funeral was attended by the leader and his wife. Ingrid asked for his body to be baptized, but all priests declined. She approached the man's body and nimbly made a cross on his face after dipping her hand in a jug of water. 'Man, rest in peace,' she said softly and asked for the microphone.

Reflecting on the construction of the bunkers, Ingrid said the dead man had been a hero. She then walked back, whispered to her husband and returned to the microphone again. 'Birds get up in the morning to eat insects flying in the morning, so is this folly by the insects, or are the birds lucky?' she asked. 'For I say to you, fellow citizens, that what we see as stupid is merely beyond our understanding.'

Ingrid continued by calling Dunia a battlefield where the children of light were locked in mortal conflict with the sons of darkness. The lady priest ended her main speech with an allegory about the sheep and the shepherd; the good and the bad; the wide and the narrow; and the chicken and the egg. After humbly asking Almighty God to rest the dead man's soul in everlasting peace, the first lady returned to her seat.

# Chapter 44

Newspapers and schools had made learning the northern language a priority, but it was not easy to break away from the local language entirely. Some individuals continued to label the advanced man's language, as the northern tongue was known, as alien and commanding. There were members in the House with such a mentality, which caused the House to split into two camps: resisters and modernists. The former were mostly people of advanced age and the latter, mainly youths.

Developments in the House of Commons worried the ruling family. On the day before President Fox's inauguration they sat after dinner and talked about it until well into the night. It was agreed that the mayor, who was an honorary member of the House and an elderly statesman, should arbitrate.

The House of Commons chose to listen to the inaugural speech by President Marshal Shroud Rough Fox, even when some members could not follow what the man was saying. Northern State was a model for development, and what went on there was crucial in the south; something that even those who barely understood the language spoken in the north approved of. Members who knew the language fully were always eager to explain it to their colleagues when in doubt. It was because of such an atmosphere that the phrase 'everyone is everybody' became a motto of the House.

Abraham said something about the mayor's role before Fox began his speech. The mayor was still talking when the entire House exploded into 'Ja, ja, ja!' When calm returned, it was amicably agreed that the press should translate the speech.

'Honorable members,' the mayor began, 'we all know what the arguments about the language to be used in this House are causing. However, if today's speech is to be translated, when being delivered, some parts of it may be missed. We wouldn't like to miss a word...'

Speeches by Savage and Fox were coming last, and the resisters and modernists were making many conflicting guesses of what the two men might say.

In the meantime, the aide to the incoming president was being interviewed on TV. Fox's right-hand man tried his level best to evade commenting on the newspaper headline of the week, which stated 'Aan Savage Included in Fox's Line-Up!' But the interviewer put it to him repeatedly until the aide found dodging the question impossible. 'Well, the post itself is not a cabinet post,' he said, looking up at the roof of the studio. The powerful lights hit him directly in the face, showing everyone that he was tense.

'Since when?' asked the interviewer.

'I am not here to talk on the president's behalf, sir,' intoned the aide, blowing out a mouthful of air.

'So, the president has made the decision alone?' asked the interviewer, moving his face closer to that of the interviewee.

'I will not answer that. I am sorry,' responded the aide, looking away from the camera.

'What can you tell the nation about it then?'

'I personally think that leaving the Savages out of politics can be detrimental,' reacted the aide with a giggle.

'Why?'

'They are the political icon of our era, don't you think, mister?' The aide said his last word with his eyes wide open, and under them the flesh had swollen like small bags.

Meanwhile, the Savage family had held a long discussion about their daughter's new appointment. As soon as she received news about it via the house phone, Aan's mother told the girl to refuse. However, when Aan told her father about the news, he advised her to take the post. The girl was in limbo.

After many family allies called the house, welcoming the idea, Savage, who had given up trying to convince his daughter, warned her against future political alienation. The mother's reluctance weaned after the interview on TV. She held her daughter's hand in the air and said, 'Go and fight even harder, my dear girl.'

'Given time, Mother,' Aan answered.

==

It was time for the outgoing president to speak: 'Allow me to congratulate President Fox for succeeding me, and may I also take this opportunity to thank and even congratulate my wife for coming second. Ladies and gentlemen, this is what we mean by democracy. History has a lot to tell us about those ancestors of ours. Please, I ask you to join me in thanking Mrs. Savage...'

The speech by the outgoing president was not long. It was generally soft, although he later changed his tone when talking about the relationship between north and south. Savage said Southern State had a right to exist, but not as a fully flagged state. He asked the incoming government to neither colonize nor allow the south to secede. After that, he uttered the slogan, 'For God and our creativity,' which he had not said for many years.

While holding the Holy Book in a rather usual manner of not lifting it high above the shoulder, as custom demanded, the incoming president took the traditional oath and then began his speech. 'At last I am your president,' Fox said and then paused. 'Before I say anything else, allow me congratulate you in this way. Fellow countrymen, I promised you a summer province during my campaign, and that you'll have. Let me...'

The Marshal President could not continue because the crowd went mad with excitement. It was only after the five-minute sound of guns, drums, and people clapping and ululating had faded away that Fox came back on air.

'Fellow countrymen, as you might have known, a potential modern army is now undergoing intensive training," he continued. "I promise you that the marines – the name of those training – shall bring the summer province under our control. Many of you might be wondering why we shouldn't use the army we already have, but let's make no mistake here; those who escaped after conspiring in the failed coup attempt crossed over to the other side to make a well-mechanized army. We have to attack before we are attacked. After all, we shall be fulfilling the military code of getting our servicemen back.

'And, of course, not forgetting that chocolate girl whose cognitive development we paid for, and continue to pay for with yet a higher prize. You all bear witness to this first lady of the so-called sister state, a woman of charisma and character, who turned us down only to go and assemble an army, both in text and troops, to eliminate this very prosperous state of ours.

'For that matter and a lot more, I shall not narrate due to limitation of time. I say no to a group of bandits in the name of a state next door. My appeal to you is to help the state build the capacity to eliminate this terror,' he concluded.

=

As the crowd attending the inauguration grew euphoric on TV, silence swept through the House of Commons in the south. It was true that the members expected Fox to be malignant, but the tone he employed went far beyond their expectation. There was nothing that could answer his speech, but to rename the only airfield in the state.

A vote was taken and the outcome was overwhelmingly in favor of renaming General Fox Airbase. However, agreeing on another name prolonged the angry sitting. Members discussed the issue for hours into the night.

Ingrid, who had her children to attend to, asked to be excused. The House tried to push on without her, but what President Fox had said haunted every suggestion they came up with. They chose to adjourn.

# Chapter 45

At Ingrid's home, her twins were playing with their relatives and Esther. The party to baptize the children had united the family in feeling and deeds. Possibly, the mother had not come to believe it, but on this evening when she came back from the House of Commons panting and cursing about how her children were lonely, her sister-in-law, Deccent, who had inherited her name from Mrs. Knots, had dressed baby Barbara in a coiffure. Mrs. Knots was also present, conducting violin lessons for the family.

The color of David and Ingrid's children excited the whole family. During the first three months the twins resembled their grandmother, and then they turned to resemble their mother, but nine months later they were changing again. The kids' hair was unlike either parent; their legs were brighter than their mother's; and their complexions were between dark and brown in color. Even then, the twins' general appearance was more like chocolate. Aware that their grandmother was against her grandchildren being called chocolate, the family chose to refer to them with the local word of mixed race, which was mareto.

Barbara was, however, very sensitive to what her grandchildren were being called. She made a frantic effort to know what mareto meant. No one told her what it really meant or its true translation for fear that she would get angry. Somehow she knew it and begged the family not to call her grandchildren what she defined to be nicknames.

The friendly atmosphere at home made Ingrid sprawl in a long chair. Esther, who had been following the handing over on TV, would not allow her to rest and demanded, 'Now that you've heard him, what next?'

Ingrid screamed, 'I have to talk to the pressmen before the morning paper is made!' She couldn't say why, but she continued to look uneasy and appeared to be thinking very hard.

'What's the matter?' Esther asked her.

'I'm concerned with how the press may cover the broadcast,' Ingrid responded.

'Why, are you worried they might have misunderstood?'

'Not exactly,' said Ingrid, 'but if they happen to report the deserters' part of it, then people will definitely blame us for the consequences.'

Esther was equally perturbed as she considered how the army in the south was formed. There couldn't be anything to make one more wary of Fox's legitimate intervention than the recent promotion of deserters within the southern army. Many departments had been opened up that were headed by them.

Most ironical of all was that of intelligence, which the army commander, Brigadier Knots, opened without even consulting the people at the top. He went ahead and appointed his brother-in-law, the one his wife followed, to head the department as director general. While Knots sent the mansion a letter announcing the appointment, he did not say much about it.

Ingrid, having seen that things were going astray, asked David in his capacity as commander in chief to revise all military appointments. He summoned the commander and asked him for a list of all heads of department in the army. David thought he need not make any changes because the list agreed with what he had in mind – everyone on it was an indigenous, dark-skinned officer in acting capacity.

The commander in chief did not know the abbreviation Agd, which the army commander had used against every name, meant acting deputy. David signed the list, confirming the appointments. Soon after, the army commander sent him another list of officers who had deserted from the north; one against every department. Together with the list was a letter explaining how confirmation of the names would make the army a well-balanced and disciplined army that was easy to command. David signed it.

Brigadier Knots, following the death of the retired security chief, knew his worries had finally ended. It was actually around this time that he appointed his brother-in-law as director general of intelligence. He knew that the person to make a follow-up, Ingrid, was busy attending her children.

Coincidentally, the lists of appointments reached the mansion when Ingrid was attending to one of her twins, who had developed a temperature that lasted some time. When the baby became well, a mini-party was held in the mansion to dispel once and for all the ACID-virus rumors.

Was Ingrid realizing the dangers of the deserters rather too late? The question now was whether it was possible to correct this anomaly. It wasn't the appointment or the army that was worrying her, but what the press would say about it. She couldn't stay long on the sofa, where she sat holding her head in her hands with her eyes fixed to the floor. Looking up, she instructed, 'Call me the guard!'

The guard was reported to have gone on a walk with one of her sisters-in-law. Ingrid couldn't stand it and chose to return to the House of Commons, but she could not find anyone, let alone the pressmen, who had left the moment she did, according to the sentry at the gate.

Turning back immediately, Ingrid got into the newly bought car for the mansion and ordered the driver to find the address of the chief editor of the local newspaper. Although it could not be discovered, the place where the paper was printed was found with ease.

Walking inside the building, she demanded, 'May I talk to the person in charge?' because everyone was giving her equal attention.

The answer by the person very close to her was that no one would be in charge until tomorrow when the paper came out, which made Ingrid order a halt in printing. Although they told her where the chief editor lived, either because she was too tired or due to her being sure the paper would not be printed, Ingrid told the driver to take her home.

What greeted the chief editor at his office in the morning was enough to suspend the sub editor responsible for printing the day's paper. The woman tried to plead for her job, explaining that it was an order from the first lady that stopped the printing, but her boss insisted that the decision was hers, and hers alone, to make.

=

The Millennium, with a majority of new faces, was busy trying to carry on from where the Savage era had ended. Although they need not follow in the footsteps of their predecessors, as the Speaker of the House put it on the first day of opening the House, issues such as the word-by-word perusal of Twege had to continue. The president was equally pleased with the idea, and the panel, whose members happened to be permanent workers within the Millennium, would give details of what they had come up with so far.

The head of the panel rose to give their view on Twege. Mrs. Slots Snake, for that was her name, made a very dull presentation, which made many deputies fall asleep. When the snoring by her audience overwhelmed her speech, Mrs. Snake rose her voice: 'Friends are neighbors, death is eternal life, heart is soul, children are offspring, sex is relationship... and I think the book is fine so far. However,' she paused and put her mouth close to the microphone, 'snow is replaced by cotton in all similes we know,' she said.

The snoring stopped and the House was thrown into silence. A land that had made snow a culture of tradition was shocked to hear it was not mentioned in Twege. According to the deputies, it seemed to address the writer's natives as its sole audience.

As the wrangle about snow went on, one returning deputy asked to know how the issue of homosexuality was treated in this very book. With the new House having more gay men than the former one, the Millennium realized it was leaving some stones unturned. A vote to ban the book engulfed the House.

Fox, a heterosexual known to have had only one sexual partner, who also happened to be his wife, was a staunch opponent of homosexuality. Using his veto as president, he asked the House to tackle what he called 'more stately issues.'

Then the Speaker asked the House to adjourn.

# Chapter 46

Barbara could not forget aiding many deserters to cross over the dividing sea and even getting them recruited into the southern army. Seeing that her actions, designed to help her daughter's effort, brought the very opposite made her think quite a lot.

One evening she chose to talk to Ingrid with a view to asking for forgiveness. As always, the girl embraced her. 'You did what was right at the time and I'm proud of you, Mother. We only need to make this army understand the value of the creator, the authority to guide them in the battles that face us now.' Both women had tears coursing down their cheeks.

Barbara began to read a prayer and asked her daughter if she had something to ask. Taking her turn, Ingrid asked God to keep the state firm and clean against what she called 'malignant infiltrators.' She asked Almighty God to turn the détente into entente. Then she caught fire with zeal, sounding like a frontline commander ordering troops to cease fire. When Ingrid ended the prayer, Barbara absentmindedly did not join her daughter in calling out the orthodox end word, Amen.

=

An atmosphere of war continued to hang over Southern State, and the church asked for dialogue. Although it was expected of her, Ingrid, unlike her fellow priests, never called for dialogue with Northern State during her sermons. Instead, she always called upon the army to take up God in whatever scenario the superior state would choose. '...Should they choose war, let there be war,' she often added.

Many people could not understand why a woman with such faith should react in such a manner. Some thought it was stress; others, however, felt it was a vendetta  for particular incidents she must have encountered in the eight years she spent in the north.

As if aware of what they were thinking, Ingrid quoted many bloody wars written in the Holy Scriptures. Her audience was stunned as to why God had allowed such things to happen. With the church quiet in shock, as if the speaker had just announced news of the Devil's army having massacred all the angels, Ingrid charmed her listeners by saying big armies were always the losers. The church could not help cheering after that utterance, and it always took a long time to get order back.

With the return of calm, the lady preacher would announce that 'Small is that of God,' which was always followed by, 'God created everything minute, but things came to multiply, seeing a disorder that in most cases offended him.'

Ingrid would prolong her sermons, telling her audience how nice it sounded to say something was small rather than big. Acting like a class of infants, the audience would start calling things small or big loudly. It was as if they were realizing for the first time that 'ka,' meaning small in their language, also meant beauty.

==

The House of Commons was to go into recess after the inaugural speech by Fox, but not until it had concluded its agenda. The first item to tackle was the renaming of General Fox Airbase. Yet, even before discussions could begin, members were already at each other's throats.

Some representatives refused to call the item 'renaming,' insisting that the current title had not been chosen by them, after all. This caused a row until everyone in the House was too tired to go on. Eventually, it was seen as pointless to carry on, because there was neither attention nor understanding. The only common thing between the resisters and modernists was short breath and sweat.

Ingrid, who happened to be neutral in this case, tried in vain to make the members understand that what they were arguing about was irrelevant. Such incidents had become routine in the

House, and it nearly always rested squarely on her shoulders to settle them.

She had wanted to bring up the issue of there being too much work on her head and that she needed an official helper. But with the House failing to decide even the simplest of issues, the only plausible thing to do was to go back to square one – the first family had to decide national matters.

It was after dinner that David, Abraham, Barbara and Ingrid sat around a table to discuss the agenda for the House of Commons. Basing on the arguments in the House, the family was faced with very many choices of names General Fox Airbase should be called. Yet Ingrid, in presenting the subject to the House, could come up with no more than two names. The family wanted the issue settled by a show of hands to avoid a prolonged argument. In the event of a tie-break, the trio, David, Abraham and Ingrid, would cast the deciding vote in the House. The family's chosen names were Portdown and Downingport, but in the case of a tie, they preferred the former, because in their view it was simpler for the local people to pronounce.

In the morning, David opened the House and read out the day's agenda to everyone. Society had not developed its writing talents to suitably mean one concrete thing, so reading was more of a clarification since the reader always added something to accompany it. Some representatives were poor speakers, and, as a rule, someone had to clarify what they said; a task usually conducted by Ingrid.

Today, she asked the House to appoint someone to assist her. It was soon agreed that the chief editor should lighten the first lady's workload.

Ingrid announced the two names to replace General Fox Airbase, as agreed by the first family. The debate did not last long. The House settled on the name of Downingport. Ingrid glanced around as she asked for hands to be raised again. The second count saw David and Abraham also count. The House had decided by a big margin to rename General Fox Airbase Downingport, and it remained for the press to make it public.

A clear message had been sent to Fox: We don't care, and you should know what the people's representatives think of you here. The first question was what action the retired marshal would take. The second was what courses were open if he responded in the way everyone in the House was predicting – flying in his super jets filled with battle-hardened men!

The eventuality hit all of the representatives in the House like a scorpion sting. It was decided to keep the renaming of the airport out of the media until the army commander had been contacted for advice.

# Chapter 47

It was the day to decide the fate of Twege in the Millennium. Many people guessed it would be banned, which reflected the panel's position. Anything to avert that would be a miracle, Mrs. Snake had told the minister for religious affairs in an interview on her request.

Aan Savage had begun her career very tensely indeed. By meeting the head of the panel, she wanted to acquaint herself with the book in question. It had been written by a friend, after all. Whenever she imagined Ingrid's book being banned, Aan remembered the day she accompanied the author after her studies and how they interacted in the mansion. Unable to handle it, tears flowed from her eyes, and she regretted accepting the appointment in Fox's government.

Ingrid, on her part, had counted the Savages as lost friends of the past since her failure to send people to boost Mrs. Savage's bid for presidency. It was because of this feeling that she had not sent them a copy of Twege. Mrs. Savage had been the only invited guest to have presented her with flowers on her ordination, and Ingrid felt sorry for the way she had handled her request. But one thing the lady priest had learned with time was to assure herself that everything would be all right.

It was the president who addressed the Millennium but, of course, only after the Speaker had invited him. Mister Speaker, whose real name was Wood Tiger, was a man who had won respect in the House for being authoritarian and non-aligned. 'First come, first served' was the principle by which he worked, always selecting people to speak who raised their hands first.

Early on as Speaker, Tiger had asked someone to talk, instead of President Fox, who was to answer something in a heated debate. Fox refused to sit down as the chosen deputy began to speak. Tiger rang his bell, asked the president to remain seated, and then called upon the deputy holding the floor to carry on. Fox sat down reluctantly. The entire House cheered.

From that day on, the believers always told Tiger that he was a gift from God, and the seculars called him a true tiger in the woods. Since that incident, every deputy addressed Tiger by his title rather than his name, which was the case even outside the Millennium.

Tiger becoming Speaker was something the deputies had long had their fingers crossed for. Most of them thought Fox would not accept their vote and favor his fellow soldier, a retired servicemen turned deputy, who lost to Tiger in a secret ballot. His refusal to reign in the tradesman made the deputies see what a different man Fox was as president.

However, today's decision on Twege would be Fox's real test. Unlike his predecessor, he bowed towards the Speaker before addressing the House.

'Mister Speaker, ladies and gentlemen of the House,' he said before bowing again, this time towards the four corners of the House. 'We all know why we're here today. But before I say my opinion on that book, may I inform the House that the marines have completed their course and will be conducting their final exercise in the sea around Hollyfield, where we all know is the shortest crossing into the summer province. This, ladies and gentlemen, is to send a message in word and action to our so-called sister state that we are coming, and coming in force.'

Fox quieted because the House had become rowdy. As usual, the Speaker was already on his feet, calling for order.

'Oh, yes, I promised a mandate, and I've to give it to them just like any disciplined soldier would,' the president said, glancing around the House before sitting down.

People looked at one another. A report just published on the sea had warned beachgoers of dangerous creatures inhabiting the area around Hollyfield. How then, thought the deputies, could people risk their  lives in the sea, moreover in that same dangerous area? They assumed the marines would venture into the water with special equipment, and they even looked forward to seeing it. That was when a deputy asked if the nation was welcome to watch and how the exercise was to proceed.

The commander in chief rose and replied, 'It is a national army, so why not; and after all, its formation was made possible by taxpayers. Regarding the last part of your question, we have trained them at a high cost, and it's high time we realized what we have achieved. However, I cannot answer you on how it will proceed. What I can say is that it should follow the military ethos that the more blood there is in training, the less it becomes in war. Now, turning to the book, the report before me is in favor of banning it, but I think the minister concerned should give the House her views.'

Aan took some time to stand. She was observing the other legislators who, like her, seemed to be mumbling a similar phrase to themselves, 'Goodness me, quite unpredictable, this Fox man!'

'Mister Speaker,' Aan began, 'I feel more than esteemed to be given this chance of saying something, which in the real fact has a place in determining our cultural destiny. It's more than sad that the panel had to come to such a conclusion of favoring to ban such a book. I want all of us to look at where our society, especially the youths, are going, and what we have done about it.

'Drugs are on the increase, alcohol is free in most bars twenty-four/seven, and the rich have nothing to do but compete in the roundhouses. Casinos are gambling with carnage in a new game called Dunia-roulette, which has claimed many deaths behind the scenes.

'But, above all, honorable deputies, what could bring confidence back other than this book? One could say that the Holy Book should, all right, but it doesn't reflect us directly – it reflects the man who came before us. We are detached from it by many generations, and, please, Twege is the modern-day version that goes with our times.

'The Holy Book talks about a rising sun on a daily basis, but how often do we see that these days? I agree some parts in the book go to the bone marrow, but that's the fact of the matter, so why don't we face it?

'Take, for example, sexual penetration between man and other animals. If fertilization took place, what sort of creatures would be produced by that? What sort of discipline will they bring in this already fragile society? So please, let's give our people what they deserve, rather than what we think they should have,' Aan concluded.

The homosexuals in the House booed her throughout.

Offering yet another surprise, the president said the book had to be allowed a chance in the communities where it was welcome.

=

The House of Commons followed the Millennium session closely. The closing speech from Aan was cheered, but the one by Fox was received with mixed feelings. Ingrid was to read a statement from the army commander to the House, but the unexpected atmosphere in the Millennium made her pause.

Brigadier Knots' statement vowed punitive action if the Fox army 'dared.' In the statement it was said that the latest military hardware, made in the north and capable of intercepting missiles, was in the south army's possession, ready for deployment. This was not true, but Knots had always said that in a belligerent situation, a 'war of words' can form a formidable force.

Having used statistics based on Dunia Modern Army's production line, as given by the director general of military intelligence, the statement looked believable. Ingrid did not read it, however. Instead, she told the House to have a word with the army commander first and that they would be hearing from her in the next session. It was also agreed that danger was anticipated, and the renaming of General Fox Airbase was stalled.

# Chapter 48

The partial lifting of a ban on Twege freed up the impounded consignment, and cash began to flow in via the missions, alleviating the situation in Southern State. Churches in Northern State had, meanwhile, made numerous orders. A plane that was to bring students in the south on holiday, which had been delayed, was to take tens of thousands of books back with it. The problem, however, was that demand was higher than production.

The church became impatient and the archbishop arranged for Twege to be produced locally in the north. Permission by the author was granted. After only one month of steady output from the church's central printing house, sales of the book brought in a lot more money.

The church advised Ingrid to allow its subdivision in her state, which in this particular correspondence was called Province of the South, to receive the money on her behalf. According to the law of the church, the sum was too large to be paid directly to an individual. Ingrid was reminded in this very correspondence that thirty percent of these earnings had to go to the needy.

She wanted to query the percentage, because she knew the catechism spoke of ten percent, but she let it to be; after all, the money would be going to her people.

A few weeks later, Ingrid received a letter:

Dear Author,

Let me first of all thank your efforts in putting down such wisdom. The Synod has asked me to be the bringer of more good news in letting you know how the thirty percent for the needy will be distributed.

First on the list are the people selling their bodies for survival in places like EPIC, and a lot more places of this kind that have sprung up in cities throughout north Dunia.

In the second category are the victims of the disastrous launch in Hollyfield; and third, but not least, are the poor families in the south of Dunia.

I remain yours in faith,
Dean of the Church

Although Ingrid had hoped for the cash to better the living standards of her own people, the Synod's decision had settled a debt that had become a living nightmare for her. Although she started writing her book in Hollyfield, where she was invited to stay by a school colleague, she had not contacted the family ever since.

The spiritual firmness of that household had been a pillar to the critical verses in her book about the society in the 'developed' north. She had either lost the family's address or found no time to look it up. It haunted her because they were the most magnanimous family she had known.

=

It came as a surprise to all the students who had attended courses in the only college in Adam when their graduation was announced. The occasion was to take place on a weekend in the gardens of the Covenant. David would be the guest of honor, to hand the successful students their diplomas.

The college had many disciplines, and a number of students had completed their studies only to walk away with just the word 'pass' or 'fail.' It made the failures taunt the victors with 'What do you have that I don't?' When those who had passed their exams asked how they were to show their performance when searching for jobs, staff told them to ask their employees to contact the college when in doubt.

In this way the failures were given a lifeline; they simply turned up claiming to have passed. The college was informed of this fraud, so it began handing out recommendations to the successful students in which their discipline, general achievements and behavior were stated.

The fact that no mention was made of the student's level of achievement was good news for employers. Employment law stated that the higher the grade, the higher the salary, so the employers paid their workers a flat rate.

Things were very hectic for the mansion family as the graduation ceremony approached. All of David's brothers and sisters were graduating, but the youngest, Fredrick, who had studied engineering, was the most excited. Completion of his course coincided with graduation day. Fredrick had been a keen scholar since childhood. Always by his father's side, he was a boy with an inquisitive mind.

Many elders felt it should have been Fredrick who led the nation, but his father died when he was too young. When he grew up, the elders under the influence of the late chief of security approached him to challenge his brother, but Fredrick turned a deaf ear and continued to respect his father's decision while pushing on with his studies.

The other brothers had taken lighter and shorter courses such as driving, tailoring, building and teaching. Scorn was directed at the one who chose cooking. As a man, Joseph had high hopes of opening and running a hotel, but since there was no special course for hotel management, he could not go beyond learning normal cooking. Traditionally, this wasn't a discipline for men, which is why his brothers teased him most of the time, asking, 'Which woman will marry you, and who will be cooking?'

The brothers were not following the direction in which the state was heading. Although the slogan of most politicians was: We don't want to resemble the developed north, their actions were contrary, and cooking for men was gaining fame, as in the north, where men doing it were celebrities.

The story for the sisters was not far removed from that of the boys, apart from Mary who, after falling in love with a mansion guard, dropped a long course of teaching and took up tailoring instead. She was proposing to tie the knot; a ceremony that the family would be seeing for only the second time. Her decision made David and Ingrid like her, because the other sisters got involved in relationships that never lasted.

Everything had been prepared in the gardens. Graduates were assembled in various colors, according to their discipline. Engineering was the most respected, and these students took up the front row wearing red hats. Since there was no full medical faculty, the second row was for doctor assistance and teachers, who wore greenish-yellow hats. The remainder sat without hats in rows of what the organizers called recession.

It was agreed that every graduate would have his or her diploma enclosed in Twege in a development that called for the author of the book to say a word or two before inviting the guest of honor to crown the ceremony.

Ingrid was short in her words, but direct to the point: 'Everything is there for you to see. I argue you to read Twege at least once a day. Best is before beginning the day's work and at the end of it. Finally, allow me call the crowd to notice the new state slogan of: Everyone is Everybody.'

The crowd yelled back.

'Now I call the guest of honor to decorate the young trees.'

David, in his opening speech, was more dynastic. He thanked his brothers and sisters for the cooperation they had shown since the death of their father, but he gave special thanks to Fredrick as he called him forward to be the first graduate to receive his coronation.

It was during this that the 'People's Anthem' was sung. With nearly every priest choosing to keep people's eyes closed for a long time, the people preferred their anthem, which was shorter and only demanded that they stand.

The day was not long enough for each individual graduate to have their coronation, so a general one was performed. After all, the guest of honor had presented the red hats with their diplomas in person.

# Chapter 49

It was tense in Hollyfield and all the areas surrounding it. The public was talking about the government dismissing requests made by the deputies representing the area to change the venue for the marines' final exercise. And the day had finally come.

People thought their deputies were lying, only for them to be proven true at the last moment – the exercise was to be conducted in their area, and marines would be dropped from low-flying planes into Dunia Sea. A viewing glass of great size was being constructed on the seashore.

When the residents asked what it was and why it was being built, the constructors said it was a magnifying glass to shield the podium from poor visibility of the exercise. The workmen told anyone asking how the marine pass-out would be conducted. Locals thought the men were being cooperative, but the fact was they had orders to induce residents to attend the function. Area deputies had shown disregard for the matter.

'Commands will be given by a gunshot and marines will jump down into the sea to combat the fiercest water creatures. It will be nice to watch,' the military field engineers contracting the site told curious locals.

Deputies from the area had offered not to attend. They claimed the exercise, which the minister for defense had explained to the House, bore the trait of what happened when a fired launch failed.

Fox reacted by using his power of veto. 'All deputies have to attend without fail. Those unable due to health reasons should seek official leave from the director of medical services.'

There was no point in anyone trying to call on that director. The man was a retired soldier and Fox's former campaign manager, who was seen by the deputies as capable of acting rougher than the president. Therefore, everyone turned up at the event, along with a handful of invited guests that included the Savages.

Unlike most national functions, this one had speeches as the last item on the agenda. Right at the tick of the hour, as scheduled, the exercise began with a gunfire that sent vibrations through the entire area, as if the earth was caving in. Those deputies who had lost touch with time were too late for the blast, which caught them without earphones.

Neither residents nor guests dwelled much on asking what the day had to deliver. The marines were dropped from low-flying planes into the sea at random. As soon as the first detail, which involved well over 100 men, struck the water, giant deadly creatures charged for the day's meal. It was a race for their lives as the men had to swim the one-mile stretch separating them from the point of victory, ashore.

Each marine was armed with two knifes; a normal one that was rough on one side and sharp on the other, plus another that could elongate and shorten when pressed at the handle. They also had torches on the front of their helmets.

There was a contest among the men to see who made it ashore first. But when the sea monsters caught up with them, the spectacle turned into a game of survival of the fittest. Most of the crowd could not stand the sight as casualties began to fall on either side. Those who were courageous enough to watch could barely see what was going on, as the sea was full of blood.

Then the chief instructor made an announcement, 'Ladies and gentlemen, searchlights are now at work.' The man spoke with the demeanor that what was taking place was fun. After about a quarter of an hour a gunshot was fired. Soon after, a fresh squadron of planes dropped more men into the sea. Those people who had vowed not to watch were caught responding with intuition and empathy. This time there was more carnage than before. The crowd appeared to blame their eyes as they tried to look away.

The exercise progressed in the same way until the last detail. Those who managed to come ashore were dressed in blood, some missing parts of their bodies. Surprisingly, however, those with what were deemed to be minor injuries, such as a lost finger, ear or bodily cuts, had to stand at attention until the last detail, right through to the very last man, came ashore.

The man who happened to be the last came ashore roughly five hours after the start of the exercise. Then the military brass band sang the national anthem. Afterwards, President 'retired' Marshal Shroud Rough Fox, the commander in chief of Dunia Modern Army, rose to give his speech.

'Let this send a message where it is intended,' he said, 'that we are more than ready to acquire what we desire. To you, marines, there are no accidents in the army; neither are there mistakes or excuses. It's punishment for anything done wrong, which may not necessarily be wrong, but contrary to the norm...'

He was still talking when a soldier of very senior rank appeared and asked to have a word with General Wolf, who was standing next to the president. This attracted Fox's attention and brought silence. The president, nevertheless, came back immediately by asking for a pardon. He was about to continue speaking when General Wolf handed him a chit.

'Good,' Fox said after a quick look thorough the message. 'Not very many missing in action,' he said with a giggle. 'Let me thank the instructors for a job well done, and I salute all of you who have made it ashore.

'Before you take your commission, it is my duty to remind you that every step a soldier takes is a step closer to death, yet it's also a step to save millions of lives. Today you have started to tow that line. Thank you very much!'

The president saluted, and for the first time the marines smiled; they actually showed their front teeth for about a second. The military elite were led by General Wolf to begin the momentous and soothing occasion of commissioning.

Although the emblem of the army was a gun crossed against a sword, the marines got a different one. Theirs was golden with an eagle flying above the sea gripping a very large fish in its feet. Any fool could interpret the eagle for Northern State and the fish for the south.

The people of Hollyfield could not believe it when the podium and the great glass were brought down. Many asked why it was being moved, and they were told that the exercise was over. Oddly, those telling them sounded sorry, not knowing what the locals meant of it.

Many people were now planning to leave the place and find some other area to live, but the local church pleaded for them to stay.

The following morning was a Sunday, and more people in Hollyfield thronged the houses of prayer than ever before. For those with a habit of taking a walk along the shoreline, it was a marathon run back to their homes. Bodies of humans and water creatures had swept ashore in great numbers. The stench of rotten fresh covered all surrounding areas and the city of Hollyfield itself.

News of what had happened during the pass-out exercise for the marines was being followed live in the well-to-do homes of Southern State. Shock and disbelief made most of them switch off their television sets. As for the army, they feared these men that they would face on the frontline.

The commander in chief at the mansions summoned the army commander. David wanted to know what to do, but Brigadier Knots couldn't think of anything. The army commander was now sure that war with a superior force in the north was inevitable. Knots sat silently facing his boss as if he had been struck by lightning.

After hearing her husband bang the table and talking at the top of his voice, Ingrid rushed to find out what was happening. David was talking to himself because Brigadier Knots was still like a statue whose face is fixed to the floor. 'Tasks need to be allotted to people nationwide,' she said when her man paused his erratic actions.

'How?' Her man asked.

'Call the House of Commons immediately,' she answered.

# Chapter 50

As the House of Commons was struggling to limit the fear caused by the marines' pass-out ceremony, the people of Hollyfield were being presented with the thirty percent sales from Twege. The money was to be used to build a house of God on the hill overlooking the home where the author had lived when she started writing her book.

However, corpses continued to sweep ashore and residents called the council to do something about it, but all calls went unheeded. Air became too contaminated to breathe.

A group of elders approached the church leaders and asked them to use the money donated by Ingrid to clean the shore. The church agreed, but the final say had to come from the writer. Two weeks later, an answer from Ingrid granting the go-ahead was received. Unfortunately, many people had left the city and its suburbs that were most affected by the stench.

The issue at stake in the House of Commons was to appoint representatives to specific tasks. The session began with a row between the resisters and modernists about what the appointed representatives should be called. All those who had been educated in the north had the term 'government' in mind, only to be shocked by the number of hands rejecting it.

One old man from the resister camp called Isacliot was very vocal indeed: 'We did not take you there to copy things, but to learn and invent what suits us from what they have. Why can't you copy our daughter who came back with our own version of a book written by them?'

This wrangling went on for some time until the mayor asked to say something. 'I should be excused for taking so long to revisit this matter, but surely, fellow countrymen, we shouldn't be arguing at a time like this. We have enough on our plate, and disagreement has no place on it. I ask you that we sort this out once and for all.'

The House heckled.

'One thing I have realized, comrades, is the failure to merge two rival parties. Politics is about rivalry – without it, it is not politics. One thing we have to remind ourselves though is to be humble when presenting our grievances. Without saying much, I want to tell you that we are not so different from the so-called democracy in the Millennium. They argue their brains out. However, the difference is that they later come to a compromise,' said the mayor.

There was a murmur in the House.

'Yes, how do they do it? I think we should have our House conduct business with ranks in mind. Our counterparts in the north call it veto when someone has the last word in the case of a stalemate. It is what we should work towards, I beg you, my fellow citizens.'

A recess was called, and when the House resumed it was unanimously agreed that challenges were dragging things. The People's Anthem was sung and then the first lady led people into chanting: We the common people... come let's build it together... let's put our noses to the grinding stone... on our guards... everyone is everybody.

People chanted loudest on the last line. Twege was then sung over and over, after which the session officially began and David was invited.

After thanking the mayor and the House for making what he called a historic political breakthrough, David appeared to have nothing left to say. Silence was slipping into murmuring when he asked his wife, whom he introduced as my lady, the Speaker, to say something.

'Due to lack of time,' Ingrid began, 'our leader, along with a number of members chosen by the people, came up with the issue of taking on individual tasks. They hope this will enable us to function efficiently - a view shared by most of us. Even if my job is only to read what has been set before me, this, honorable members, is a great challenge that I feel duty bound to take part in too.'

The representatives heckled.

'We shall have a body that will come up with solutions to our problems in a shorter time, and it will be called Lukiko.' Ingrid paused, perhaps to gauge the reaction of the House. After all, the word Lukiko meant high-powered gathering. 'The head of that Lukiko, gentlemen, will be called minister-president, and the people under him will be called people's assistants.'

Although she paused, there was no murmuring this time; the representatives were too busy looking at one another. The list that had taken the mansion family, together with the chief editor and army commander, days to compile had twenty-four names on it, half of which would be deputy appointments.

Ingrid could not wait any longer and started to read out the names, beginning with David Ngobi Waguma as minister-president. People cheered, which did sound as if to mean that no wonder. It nonetheless lasted quite a time. The statement that came after it – 'The minister-president will have no deputy' – brought a cold breeze through the House.

Ingrid sensed it and quickly returned to reading the list. Clapping followed every appointment until the last one. When Fredrick's name was mentioned, every representative turned to see whether he was around. Fredrick, who would be the people's assistant for renovation and reconstruction, stood up and waved his hand. The House spent some time silently observing the young man. Murmuring was cut short when the announcer invited Moses the Shepherd to lead the people's assistants into a swearing-in ceremony.

There was a moment of absent-mindedness as to what would come next. Ingrid approached the minister-president with a whisper, and David announced that the members of Lukiko should remain behind after the rest of the House dispersed.

Politics was beginning to claim grudges; some representatives were heard murmuring words on their way out that could only be interpreted to mean that they had been thrown out. No one felt the depth of it more than Ingrid. Yet she had no time to comfort disgruntled colleagues. The feeling in this priest lady was spiritual – God had chosen his few.

Moses the Shepherd was going around the appointees, chatting and looking unwilling to leave. Barbara had told Ingrid how the man had resisted her book coming into print and the girl noted it, but since Twege was doing better than expected, she had forgiven the priest. However, this was a meeting designed to discuss security matters, and military intelligence had warned the mansion of Fox's moles living under the cover of missionaries.

Barbara's story about this man and her book came back to Ingrid's mind, and she announced that the Lukiko was late already and asked everyone to speed up. Moses the Shepherd turned and looked at her with a sneer, but they later smiled at one another as the male priest walked out.

As soon as he left the House, Ingrid announced that the security meeting was open and invited the minister-president to deliver his speech. David, who had almost nothing to say, asked his brother to stand. Pointing a finger at him, he said, 'I find it right to ask this newcomer to the House to stand before I tell you something about his appointment,' he began.

'Lady and gentlemen, this highly schooled, technical young man is to work hand-in-hand with our army commander to ensure the safety of our bunkers. As someone who has studied engineering at the highest level, we couldn't think of anyone else. I don't need to tell you how much we need these bunkers upgraded. Fox is more than determined to wipe us off the face of Dunia, and these bunkers should be the place to offer us a breathing space.'

After thanking his brother for appointing him, Fredrick made a request. 'I need a few colleagues out there to help,' he said.

It took the House little time to grant his request. The salaries of the engineers working on the project would also be revised upwards, the House agreed.

Brigadier Knots was invited to say something before the Lukiko ended. 'Training the army to counter the eminent threat of Fox is a long-time strategy,' he said and continued, 'I therefore suggest bunkers, but for fighting purposes.' There was a murmur in the Lukiko, which the Brigadier had to address as soon as it died down. 'I suggest that underground trenches, bunkers as you prefer to call them, be constructed along the enemy forward arc.

This provoked the sitting to ask him what he meant by 'enemy forward arc,' which had left his listeners rather stupefied.

'The coastline overlooking the place where the marines would strike from.' Knots answered.

'How sure are you about this route-in?' One curious member asked.

'Simple,' Knots said and without taking long to think. 'Of course, it has to be from Hollyfield, the narrowest sea crossing.'

The sitting evaluated the cost of building underground trenches, which was found to be very expensive and even unaffordable. The Lukiko decided to enhance the bunkers to suit a long-term stay, and the technical men in the army were asked to join hands with Fredrick.

The minister-president closed the meeting with a short speech. 'Since I now have the task of running the Lukiko, may I suggest that the army commander might need me at times when I am busy. For this not to happen, may I take this opportunity to announce Mrs. Ingrid Ngobi (Reverend) as the new commander in chief of our armed forces. Thank you very much, lady and gentlemen.'

# Chapter 51

It was winter in Northern State, but a different one this time. There was no snow, even though temperatures were very low, keeping people indoors all the time.

The population was used to snow and liked it. Children had made a habit of chasing one another while making balls of the stuff and hitting each other with them.

The authorities had learned how to manage it. Trucks sprayed roadways with salt solutions whenever snow became a driving hazard, and within minutes the snow melted, becoming flowing water. Technology had also mastered it: wheels with special grips that held firm on slippery surfaces were a must for vehicles to dress in during the winter. New cars had a system whereby the driver pushed a button and the vehicle could not skid or slip.

The industry of culture and design had also come to master the art of making statues from snow, which attracted many viewers and cash prizes. Many games had been introduced, which were claiming championships. People could have fun skiing, too.

Yet snow was nowhere to be seen during this winter.

Meanwhile, the church was putting the thirty percent of Twege's sales to its intended purpose. The EPIC village of Eden was the one to benefit this time around, having come second on the list after the Hollyfield marine pass-out disaster.

The cathedral in the middle of the village was being fitted with a place where free food could be served to the homeless and drug users who had started living rough on the streets of the city. The house of prayer was to employ social workers who would provide prostitutes with counseling; they hoped to help these women and men to get better jobs elsewhere.

Moreover, the authority had another plan altogether. It had instructed its paramilitaries to collect all those living on the streets because they had started to die from the harsh weather. The operation also collected prostitutes on night errands.

It wasn't long before the custodies (tiny, cold rooms, commonly known as cells) were packed beyond capacity throughout the city's stations. The screams and yells of inmates could be heard by passersby. Fortunately, there were hardly any people walking the streets, but the situation turned security personnel on each other.

'We shouldn't be doing this,' the paramilitaries began to tell one another. Such talk became common, and in one particular incident a man and a woman exchanged blows.

The two were planning to get engaged, but the woman felt sorry for one of the gay drug addicts whom her fiancé had locked in a tiny cold room they called cell. After her fiancé left, the woman took the man outside and gave him a hot drink. By the time the fiancé returned, the 'jonkie' (a term the security personnel used to mean drug addict) was taking a shower.

When the fiancé (who was of senior rank to his spouse) asked what was going on, the woman told him to back off in a rude tone. The man slapped the woman, which was when the close combat began.

＝

The Millennium convened and agreed that the matter of dead bodies on the city streets be tackled expeditiously. Funds and resources were needed, and yet the House was bickering because of bureaucracy. Whenever the issue seemed to be getting somewhere, someone's signature was always needed, and that person was often hard to reach. The whole thing was like sabotage. So, the House agreed that a smaller body of people, readily available, should handle the matter.

In the meantime an army of volunteers, organized by the cathedral, went around providing winter clothing to those who needed them, but this was a different sort of winter. No cloth ever made could keep someone warm outside at night. Human corpses became a common scene on the streets of Eden, however much effort was made to remove them.

Cabinet convened with the issue of 'mushrooming bodies' all over the city as the only item on its agenda. The matter was sensitive and tricky, because the only answer was to get new linen to produce better coats. With nearly all the animals that provided the raw material now dead and many fabric factories closed, the questions of how and from where kept ministers whispering in groups.

Unlike Savage before him, Fox spent no time chatting with his ministers before or after cabinet meetings, which made them nickname him 'No Nonsense.' Although the ministers were sure he would order the bodies to be eradicated, or gassing as they called it, the cabinet waited nervously.

It was during the meeting that the paramilitary commander was asked to tell his story. Although the cabinet and even the president had thought of combating the situation in Eden, the commander cited other cities with similar problems. Hollyfield was reported to be the worst hit due to its nearness to the sea. The deadly cold was said to come from the currents hitting the land.

Just as expected, Fox ordered for the bodies to be dealt away in a way that would not require a lot of government spending. It was agreed that they should be put in very hot chambers, burned, and any remains to be gassed with acidic steam.

Next, the issue of overcrowding in the cells arose, causing a very tense debate indeed. The president wanted those in custody to be thrown into the hot chambers with the dead, until the minister for health said that long-time drug users could be helped to drop their habit. He managed to convince the House, but money, and a lot of it, would need to be injected into the project. Fox called it Plan B and ruled it out.

The meeting dragged on without agreement for a time that everyone perceived as too long, and it was left to the president to decide. All of the cabinet members expected Fox to decide on burning, but to their surprise the retired marshal reminded them of the concerns of the church in such a crisis. Cabinet adjourned, with the junior minister in charge of religious affairs being summoned to attend the next meeting.

Aan Savage was shocked when she received a memorandum from the Speaker, inviting her to the next cabinet meeting, which was to take place in two days' time. He asked her to contact him at his office for further details. On learning what the meeting was all about, Aan chose to contact the archbishop for advice. The prelate revealed to her the thirty percent Twege book sales, saying the collection could help the homeless.

At the cabinet meeting, Aan was asked to say something about the issue of homelessness. Many ministers had called it a waste of time, probably because she chose not to let them know what was in the offing. So, when she rose to speak, most of the audience were daydreaming or not interested in listening. However, when Aan mentioned that her ministry, in conjunction with the church, could help out, everyone in the House wanted to know how.

'Sales of the book that the Millennium authorized sometime back have accumulated enough funds to tackle such deficiencies,' Aan explained. 'The author, Reverend Ingrid Ngobi, donated thirty percent of her book sales, which have been used, among other things, to clean up the coastline at Hollyfield where bodies continued to sweep ashore after the marine exercise. Currently, however, the fund is enlarging the cathedral in EPIC, where prostitutes will be helped to find alternative careers, and the homeless and needy will have free meals and somewhere to sleep.'

The president thanked the minister, and there and then he upgraded her ministry to cabinet status.

The next morning, the newspapers in Northern State contained some news beyond the ordinary. Although the theme would be the same, which was the weather, Daily Snow sought another way to report. There was no headline apart from a big, smiling picture of the daughter of a former president holding a book that was considered dishonorable among northern politicians. The introduction drew full attention to the day's story:

God's promise is never late, even if the people to receive it always see it in that light. From rewriting God's Testament, the only woman priest of mixed race has become the savior of the dying streets – the homeless, prostitutes and drug addicts – in a state that calls her a leader of bandits.

No article had sold more copies of Daily Snow than that one.

# Chapter 52

Ingrid felt that David had appointed her on purpose to acting commander in chief of Southern State's army when closing the Lukiko. She had often reminded her husband of the racial imbalance in the army, which he had tried to address in vain. Ingrid hoped to use her tenure to do what her husband had failed in.

At first the first lady thought that turning the army around was a matter of drafting a message, saying that so and so should do this and that, and then send it out. But when she sat down to do it, her sixth sense told her to seek advice.

Ingrid therefore approached her father, whom she believed would offer the best advice, given his experience as advisor in situations of military nature. Abraham's response was reprimanding, however: 'Don't even begin!'

When she asked him why, the father talked her through army ranks, which lasted well over an hour. Ingrid learned that the army was a very sensitive institution, triggered by promotion and change in its hierarchy. She abandoned her plan.

The only legacy that Ingrid's tenure as commander in chief left behind was that of introducing faith into the army. By the time she handed things back to her husband, half a year later, the GOA, as she felt the southern army should be called, was truly an army of God. Every unit was on course to have a chaplain, and religious functions such as baptism and marriage would soon be taken care of inside the barracks.

=

There had been tough days for the leadership family, but an air of change was looming. David's sister, Mary, was to marry her soldier boyfriend, and Ingrid's twins were to sweep ahead of the couple. It was a moment for Fredrick to rest from the demanding task of supervising the renovation of the bunkers. He would be master of ceremonies at the wedding, which was scheduled to take place in a week's time in Southern State's biggest house of prayer, called All Saints Cathedral, within the capital, Adam.

The twins had been rehearsing their drills for quite some time. At the age of three they were not to be left entirely alone and someone was always to be walking very close, directing them. The girl would walk on the bride's side and the boy on the groom's. The children progressed well in their drills.

Sunday was sunny and scorching hot when Mary turned up to find Sam, who was in the company of another brown-skinned soldier like him. They were both smart-looking officers of equal size and height dressed in well-pressed military attire.

Golden embroidery covered the edges of the soldiers' hat shades, and swords hung by their sides. On their shoulders were three golden stars. As it was not common to see soldiers dressed in such a way, the locals thought the army had bought a new uniform for them. The truth was that Sam and his best man were army captains in ceremonial dress.

Mary was escorted by her sister-in-law Ingrid into the cathedral. The two women walked down the aisle to where the groom was already waiting. The bride had to walk very carefully, as Ingrid minded the dress that spread out four feet behind her. When Mary got to the altar by her groom, Ingrid arranged her children in their right positions to execute their task of escorts.

Esther was conducting the ceremony, assisted by a military chaplain. Moses the Shepherd, an invited guest, was to say a word to the newlyweds. Esther began the function by asking whether anyone had a reason to stop the couple from becoming wife and husband. There was silence.

Esther then asked Mary and Sam whether they would still love each other when faced with life's absurdities of poverty, sickness, age and ugliness. Each one answered, 'Yes, I will,' while holding Twege in their hands with smiles on their faces.

Then the military chaplain took over and asked the couple to step forward. About six men dressed in military uniform sprung up from the pulpit and formed two ranks, facing each other. Acting silently in unison, they drew their swords, kissed them and crossed them above their heads in an arch.

Ingrid led people into cheering as her twins led the newlyweds through the arch of swords towards the cathedral exit. The performance was utter perfection: the soldiers were smart and orderly; the newlyweds elegant; the best man and matron were accurately matched; and, perhaps most alluring of all, were the three-year-old twins who matched their movements so gracefully to the rhythm of the band music.

It was Fredrick's turn to perform at the mansion house. Many uninvited people, and the seating arrangement couldn't cope. It would be very ungodly to ask the gatecrashers to leave, advised Ingrid, so additional seats were quickly put out in the scorching sun. Fortunately, there was food in excess.

Speeches were planned after eating. David would speak for the bride and Brigadier Knots for the bridegroom.

According to custom, it should have been the bride's side that spoke first, but the arrangements for this marriage were not normal. Usually, both sides funded the wedding, with the groom's family making the biggest contribution. Yet, in this case it was the bride's relatives who paid for everything. Therefore, Sam's side was asked to speak first.

The army commander didn't say much, although he told the people what a disciplined and smart officer Sam was. Maybe the part regarding discipline was useful to know, but no one needed to hear about his smartness because it spoke for itself. After calling marriage a difficult yet simple journey, Knots briefly mentioned the passing of the couple beneath the swords.

'We carry the book all right, but without this custom being done, a marriage isn't yet done,' said Knots. Then he sat down, leaving people to evaluate his brief speech.

Fredrick asked the bride's side to take their turn. Her side would have a lot to say. Since the death of Mary's mother, roughly a year before this day, people had not gathered for a public function. There were no speeches at the funeral of Esther Ruth, who happened to be David's mother as well as Mary's. It had been a time of total grief. Adhering to custom, life had been taken away and speeches were unbefitting.

However, the wedding of the youngest daughter of Esther Ruth was a suitable occasion for some words to be said about a mother who was so kind and loving. Ingrid had written the tribute. Abraham, who had said a few words at the funeral of Esther Ruth, was also asked to speak, but he chose to be silent. Nonetheless, he asked his son-in-law to thank the people for the spiritual and moral support they had given during the time when the home missed its irreplaceable mother.

David thanked the people for turning up in such great numbers. He then congratulated the couple, in particular his sister whom he called 'a patient girl of indigenous morals.'

'If she is to change from that, then we wouldn't like that to happen and we don't expect it,' he said. 'We've given you a girl with one heart, so please treat her with one heart. Sam, you might have done it in secrecy, but now is the time to do it in public.' He paused for a bit, as if to remember what to say and coughed. 'Yes, it's about a year, if not slightly more than that, since we lost a mother in this home.

'As you all know, time to grieve is time for grief, although a remaining father in this house had to say a few words. I find it incumbent upon me to say something about our departed dear mother. In her days, Esther Ruth had known of the relationship between Mary and Sam, and she hoped to see this day. Unfortunately, she hasn't, but she told me something to say to both of you: "I love you and I'll always be by you, on your journey of love and tolerance." As a messenger, I have delivered my message. It's up to you… will you appease or offend the dead? Thank you very much. May God bless us all.'

# Chapter 53

The weather in Northern State had deteriorated so badly that the resulting death toll was the highest level in living memory. House-conditioning devices, commonly known as central warming systems, had been rendered ineffective. What continued to puzzle scientists was the failure of snow. Many hoped it would fall, but it had not happened for six months.

Research to discover the truth had become a hobby for the scientists. The answer was always the same: blame the launches, which cause air pollution. Some researchers went a step further by explaining how the launches had brought a blanket of smog in space that was hard for the sun's rays to penetrate.

The people got fed up of hearing the excuse. 'Is this an answer to a local taxpayer whose latest central warming system cannot cope?!' many asked.

Amazingly, the politicians continued to shy away from discussing the matter. The rich didn't have much to grumble about, since they could afford trips to sunnier places. However, the majority of them died because their bodies could not adjust.

Most of the deputies had returned from a newly introduced leave called winter vacation and would be having their first sitting in months. The issue at hand didn't need them, though, according to President Fox. Instead, he chose to call a cabinet meeting, which was to be attended by a number of weather specialists. The issue was to determine the amount of money needed to avert the situation.

To the scientists, the answer wasn't money, since the land would not respond to artificial catalysts. 'We made the mess and it's too late,' they told the cabinet openly.

It was up to the president to decide on the next step. Cabinet waited as Fox held a meeting with a smaller group in his office. Named Inner-core, it had three active members: President Fox, minister for defense and commander in chief of the armed forces, who was its chairman; the joint chief of army staff, General Wolf; and Dr. Spider, the minister for scientific research. Also present at the meeting, but with only observer status, was the Speaker of the House, Wood Tiger.

With journalists locked outside and the only minister in attendance being the man behind the NEDO project, speculation about the president sending his marines south to expand his territory was rife among cabinet ministers. It was after a marathon talk of six hours that the chairman allowed the Pool (journalists affiliated to the Millennium) into his office.

The public waited in vain. News had also reached Southern State where people sat in front of their televisions and radios, waiting anxiously.

In the morning the Daily Snow, using an anonymous source, stated: After a marathon meeting with a clique of his security team, the president, who is also the minister for defense and commander in chief of the armed forces, is ready to grant his election promise of turning Southern State into a province of Northern State. Individuals willing to settle in the new province may contact their deputies to get the necessary papers for proper passage there.

The atmosphere was ecstatic as people thronged the offices of their deputies wanting to fill out the forms. Unfortunately, nothing of the kind was available. Fox saw the Daily Snow as committing the harshest crime by any media and he ordered the press to never again report anything pertaining to military duties. It was a state secrecy, he warned, promising severe consequences on any press that violated the decree.

The president went on to warn of a state of emergency in the days to come. The nation was confused. Should they blame the press for the early warning, or Fox? Whatever was to come was a situation that kept the population in limbo.

As deputies lobbied cabinet ministers to know how the province would be annexed, nearly every minister had no answer. The situation provoked rumors of the marines being sent to attack the south. The Millennium quickly dismissed this. 'All this is wolokoso,' said the national spokesman somberly. 'The marines are up-country camping, and they will be there for some time to come.'

For an evacuation into the south to work, it had to be well arranged, and the marines were in the middle of the sea doing just that. Enabling a nation's population to cross the rough waves would require commitment and good planning. The marines had been teamed with civil engineers for the task of assembling big ships, measuring almost a mile long.

Four ships had been completed when disaster struck. A strong storm sunk all of them. For months, rescue efforts tried to float the ships without success. On each attempt the exercise claimed more men, and the project manager eventually called it off.

Fox made many trips there, desperately wanting the doomed ships refloated. Each visit was a pressured moment with poor, desperate decisions. The president's language was so tough that after his last visit, the project manager decided to follow the many young men he had seen perish in the daunting exercise.

The task of finding another project manager with the ability and empathy of professor Webber Hechoog was difficult. Civilian personnel working on the job had to be unmarried or married to fellow engineers who would also be involved in it, because no one was allowed to leave the site until the project was finished. The fact that the task would take years was so secret, those people who knew about it were sworn to keep quiet.

Monitoring of the project was a minute-by-minute task inside the president's inner office. Having realized that it was impossible to float the sunken ships, Fox came up with Plan B, which was to dig a tunnel under the sea. Shipbuilders were not tunnel diggers, so a new wave of engineers had to be found, even when Fox was told the project would take years and required too much money.

To the president, there was no turning back. 'The state has to use a recruitment drive that can cause no alarm or question,' he declared.

It being a time when underground transport was the safest and most common means made things easier. Many tunnels needed renovation due to too much usage that was in true sense over usage, so engineers were called upon under the pretext of repairing existing transport networks. The pay was very appetizing and engineers came in great numbers. They were to work in the south of the state where temperatures were slightly better, after all. The task was to join Hollyfield with the south of Dunia by tunnel.

==

Meanwhile, an airplane to pick up more copies of Twege had left Southern State for the north. The new national newspaper of the south, The Hot Sun, mentioned it the following morning in an article, which began: A big cargo plane full of Twege left Downingport airport yesterday for the north...'

Fox got the news in his office as part of the presidential situation report. Though aware that the south had only one airport, he called the minister for transport and aviation to confirm. 'How many airports has the south?' Fox asked his minister.

'Only one, sir,' the lady minister replied.

'Thank you,' Fox said and hung up. The president was now aware the authorities in the south had renamed General Fox Airbase. He looked around his office, gritted his teeth and hit the table.

The Lukiko called an emergency meeting, and the chief editor was accused of an inside job. The man called his accusers dictators who wanted to gag the press. The House became rowdy when David pointed a finger at the editor, telling him that he should have known better than anyone what the consequence of his actions would be.

Ingrid approached her husband and asked him to play things calmly. At first David could not be silenced, until his wife told him how the House was unable to differentiate between the two of them.

The matter ended with a vote in favor of suspending the chief editor. News about it appeared in the media that evening. The man's deputy, the lady he had sacked following the saga about reporting northern army deserters, was the one to replace him.

# Chapter 54

Newspapers in Northern State strongly condemned the sacking of the chief editor in the south. Daily Snow was extra vocal, calling the first family a gang of dictators who were all out to censor the media. A few days later it reported surging bodies along the beaches of the north.

What Daily Snow did not know was where the bodies were coming from, but their dress could not escape the reporter's eye. The article mentioned the copses wearing combat camouflage, blue belts and an emblem of an eagle flying with a fish caught in its craws. The description matched the marines, and Fox gave an order to close Daily Snow.

Meanwhile, paparazzi were running after the joint chief of army staff, asking him whose bodies were filling the beaches. The nation had been told earlier that the marines were camping up-country, and there was no way the general could state otherwise.

Newspapers responded by calling General Wolf an arrogant commander who did not care about his men when they were in peril, and they unanimously demanded his resignation. That was when the general asked his commander in chief what he should do. Fox advised him to deny everything through what he called 'the channels at your disposal.'

'It is with great concern that bodies dressed in our code are sweeping over our beaches,' said a military spokesman. 'They cannot be marines, as they are up-country. Our doctors are working around the clock to find out whose bodies they are. I don't want to speculate, but I have a feeling that deserters have tried to infiltrate us, but their attempt ended in doom. We shall keep you posted.'

The statement sent shockwaves throughout Northern State and beyond. The population could not imagine deserters daring to come back when the strong army they had fled was preparing to follow after them.

The task of clearing the coastline of bodies was happening around the clock. The entire beach was under army patrol and areas with corpses were cordoned off. Fox had instructed the joint chief of army staff to take charge of the operation, and Wolf was doing the job with all his heart.

Meanwhile, journalists were traversing the country, trying to find out whether it was true that the marines were camping. It was daunting. The army had deployed soldiers in strategic places, where visitors were denied access without clearance from the joint chief of army staff.

The end game came when some marines who had survived the accident appeared on national TV and called the sweeping of their colleagues on beaches 'wolokoso.' What intrigued people the most, and especially journalists, was the setting in the TV clip – isolated smoke spots and various tents with a color like that of the marines were visible in the background.

Rumors of marines dying so tragically were received in the mansion in the late hours of the evening, and David looked confused. Barbara, who was having some fun with her grandson, watched her son-in-law sink unusually low in his chair after exhaling a deep breath. David had just recovered from a chest infection and Barbara was concerned. 'Call Ingrid,' she yelled at the housekeeper.

'What's the matter?' called Ingrid, running ahead of her daughter, whom she had been teaching to sew on a machine in the adjoining room.

'I think they are on their way,' Barbara said while staring at David.

'Who?' asked Ingrid, rushing to her husband.

David tried to speak. 'The marines... uh, anyway, they were, I should say...'

'What are you talking about, David?' Ingrid demanded.

'Couldn't cross the sea, dead, maybe all of...'

'I don't understand, David, please, don't!' Ingrid begged.

'Try, maybe...' Barbara was unable to complete her sentence.

Ingrid turned to her and asked if she knew what David was talking about, but Barbara pushed her lower lip forward and shot her shoulders upwards at the same time.

Abraham walked into the room and asked, 'What's the matter?'

'I cannot actually tell,' Barbara told him.

'Call the commander,' said David, speaking as if he had just awoken from a frightful dream.

His wife was about to ask what the problem was when David began to tell them what the military spokesman of Dunia Modern Army had said. The first family was still pondering what to do when Brigadier Knots entered the room. 'It is good. Our worries are far less now,' he said before taking a seat.

'What do we do now?' Ingrid asked.

'I have to dispatch a force to secure the coastline,' Knots replied.

There was silence.

'Are you sure of your reaction, commander?' Abraham inquired.

'We have no other option; besides, it appears all his well-trained men capable of scaring us are gone. We need to act and act at once before he calls in the reserve to occupy our beaches. I know that was his plan, and it still could be.'

'Then do it now,' David said.

The commander stood up, saluted and left.

That night Brigadier Knots dispatched one brigade to secure the narrow stretch of water between the two states. He had a reputation for calling native soldiers cowards, and the force he assembled lacked any native dark-skinned soldiers. Surprisingly, however, the commander, Colonel Semei Muna, was a native.

The colonel wanted to refuse because he was the deputy commander of the army, but Knots told him that he was taking the best soldiers the army had. There was an argument between the two most senior commanders until Knots threatened Muna with a charge of insubordination. The penalty on conviction, Knots reminded him twice, was death by firing squad. The colonel left immediately with 3,000 men and 125 officers.

# Chapter 55

Ingrid woke up early to go to the bishop's office for her payment check. After breakfast, Ingrid asked her mother to accompany her, and the two women left the mansion on a ten-mile journey to meet the dean of the southern region.

'Come in,' said the smiling, light-skinned man in his spiritual attire.

'You must be new,' said Barbara.

'Oh, yes, been here a couple of weeks now.'

Silence.

'Anyway, here you are,' said the dean, handing Ingrid a check for her books.

The figure was appetizing and the female priest could not hide her happiness.

'By the way, about the project to aid this time... the local community here, I was wondering what we should do,' he asked.

Ingrid looked at her mother. Barbara said the matter was rather sensitive and they would need to do some research, as society was changing very fast.

'Yes, the needs of yesterday aren't the needs of today,' said the dean.

Silence.

'By the way, I was struck by the many missions we saw on our way,' Ingrid said.

'Oh, yes, this is turning into the promised land of Dunia. Not many churches are operating back home, you know!'

'But, why?' Barbara demanded.

'Well, there are many factors, but it seems nature is turning against us. Might we be paying for our iniquities? I wonder, but it looks so,' said the dean.

'Politics, I suppose,' said Ingrid.

'Well, plus many other things. For instance, power is regulated so much that most houses of God are in everlasting blackout. Such houses do not operate anymore because no staff can survive there. The Archbishop suggested moving his headquarters south to Hollyfield where conditions are more humane. The north of Dunia isn't a good place to live anymore. Of course, together with an inadequate spreading of the Word, bad weather is playing a negative part, too.'

'You must be happy with your posting then?' Barbara asked.

'Oh, yes, of course. By the way, call me Elijah.'

'Thank you, Brother Elijah,' said Barbara and she got up to leave.

'By the way, I am sorry, but this is my mother, Barbara.'

'Thanks, Ingrid,' said Elijah, 'a chip off the old block.'

On the way back home, Ingrid asked her mother what project the thirty percent of her book sales should aid.

Barbara thought for a while before replying, 'I'll never forget the circumstances under which you came into being. It has always been my wish to tell you how it really happened, but, again, I found myself tight-lipped. Now I feel free to say. I did not give birth in hospital, as it should have been...'

'Why?' asked Ingrid.

'There was no such facility around,' said Barbara.

'I thought I was born in the mansion,' Ingrid intoned.

Barbara looking alarmed said, 'Yes, of course you were.'

'The mission clinic isn't far away,' said Ingrid.

'It wasn't there then, and I was in labor for an hour until you helped me and came out without any complications.'

'Who, I mean, how then?' Ingrid asked while looking her mother in the face as if to mean that she was lying.

'That late father-in-law of yours was a nice man. He allowed people with experience of delivering children into his house. Anyway, the circumstances themselves were... what I can say, well, I had just arrived and almost immediately a daughter died inside the house.'

When Ingrid and Barbara got home at around midday, Mary was in the sitting room crying. She was due to give birth, and the two ladies became concerned that she was going into labor. Ingrid, who had started panicking and rushed to the phone to call the emergency services, was cut short by her husband.

'Something has gone wrong,' David said from his chair near the house phone.

'I can see,' Ingrid replied while stretching her hand to pick the phone.

'Sit down first!' he instructed.

'Have you called already?'

'It is not about that,' he answered, sounding tired.

'Divorce, eh?' she inquired putting the phone down.

'No, her husband was sent to the north and she is alone at home.'

'I thought Sam was a battalion commander.'

'Yes, of course he is, and his battalion is one of those that left.'

'Pathetic, eh?' Ingrid commented.

'Yes, even Colonel Muna is there, so I am told,' David said.

'What?'

'I am just speechless.'

'What are you going to do?'

'That's the question I was about to ask you.'

'The commander should be the person to explain, I suppose,' said Ingrid.

That evening Brigadier Knots arrived at the mansion after being summoned by David.

'How have you handled the threat so far, commander?' David asked him in the presence of Ingrid.

'Everything is fine, sir,' answered Knots confidently.

'I should think so, of course, but don't you think I need some feedback on how you went about it?'

'Oh, yes, certainly. Anyway, I'm sorry sir, I should have done that already, but as you know, things are happening so fast, and time is not on our side...'

'I suppose we have time now, don't we?'

'Sir, I hope you don't mind if I return later for the briefing.'

'Why?' asked David.

'It is just that I'm not ready, sir.'

'Missing something vital, commander?' Ingrid commented.

'Surely, ma'am,' Knots replied as he rose to go.

'One moment, will you?' said David, moving his hand to direct the commander back to his seat.

Knots tried to explain while standing, and Ingrid told him it would be better if he sat, so he returned to his seat.

'Now tell us how you made the deployment. Surely you know in your head who and how you did it – number of troops, officers commanding them, and the like?' David asked.

Brigadier Knots cleared his throat. 'Well, sir, I took the threat very seriously indeed and dispatched the most elite of our army to block the likely enemy route in which, of course, is the narrow water crossing.'

'Brilliant idea,' David commented.

'Yes, of course, and that is why I had to put the force under the best officers, because I know that is the only place we can put up a meaningful fight. If the enemy can cross over, we stand no chance.'

'Who are the commanders in charge?'

'My second-in-command, sir,' Knots replied.

'Do you really have the power to deploy the commander of the army without consulting the commander in chief?' Ingrid asked.

'Well, ma'am, it depends on the situation.'

'Situation?' asked David. 'I want you to call back Colonel Semei Muna, because he should be going through the locals to convince youths to join a juvenile force. I think he is best suited to doing that than you.'

'Okay, sir.'

'And I'm promoting Captain Sam to major and appointing him commander of the guard garrison.'

'Understood, sir.'

'Who is going to command that force then, commander?'

'I'll find out, sir,' Knots replied.

'And all senior appointments must be approved by me or someone acting in my place before they take effect,' David insisted.

When the Brigadier left, Ingrid asked her husband why he did not do as they had agreed and send Knots to replace Muna, but David said he had seen enough scare in the man's eyes.

# Chapter 56

All of the bodies recovered on the beach were burnt and the ashes dumped into the sea in accordance with marine burial rituals. Fox was a wounded man, because the disaster had wiped away ninety-nine percent of his trusted battle men. Those who survived were traumatized, unable to operate as a military unit, let alone a fighting one. The only way for the north to force its way into the south was to train a new batch of marines. Time was not on Fox's side, so the tunnel became his only hope of launching an attack.

A survey was carried out and the geologists learned that the task of building a tunnel would take at least ten years and perhaps even more. Ever since the weather changed, most industries were operating at very low capacity. The companies capable of producing the type of tools required for the job had been shut down because of the amount of power needed to run them. The little power that was being produced in Northern State went into running homes, hospitals, schools and light industries producing basic needs, such as food and clothing.

When the survey reached Fox's office, everyone feared presenting it to him, because he had hoped the tunnel would be completed within months. The president often sat his staff down and spoke at length about his wish to get the population into the south. He was always smiling, and appeared to have recovered from the disaster with the ships and the deaths of the marines. Fox had even started planning where his office would be located in the south.

Even so, keeping Fox uninformed was no option, according to his senior aide. 'The report about the tunnel is in, sir,' said the aide after saluting.

Fox replied with a smile, 'Good, just in the nick of time. Let me see it.'

The aide was confused whether to show or tell. After a moment of thought he felt that showing would be the best option. He walked to the corner of the oval office, switched on a computer, inserted a USB stick into it, and backed away a few steps. He then operated the gadget with a remote control.

The project manager appeared on screen first. After thanking his team, he called upon the senior geologist.

Professor Zuman was nicknamed Rocks because of his knowledge about them. 'I have the honor to be part of this team,' he began. 'I should be thanking you individually, but I'm aware of the curiosity we all have about what we have found. The rock we have to penetrate is a young one, which is good news, but I was astonished to find that it is not as porous as I first thought. The rock is so compact that we need very hard blades. By using the type of blades we currently have, it may take us many years to do the job; that is, if they will be able to...'

The president ordered his aide to switch off the computer. Sinking into his chair, he inhaled and exhaled, and placed his hands on his head. 'That cannot be,' he groaned, and asked to be left alone.

In the morning, Fox was to tell the Millennium of the progress he had promised. That night he could not sleep, knowing it had to be told something. Time was running out, because the Millennium was even advocating for sittings to be moved to Hollyfield where the weather was more permitting. Many deputies couldn't stand the constant blackouts in the House. Only a couple of minutes of darkness made the huge hall a living nightmare, and some deputies had stopped attending sessions. People had started to see no difference between their representatives and the weather, both appeared to be one and the same living nightmare.

Fox began by thanking the deputies for heeding his call to attend the day's session. The Millennium was silent and divided.

Most deputies had lost hope in Fox providing an answer to the ongoing problem. In their view, it was a cataclysm they were facing. Some, however, still felt that the ex-marshal had the capacity to rescue the state. He had always spoken with a lot of vigor and seemed to know how to achieve his goal. Many deputies were even saying it was a good thing the situation had happened when Savage was gone. Today they were all ears to hear what their 'savior' would tell them.

Fox began, 'I understand how we all feel, but I should ask you to understand that none, no one among us, is the cause of all this. Forget what some scientists are saying. All right, let us pretend it is true that we caused this; so then, who do we expect to correct it for us? Please, I ask you not to be like some people who think that prayer turns misery to hope. They have prayed and prayed, and what change have we got? The situation only gets worse by the day. The question now is whether we should continue with hope, or do something to help ourselves.'

The House was becoming inattentive.

'Right, honorable members, in the army when things get tough the tough get going. How do they do it? By going back to square one,' said Fox. 'We should remobilize our army. And after we have done that, it will be my duty to proceed. Remember, we don't have time to waste.'

# Chapter 57

The directorate of military intelligence was working closely with the authorities in Southern State. Fox's speech was followed word by word by the leaders in the south. There was an argument in both the Lukiko and House of Commons as to what action should be taken.

All of the politicians in the south agreed that Fox sounded like a finished man, and making noise of what he said would only amplify his words and make him a threat. With that general assessment, they ruled out letting the public know what was going on in the north, although fear of them misreading it was also imagined.

Fox's words reminded David of his meeting with Brigadier Knots earlier in the week, and when he got home the first thing he did was to call him.

'Speaking, sir,' said Knots after realizing it was David calling.

'What do you make of Fox's speech?' David asked.

'A very frustrated man indeed,' answered Knots.

'And how far have you gone yourself?'

'I am sure we're in a far better position than him.'

'How far has the colonel gone with the recruitment drive?'

'I cannot say officially, but unconfirmed reports are positive.'

'Where will the training take place?' asked David.

'As you know, sir, these are vigilantes, so I suppose keeping them in their respective local areas would be better. However, we intend to pick some good ones whose training should not be done far from the coastline...'

'Why?' David cut in.

'To maximize efficiency, in case of reinforcement, sir.'

'Nice idea, commander, eh. By the way, has Sam reported?'

'Yes, sir, and his promotion will be coming out in Part Two Orders shortly,' Knots said and exhaled.

'Nice to hear. Is he already wearing his promotion?' David asked after the noise by Knots' hard breath died away.

'Certainly, sir, once you say the word it will take immediate effect. Part Two Order is merely for record purposes. But, yes, he's happy on his major peeps. By the way, how is his wife?'

'What do you mean?'

'I understand she was taken to hospital this morning,' said Knots.

'Thanks, we hadn't been informed.' Seeing a messenger waiting, David put the receiver down.

'Congratulations, sir, Aunt Mary has given birth to a baby boy,' said the messenger.

'And how is their condition?' he asked.

'The message made no mention of it, but there was nothing more to report, sir.'

David called for his driver and left, along with his wife, to check on his sister. Mary had undergone a cesarean. Both mother and baby were in good health.

Brigadier Knots had been awakened. Soon after talking with the commander in chief, he sent a message to all units in which he mentioned the recent promotion and appointments in the army. The army commander had appointed Major Benjamin to replace Colonel Muna at the coastline, which was now known as the frontline.

Knots' message gave Colonel Muna a stomach ache. Benjamin was an artillery commander, attached to the force for support. The decision for him to be replaced by such an officer would leave the force under poor command; moreover, it left the support unit being overseen by someone with no knowledge of artillery. The colonel thought of advising the brigadier, but recalling what had happened between them prior to the formation of this particular force made him rethink it.

Moments later, however, thoughts of what the reshuffle could do to a force preparing to confront a superior enemy overwhelmed Muna, who knew the army's success depended on that force. Its failure due to insubordination, as he foresaw, would ruin the army, the state and its people. He left to meet the commander in chief at his mansion.

David refused to give Muna audience, but Ingrid became concerned and pleaded with her husband until the colonel was accepted.

The chemistry between the two men started off slowly. All along, David was thinking that Muna was not happy with Sam's promotion, but with no mention of the man, he realized Muna had something else to say. The colonel, after the formal courtesy, began to explain the command structure at the frontline. David began to see his army disintegrating at the hands of Fox's men.

'What do you suggest, colonel?' Ingrid asked.

'Either I go back, or someone else is promoted above all the ranks in that force and appointed as overall field commander.'

'Do you mean to say, you're not comfortable with the task of recruiting?' asked David.

'Not really that, sir, but what is the point of recruiting when the army at the frontline is not up to the job?'

'Surely they are – the commander told me.'

'Sir, I don't mean the troops, but the command structure. I'm certain that intrigue and mismanagement will emerge,' Muna replied. 'It is not what we want, sir.'

There was silence. David observed his wife, who fixed him with sympathetic eyes, which she normally did when asking him to concede.

A signaler walked in and delivered a message from the army commander. Ingrid, while passing it over to David, managed to read what it was vaguely about.

...I wish to report desertion of Colonel Muna from his post without leave. I shall take action once found. You'll be informed accordingly.

David held out the message to Muna after reading it, but Ingrid acted faster than the colonel.

'Not his, of course,' she said, grabbing it.

The atmosphere in the room became silently tense as furious glances were made. Ingrid inhaled.

At that moment Abraham entered the room with his grandson running alongside him.

'How do you feel now, Dad?' the twin son asked.

'A lot better, and you?' David answered calmly.

'We are fine,' said the boy.

'Ma, Ma, dim called and… and,' the boy said and then glanced at his grandfather.

'Say what he said, Stephen. Go on, tell Mama,' insisted Abraham.

'That… that, ah…'

'What is it, Dad?' requested Ingrid.

'Yes, the dean of the church called that you know why,' announced Abraham.

'Oh, yes, sorry, he must have waited long, poor shepherd had to call. Anyway, we have been very busy,' Ingrid said while walking towards the house phone. After dialing a number, she said, 'Pastor Ingrid, may I talk with the dean, please? Oh, I am indeed sorry. We have been very busy. Anyway, I have a plan. I would like a maternity center in one remote area of the city.'

'What was that about?' David asked his wife when she hung up.

'Church project from the book sales,' she announced.

The meeting between the commander in chief and Colonel Muna ended with a promise from the former. David would see to it that the army was in conformity with its establishment.

# Chapter 58

The army in the north was not ready to forgive its paymaster, the state. Since the launch of the marines, many regulars had received no pay and decided to desert. Some tried to go back to their former careers, but it was impossible. Although their former employees used the phrase 'bad times' when they meant that the economy was not doing as good as before, the fact of the matter was that they could not entertain them. Either due to stigma or lack of therapy, most of the army men had turned to drug abuse. In the absence of drugs to keep them high, life became meaningless and many decided to take their own lives. No wonder the call from the deputies for them to return and serve passed straight through their ears.

When Fox heard back from the deputies, the general statement, the servicemen we contacted showed no interest to serve, did not make him as furious as they had expected. They thought his failure to deliver had turned him into someone needing friends rather than foes. After all, rumor was rife of the president having been diagnosed with severe conditions related to over-thinking. It was therefore logical for the deputies to think their leader had heeded his doctor's advice and turned himself into a happy man.

What the deputies did not know was that Fox's happiness was because of something a childhood friend had told him recently. The president's wish to occupy the south had driven him to seek advice from anyone he knew and could hold a conversation with. This childhood friend told Fox that he was a marine engine designer, but had lost everything due to bad weather. The man said things were so bad for him that he didn't have the money to buy fuel to run his home generator.

After recalling who his guest was, the two men talked casually about their childhood. Fox was made to understand that his friend was a shipbuilder, and he became more open and told his guest of his dilemma. The man expressed his ignorance about building big ships, but told the president that he knew someone who was capable of doing it.

The next day, Fox entered his office whistling a military tune called 'Reveille,' which usually sounded to wake soldiers for the day. 'I want you to find me an engineer called Formula,' the president asked his senior aide the moment he sat down in his office chair.

The aide began to check the name in the list of engineers, but he could not find it. Thinking it unwise to report back so soon, the man widened his search. After an hour, he gave up and called the faculty of engineering.

'Real name is Webber Hechoog, sir,' said a female voice on the line from the faculty of engineering.

'Thank you very much, madam,' replied the aide.

The man was about to report his findings when the name Hechoog rang a bell. He stopped. After thinking a little, he realized that the man was the project manager of the disastrous ship project. The aide decided to find out whether the project manager survived.

'Hello, Office of the President calling, can I speak with the joint chief of staff?' said the aide.

'Moment please, connecting you, sir,' answered someone on the other end of the line.

General Wolf picked up the phone. 'Hello, joint chief speaking.'

'Sir, this is the senior aide to the president. I would like to know the whereabouts of Professor Webber Hechoog, sir.'

'Who wants him? Is it the president?' asked General Wolf.

'Yes, of course, sir,' answered the aide to the president.

'Is the president around? Can I have a word?' asked Wolf.

'I'll find out, sir, hold the line, please.'

'Wolf, what do you say?' The president said.

'About this engineer, sir...' said Wolf.

'Which engineer?' asked Fox.

'Formula, sir?' said Wolf.

'Oh, yes, where is he?' said Fox.

'I am afraid he is dead, sir!' announced Wolf.

'Dead?!' Fox wondered.

'Yes, sir,' confirmed Wolf.

'How?' asked Fox.

'Suicide, so we were told by the survivors,' said Wolf.

'Okay, thank you, general,' said Fox and hung up.

=

For some time, David weighed what Colonel Muna had told him. On many occasions he sent for Knots, but the brigadier was always in the field. When he asked his wife what was to be done, Ingrid advised her husband to send a message to Knots, asking whether the colonel had been found. David wrote a message and asked his wife to check that he had addressed everything.

Ingrid made the message shorter. Let me know more about Colonel Muna(.)///

The army commander replied to his boss without delay. I am currently sorting out a few things at the front, sir(.) I shall call on you as soon as I return(.)///

David showed his wife the message, and the couple looked at one another with Colonel Muna's concerns beginning to resonate in their minds.

After three days, Brigadier Knots arrived at the mansion.

'Tell me what it was that you were sorting out at the front?' David asked.

'Not really much, sir; you know some of these young officers tend not to understand how the army works,' Knots said.

'Not taking orders?' David asked, looking very inquisitive.

'Oh no, not really that, sir.'

'What is it then, commander?'

'Just routine field matters, but anyway, I have it sorted,' Knots said, looking relaxed.

'Don't you think, as commander in chief, that I need to know?' David bounced back, killing Knots' mood.

'Of course, if it requires your attention then I am obliged to, sir, but as things stand now, not really – actually, everything is all right.'

'Let me get this straight, who is commanding that force now?' David demanded.

'Ah, actually, that is why I went there. And I was going to address that. I made changes to suit the situation...'

'Again, without consulting...?' David spoke while pointing at himself.

'I should admit that the first appointment was done hastily and the command wasn't going smoothly. Anyway, I made some kind of professional mishap, but it is all sorted now, and the force is happy and morale is high.'

'Do you mind telling me that mistake?'

'I had appointed the artillery commander to command the force, and I admit that was wrong, but now everything is all right,' said Knots.

'Who is the commander now?' David asked.

'Major Barks, formally commander of First Battalion, sir.'

'I also understand that all troops are of one skin color – is that true?' David demanded.

'Well, sir, apparently it happens to be so.'

'Why?'

'Originality of units, sir,' said Knots.

David exhaled and said, 'Colonel Muna, I saw the message!'

'Oh, yes, he returned almost immediately. He is now busy recruiting.'

When the meeting ended, Abraham, who was listening from an adjoining room, walked in and advised his son-in-law to visit the troops at the frontline in order to gauge the situation himself. Ingrid objected, but David insisted on going.

'Weighing the tone of Colonel Muna against that of the brigadier, I can smell a rat. I advise for the matter to be taken to the Lukiko,' said Ingrid before bidding the two goodnight.

# Chapter 59

To the amazement of everyone, the weather in the north eased. Temperatures rose and people began to walk their dogs. Some regular soldiers were showing renewed interest in their careers, and the paramilitary, which had disintegrated due to severe weather, was reorganizing itself.

The problem, however, was that no individual force could operate as a single institution any more. The marines were very few, the army was badly demoralized, and the paramilitaries had resorted back to civil life. All three sectors, which once made the north a security giant, needed reorganization, both physically and mentally.

Fox directed Wolf to merge all three into a single force. A month later, the joint chief of staff had made considerable progress. The issue now was to get the Millennium to endorse the new formation.

The first session in the House since the weather had improved saw many issues to address. Some deputies had passed on, and a by-election was the first thing on the agenda. The economy that had taken a battering due to power failure would follow. Infrastructure, too, had a slot, but most daunting of all was the issue of the bodies on the beaches. Some deputies wanted to know who they were and what had happened to them.

Fox spoke about the bodies first: 'Mister Speaker and honorable members, I hope we all know what loose talk can cause when it comes to the security of our...'

The entire House echoed with booing. The Speaker rang his bell for order, but there was no immediate silence. When calm returned after a long while, the Speaker asked General Wolf, the joint chief of staff (who was in attendance for reasons only known to Fox), to tell the House why the bodies were in a uniform similar to that of the marines.

One deputy raised his hand before the general could speak. Given the sensitivity of the matter, the Speaker was obliged to allow it.

'Honorable members,' the deputy began, 'it seems we're interested in the Queen Ant being responsible for the ills in the anthill. Perhaps we should narrow the picture.'

The House heckled.

'I-I, for that matter, ask for the chief of staff for the marines to be the person telling the House what really happened.'

There was silence. The Speaker asked General Wolf to return to his seat and a recess was called. When the House resumed, it was deemed necessary to hear from the marine chief of staff.

Fox stood up, even though he had not been called upon, and said, 'Mister Speaker, before us is the overall commander, and in my view, which is the view of all servicemen, the joint chief of staff will refer us to this very commander.'

'We shall, all the same, hear from this officer,' answered the Speaker.

There were whispers that eventually became noise, and the Speaker rang his bell. There was silence. 'I shall, for that matter, call upon the marine chief of staff to appear tomorrow promptly,' he added.

—

Speculation about the marine chief of staff had been mounting. One deputy claimed to know a man who knew all about the officer in question – one of the few civilians to have survived the shipwrecks. According to the deputy, the man, who was a gay partner of the project manager, Professor Webber Hechoog, was totally traumatized and feared everything, including his own shadow.

When other deputies asked what the man had to say about what really happened, he said something that left everyone speechless: 'All of the marines perished, including their chief of staff.'

The gay man, whose name was Denis Perim, lamented often in the legislator's home where he was living: 'The raging storm brought with it howling winds and fierce lightning as the workers looked up at the angry skies with alarm. The floating home where the marines camped was precarious, but Fox brought more men almost daily until the damn thing could not cope. My dear Formula knew a disaster was looming; the poor man bought time by switching the marines between ships being built. But the storm tossed the structures over and over like empty cups. I'll never get a partner like him again!'

The man broke down crying, and then repeated the tale again and again. On many occasions he rejected food until the host deputy, who happened to be Perim's cousin, threatened to throw him out of his house –the only thing that scared him.

The marine chief of staff did not appear as requested by the Speaker. The president gave an excuse: the relevant authorities were still trying to contact the officer. The House adjourned for yet another day.

The next day the marine chief of staff still did not show up. This time Fox had run out of tricks. 'I should advise the House to move onto the next issue on the agenda as we trace the officer,' he requested. The House heckled and called the president a man with blood on his hands.

The failure of the marine chief of staff to appear was a big blow for Fox and his regime. The media interviewed the traumatized man who was staying at the deputy's residence. A giant picture of him with tears larger than his eyes coursing down his cheeks made front pages in all of the northern newspapers.

—

In Southern State, the opening of the Lukiko began with the issue of bunkers. Fredrick talked at length about his progress. Building bunkers throughout the state was not possible, he admitted, but he hoped that many individuals had personal ones under their houses. Frederick said the focus for his team was to make bunkers in the urban area that were missile-proof, to which the House applauded. He went on to promise that his team would give lessons to individuals on home bunkers. When he was asked how, Fredrick, after a long explanation, said it would be done at the community level.

David introduced the next issue, which urged politicians to support the current troop deployment along the coastline. Most of the people listening had not known the army was on alert. To muddy the waters further, the minister-president revealed the animosity between the deputy army commander, Brigadier Knots, and his deputy, Colonel Muna.

Ingrid moved closer to her husband and whispered something in his ear.

The commander in chief then blamed himself for not having gone to check on the men at the frontline.

There was heckling.

One representative rose and asked David to erase the idea of venturing to the frontline from his head. An argument ensued. Some representatives were in favor of it, but others were against, warning that it was far too risky to send a head of state so close to a technically advanced adversary. The debate did not last long as those against conferred. Both parties agreed on the politicians analyzing the frontline situation.

The visit needed in-depth observation, and Isacliot, a politician who was denied becoming the People's Assistant for reasons most members saw as fear from the leadership, was voted to be part of the team. He was a veteran mansion guard whose views were robust and impartial. Members of the House saw him as the right man to assess the true picture of the wrangles in the force at a time of imminent attack.

David raised many issues that clearly exempted Isacliot from the team. The minister-president, after mentioning Fox's mole structure being well wired, warned against bringing in outsiders at a time of crisis. It appeared that his advice was winning support, but his wife remained reserved.

Not wanting to disagree with her husband, Ingrid quietly told him that she had a splitting headache. David asked her whether she wanted to leave, and she nodded her head up and down like an agama lizard. He closed the meeting.

Later, at home, Ingrid did not go to bed as her husband expected. 'Please, David, just allow Isacliot to be part of the visiting team. I feel the man is impartial, and with him we will get back what we really want; after all, he was himself a soldier,' she said while presenting him with a cup of tea.

Escorted by the deputy army commander, Colonel Muna, the team was in high spirits. On arrival, they managed to take snaps across the sea, and they also chatted with the natives, the majority of whom were fishmongers baffled by troops coming to pitch camp in their area. After that, Major Barks officially welcomed the political entourage, but none of them actually knew him. No wonder they were thinking why him, of all commanders.

Isacliot called Colonel Muna aside. 'Who is this guy?'

'One of the officers, of course,' answered Muna.

'Well, I should have known that, but none of us know him. Don't you think, Commander, that the army and leaders need to agree on matters like command structure at a time like this?'

'Of course I do. But it is not my duty to appoint.' Muna spoke with a slight sneer.

'Are you comfortable with this?' Isacliot asked him.

'Well, as you know, army is all but orders, and I am here to serve.'

'Even at the peril of the state?' Isacliot said.

'I hope it does not get that far,' Muna replied. Asking to be excused, he joined the rest of the politicians.

When the team had not seen any dark-skinned soldiers for hours, insecurity set in. Colonel Muna saw their fear and assured them that everything was all right.

The colonel asked Major Barks to assemble his officers. The major asked him why, and dialogue between the two men soon became a circus. Some soldiers heckled in support of the major. Colonel Muna decided to cut short the visit.

# Chapter 60

Fox went to see General Wolf's men many times. On every visit the president warned against what he called egoism, and told them how important it was to regard one another as brothers with similar tasks and one goal. He reminded the force that the entire nation looked at them to deliver it from its misery.

The men seemed to accept one another, but that was only after elite outsiders like Fox visited them. The order in the camps was of hate and denial, defined by hierarchy. Marines, apparently the fewest in the group, regarded themselves as superior, and then followed the army, with the paramilitary at the bottom.

In a surprise move, Savage called, wanting to know how things were going with his predecessor.

'Great, I should say,' said Fox.

'But, Shroud, I don't think you have forgotten?' said Savage.

'Not at all, if you mean what I mean, Humane.'

'Whatever one should mean here, but, of course, Shroud, you haven't forgotten our vow?'

'How on earth can I block?' said Fox.

'Thanks, once again,' said Savage.

'By the way, how do you gauge my performance so far?'

'Excellent, I should say, except for that marine thing. I would have handled it otherwise; anyway, different men offer different approaches.'

'Certainly, although I would have called it tactics,' said Fox.

'Come on, never mind, you are doing great,' said Savage.

The door to the president's office swung open and the aide entered. Normally, Fox would have asked the person on the other end of the phone to hang on, but he killed the line instead.

Two weeks had passed since the newspapers ran the article about the fate of the marines by Formula's partner. It had been published only days after the deputies in the Millennium had heckled and called Fox a man with blood on his hands. No sessions had been held since. The issue put the president's job on the line when the House resumed.

'May I remind the House that the president can be impeached if more than fifty percent of the deputies are in favor of moving the motion?' the Speaker announced when the issue of bringing Fox to account for the marine chief of staff bounced back.

Fox had not thought of this development, and it seemed he had run out of initiatives. He asked for some time to think it over. The Speaker granted it and called for an hour's adjournment. Fox went to his office, called Savage and told him what was going on. There was a brief moment of silence on the other end of the line.

Savage had had enough time to think of what to say: 'I understand the army is run by orders.'

'Yes, of course,' said Fox.

'I also understand that you give your men leave, and if they don't show up, it is desertion,' asked Savage.

'Yes, of course,' said Fox.

'Does that apply to senior officers as well?' inquired Savage.

'Yes, of course, it does,' answered Fox.

'Good, could it be that this officer was given leave?' suggested Savage.

'Not at all, as I told...'

'I understand all that, but here is the trick: Wolf, as the boss, granted this officer leave and has yet to see him report...'

Fox cut in, 'You mean the army is investigating his whereabouts?'

'There you are, and that's why you wanted the general to tell the House,' Savage suggested.

'Thanks a lot, comrade,' said Fox, held the phone receiver for a while in his hand before hanging up.

=

The Millennium was in a combative mood when it reopened. The Speaker called order as many times as it was inevitable for him to use other methods. He rang the bell and there was calm.

'President, please,' the Speaker announced.

Fox rose.

'Mister Speaker and honorable members, it surprises me that you could not allow the man in charge of all personnel in the service to address the House. I'm the commander in chief of the armed forces, but I'm also your president; and as we all know, the last period has been quite busy. I'm actually yet to be properly briefed on the state of our forces. I believe you no longer see the patrols as before, there are fewer army men than before; so can't we ask ourselves why? I say that I must either be briefed by the joint chief of staff about our force, or we allow him to brief us about it.'

The House, which had been silent ever since Fox began to speak, continued to be so, even when he sat down. There was no way Fox could be impeached because of someone under someone. The whereabouts of the marine chief of staff fell squarely on Wolf to explain.

'I call upon General Wolf,' said the Speaker.

General Wolf began amid silence.

'Honorable members of the House, it is with profound sadness that I couldn't be allowed to come and brief you earlier. More saddening, however, is that I couldn't find time to brief the commander in chief, who has been busy around the clock. It is military protocol that we use wireless to keep ourselves informed of developments, but the power problem has rendered our technology useless. May I take this opportunity to inform the commander in chief that many servicemen have deserted the force?'

The House heckled.

Wolf continued, 'It is also sad to note that even our senior officers have deserted us...'

'Ja, ja, ja!'

'Order, order! Continue, General Wolf,' said the Speaker.

'There is no place such men could have gone; not many could have made it into the south. As for those who did, we are preparing to pursue them.'

There was complete silence.

'Could the marine chief of staff be among the deserters?' Fox asked, sounding shocked.

'Investigations to find him are ongoing but as of now, we assume so, sir,' Wolf answered before sitting down.

# Chapter 61

With the dead bodies in uniform explained in the House, Fox relaxed and began to attend to the backload of work that had piled up in his office. There were the issues of the tunnel, rebuilding the army, and many more tasks to do with the day-to-day running of the state. Fox just wasn't sure what to prioritize. For now, though, his career was not on the line, and returning to his pledge was a priority. Fox ordered the reopening of the heavy industries. The report was not promising. The industries had been dormant for several years, and restarting them required a lot of spares, because many parts had been oxidized.

Wolf, meanwhile, was doing his best to reassemble the tattered army. Training, which was called refresher courses, was ongoing in many parts of the country, away from the populated areas.

Fox had plans too: if the pride and glory of Dunia Modern Army was to be revived, the answer lay in live training. Wolf thought the commander in chief was referring to the use of live ammunition, only to be told that the plan was to attack the south.

Given the prevailing good weather and clear visibility, crossing the sea would not be hazardous, but surveillance was needed, according to Wolf. For Fox, however, time was of the essence, and the operation had to be done sooner rather than later.

Fox imagined a lot of things that would happen if their army was victorious in an attack. He knew the population would regain their trust in him, and even forget the controversial uniformed bodies on the beaches. He was also aware that the people knew the truth. Just like them, he knew his victory in the Millennium was a matter of politics, not policy. The dead were part of the community, after all, and their failure to return home was enough to explain it all. By winning a war, Fox knew the people would sweep all his ills under the carpet, and the taxpayers would gladly invest more money in the army. He feared the public would not fund an invisible or dormant army; moreover, training aids and salaries had already drained the defense budget.

=

Major Barks' force was learning the geography of the area when a message from the commander in chief arrived, placing Northern State on maximum alert. It wasn't clear whether the message was in any way connected with Fox's intentions. What had alarmed David was that dead bodies had finally swept over the beaches of Southern State. First, blue belts were seen waggling on the water. Fishermen got scared when dead bodies in camouflage followed the corresponding belts, and they sent word to the mansion. A message was given to the army commander. Brigadier Knots confirmed the belts as belonging to the marines in the north.

The south knew this was an intended attack that had been averted by God-only-knew what. David wanted to bring the issue to the attention of the people, but Knots warned of panicking them, even though stories and cartoons about the incident were already in the press. David and Knots agreed to put the army on maximum alert.

David had gained respect for Colonel Muna and he sent for him. The colonel was still recovering from the humiliation he had suffered in front of the team of politicians at the frontline. He knew no politician could explain to the commander in chief how he felt, so this call was timely.

Muna did not want Ingrid to be present at the meeting. He was hit hard by xenophobia whenever he looked at the first lady. Knots' arrogance and the way Major Barks had behaved towards him resurrected themselves in his mind. How dare they treat me like that; don't they know they would be dead if it wasn't for this state? Such were the colonel's feelings in front of Ingrid, whose skin color likened that of the northern born soldiers within the southern army.

The colonel had to endure almost half an hour with the first lady while waiting for David. Ingrid had always seen fear in Muna's eyes. She had been told how the soldiers at the frontline behaved. Why they had no regard for the colonel, even though he was second ranking in the army, troubled Ingrid, who knew the force to be the most disciplined of institutions.

'How was the trip?' Ingrid asked him.

'Which one, ma'am?' asked Muna.

'The one with the team of politicians. I thought it was you who went with them.'

'Oh, yes, that one, well it was as it was. Military things aren't exciting, of course. How did the politicians find it?'

'They have yet to report to the House. We are anxious to hear,' said Ingrid.

'Well, I only hope they report as it really was,' said Muna.

'What do you mean, colonel?' asked Ingrid, studying him for a long moment.

'Nothing, but, of course, I have my view, which might not necessarily be similar to theirs.' Muna said after taking a moment of thought.

'Exactly, perhaps it would help if we knew both views.'

'Ma'am, as a soldier, I only take orders,' said Muna.

There was silence.

'But tell me, colonel, how is your working relationship with your boss?' Ingrid asked.

'Good. What can I say? He is the boss and it is the army.'

'Surely you shouldn't, anyway, you soldiers with your profession!' Ingrid made her commented in a low voice.

'Is there anything else, ma'am?'

'Not really, but if you are fine, then it is all right. I have only been thinking that...' Ingrid stopped and observed the ceiling. When she dropped her face there were tears in her eyes.

'Have I said anything, ma'am?' Muna asked.

'Well, not really,' Ingrid said as she walked away.

David walked into the room looking serious, and Colonel Muna's heart started to beat fast. What did I do to her and what has she told him?

'Please sit down,' said David in reply to Muna's salute. 'As you know, we have a situation on our hands.'

'Yes, sir, I saw the message.' Muna said before sitting.

'Good, I was wondering if those troops up there can contain the situation.'

'What do you mean, sir?'

'A member of the political team has told me what I did not expect to hear. You know, colonel, my father used to say that a soldier with no discipline is no soldier, and I am beginning to wonder if that Barks will be able to command if he can behave that rudely to you.' David said.

'Well, sir, the issue of discipline in our army has to be addressed from the top down. I am glad you have realized it. The army is divided. Our comrades from the north don't feel part of us. They are their own. What can I say? Anyway, things are…' He paused.

'Come on, Colonel, you are a soldier and I am your commander in chief, so tell me. You know what, my wife has always had a lot of sympathy for you, and that is why I called you to find a way to tackle this.' David said.

'You know, sir, my father used to say that a bad daughter will never make a good wife. These are mutineers and deserters; yes, we are right to welcome them, as they brought a lot that our army can be proud of, but maybe we gave them a lot in return.'

'You know what? I was thinking of you becoming the army commander.' David proposed.

'Well, sir, thank you, but that only shortens the life of the time bomb. It is these deserters heading all departments within the army and even the forces we are depending on to protect the state. What makes you think they won't try a coup? Sir, just don't do it.' Muna begged.

'What should I do then?' David asked, observing the roof.

After a moment of silence, Muna replied, 'Reshuffle the army.'

'I want you to compile a list of how the army should look,' demanded David.

# Chapter 62

Reports of dead bodies wearing combat camouflage washing over the beaches in Southern State was welcomed by Fox. No army can leave its dead in the hands of enemies, he said, as soon as the news reached him.

Begging the south to hand over our comrades, albeit their remains, is out of the question, the president told the Millennium. Deputies were confused as to what the president meant. They thought he meant leaving the issue as it was.

Fox explained himself further: 'Under no circumstances, and I mean under no circumstances, can men that once carried the name of a proud state be left in the hands of foes, whether they are dead or alive.'

One deputy asked if deserters still deserved to be treated with honor. Fox's answer amused the House: 'Only court-martials are capable of stripping soldiers of their rights.'

General Wolf was forced to cut short training the remnants of Dunia Modern Army. The men were wanted and a head count was done. The marines numbered 460, out of the 5,000 that originally passed out; the infantry men were 600 out of the original 7,000; and the paramilitary numbered 720, out of 3,500. Less than half of this force could not launch an attack due to trauma. Wolf knew it, but he was tired of repeating the similar story to his commander in chief, President Fox.

$=$

In the south, Colonel Muna had made all possible efforts to compile a list for David. Moreover, the military command structure would need to change. Being one of the first military academy students, Muna had excelled well enough to become what he was now. Together with military tactics, he studied leadership, which was the political part of his training. To the surprise of the thirty graduates with whom he passed out a decade ago, nearly all of them were now under the command of deserters from the north.

The native army officers had Ingrid to blame. She was the person wielding real power when the deserters from the north swamped the army. For many years it was impossible to gain an audience with David, let alone Abraham, the man who came up with the idea of training the thirty officer cadets who led the force from a guard unit into a regular army.

Colonel Muna's new structure would have the army commander (AC) as the figurehead, and the man running the army would be the chief of staff (CoS). The officers Colonel Muna asked to help him with drafting the new structure unanimously agreed that it had to be him to fill this appointment. The team, which composed of only officers that led the force from a guard unit into a regular army, agreed that some departments had to be elevated from directorate to chieftain.

All chiefs were to take orders from the CoS, who, like the army commander, would have equal access to the commander in chief of the armed forces (Cicotaf). The biggest difference was that the CoS was the man responsible for appointing senior officers with immediate effect, but he would have to get confirmation from the Cicotaf. In turn, the Cicotaf would only confirm an officer after the CoS had given the go-ahead. Nonetheless, he still had the right to reject an officer. The idea was to give the Cicotaf full authority over the army.

The issue of promotion was rather trickier, and the officers argued a lot. Some said the promotion board should involve civilians, such as the People's Assistant in charge of security. Others wanted it to consist of only army personnel.

It was after an exhausting argument during which Colonel Muna relayed his experience with the politicians at the frontline that his training colleagues, after listening in total silence, agreed to the idea of civilians helping to determine their rise in rank.

The remainder of the matter involved putting individual names against job titles, which Muna felt like doing alone. The colonel thought that since the officers who had assisted him were potential candidates, doing everything with their knowledge would deprive the project of the key element of surprise.

＝

It took awhile for the south to decide how to dispose of the dead bodies sweeping in from the sea. Some of the people's representatives thought the bodies carried bacterial infections and preferred them to be burnt, but others viewed such a thing as ungodly. The issue at stake was between infection and tradition, and the latter won by the most hands. The minister-president, in his capacity as commander in chief of the armed forces, ordered the army to bury the bodies.

Knots sent the commander of the frontline unit a message to inter all of the bodies. The soldiers embarked on the task, but halfway through it became impossible. The bodies were literally pouring in from the sea, and a terrible stench covered the entire beach. Many soldiers became nauseous.

Major Barks had to do the inevitable thing and order the burning of the bodies. The smell that followed was worse than before and the unit withdrew inwards. With the wind blowing towards the land, they were pushed back until they were many miles from the seashore.

＝

In Northern State, General Wolf had assembled his force under the command of a two-star general, Major General Dile Croks, who happened to be the chief of staff of the army. Croks had two generals under his command with one star each, who were commonly referred to as Brigadier. One was in charge of a seemingly able force named Forward Brigade (FB), composed largely of marines. The other, named Rear Brigade (RB), was comprised of the sick.

The force was not told of its mission until the very last moment when they were in sight of the sea. Many marines fainted. It was in this very environment that they had survived death before; more than that, it was in this very place that their colleagues perished.

Many marines began to recite uncontrollably what had happened on that fateful day when the ships they were building sank. History had chosen the wrong time and place. What should have been strong men spearheading an attack on an enemy became convulsing human beings, scared by the perils of nature. The commanders were just as confused as the other soldiers from the army and paramilitary, who had been ignorant of what had really happened to the rest of the marine force.

Lieutenant General Croks radioed General Wolf and told him what was going on. The two men agreed that it was meaningless to take such soldiers into war, especially when Croks told Wolf that the problem was spreading throughout the entire force like a plague.

Wolf contacted Fox and told him what was happening. There was a brief moment of silence on the line before the president roared, 'Cross the frontier and attack. Roger. Out.'

# Chapter 63

Colonel Muna's list of the new structure of the army reached the mansion house. David called his wife and Abraham, and they studied it together for hours. The abbreviations of some appointments, especially Cicotaf, amused them.

'Why didn't we do this in the very beginning?' Ingrid asked.

'Because it wasn't possible,' her father answered.

An argument between daughter and father was emerging when Barbara arrived with her grandson. The boy asked what his mother, father and grandpa were doing together. Ingrid wanted to answer, but Barbara shooed her away, saying, 'You don't have to answer whatever he asks.'

'Why not, Mother?' Ingrid asked.

'Can't you see that the boy is asking too much already?'

Ingrid grimaced. 'So what? Isn't that him wanting to learn?'

'My dear, can't you understand that he is becoming a bully?'

The argument between mother and daughter was getting emotional, so Abraham asked his wife to let things be. Ingrid hurried out of the room and did not show up again until dinnertime. After the maid announced that the meal was ready, David got up and said he was going to call Ingrid. His son ran ahead of him and asked to go instead.

The boy came back with his mother, who was looking sleepy. When Barbara began to apologize for what had happened, Ingrid walked towards her and said, 'It was my mistake, Mother.'

Although Ingrid advised that Muna's plan be acted upon after forming a promotion committee, David said the matter was too urgent. Therefore the first family sat down and promoted the officers. A message from Cicotaf, confirming the promotions and transfers, was sent to all units in the army.

The trick of leaving Knots at the top made the deserters confused. Many had seen the new structure as a plan to sideline them, but again, they still had the commander of the army as one of their own. What they didn't know, which couldn't actually be said in the message, was that his powers had been reduced.

The message was very careful in its wording. Top of the list was Brigadier Knots, who had been promoted to the rank of major general, and then came Colonel Muna, promoted to the rank of brigadier and also army chief of staff. All of the chiefs had been promoted, but they were natives. Their deputies, who were mostly deserters from the north, had also been promoted. The biggest surprise, however, was that the director-general of intelligence was made field commander at the frontline. The force would be called Attack Brigade and its commander had been elevated two ranks, up from major to full colonel.

—

In Northern State, the members of the force under Lt. General Croks were still at the seashore recovering from their trauma, but feeling completely demoralized. Their commander was not ready to commit such troops into what he called 'black combat.'

According to Croks, the mission was suicidal. He essentially needed to know three things about the enemy: location, habits, and strength. Without these facts he was obstinate about launching an attack. Whenever he sat down to plan, there came a message from Wolf, ordering him to cross the sea and attack.

The sea was calm and the plan was to make the men cross it by floating on logs. The stretch was narrow enough for a man to see across to the southern mainland. The water appeared calm and welcoming, and the gentle breeze brought the smell of ripe palm fruits. But the men were still traumatized, so the idea of leading them into combat was something Croks had to think long and hard about.

The peaceful, twinkling lights of Hollyfield made Croks spend many hours recollecting his heyday when he sat in an oval office waiting for reports. He could not stop to think about how he escaped death. The president gave an order for all senior military officers to attend his commissioning of a marine project in the middle of the sea. They were to be there the day before the commissioning; however, Croks was busy attending a special meeting.

That evening Croks called General Wolf and asked if he could show up the next day. Wolf, who would be flying with the president on the day of the commissioning, accepted Croks' request, and even welcomed him to accompany them. The next day there was a lot of turbulence, and the sea was like a raged terrain. The pilot made many attempts to land, but he was unable to see the landing pad that was a floating deck half the size of a football field.

Fox ordered the pilot to land on the nearby island of Directionland. A storm was still surging and the man advised that it might not be wise. Fox roared with his finger pointing down, so the pilot lowered the chopper. As the machine neared land it started to wobble, and all of a sudden it made a dive towards a flat rock. The pilot fought with the controls. With only hands to go before the rock, everyone in the helicopter closed their eyes. When they reopened them the rock was under them. There were nervous glances all round, and Fox changed his mind. He made a hand signal for takeoff. That evening, news of a strong storm sinking the marines at sea was sent to all units.

With all this haunting him, Croks came up with a weird plan that night. By morning, the burnt fumes from an uncoordinated bomb explosion the previous night were forcing people to flee Hollyfield. All roads in and out of the city were jammed with millions of stranded residents looking edgy, disgusted and confused.

With the entire nation fearing where the next bomb would go off, the media had this to say:

A terrorist attack has left twenty civilians dead in a nighttime bomb explosion in the center of Hollyfield. Frightened, fleeing residents, unsure where the next attack will take place, have chosen to return and wait for their fate in their homes. With hospital generators finding it hard to cope, schools and factories have joined the list of recent closures in the industrial hub of the nation...

Fox called Wolf to find out what had happened. The joint chief of staff expressed total ignorance.

There was no way Dunia Modern Army could launch an attack on the south when its home soil was being attacked. Fox ordered the joint chief of staff to establish the cause of the explosion and report to him immediately. Wolf spoke of combing the entire city, which would involve a lot of men and the evacuation of the city. The task of evacuating millions of people would require a lot of manpower and resources.

Fox told Wolf to use vigilantes to boost his manpower. When the joint chief of staff asked the president where to get these willing people to assist, Fox threaten to fire him. It did not work.

Wolf continued to ask odd questions. The president calmed down and asked him to take a deep breath. After a while, Wolf saluted the phone receiver and hung up.

The issue of what had happened in Hollyfield dominated the Millennium. Many deputies believed the state was immune to such attacks. Given the North's military superiority, the likely suspect, Southern State, would not dare to do such a thing, they thought. The deputies knew it was suicidal for deserters, the backbone of the southern army, to provoke the north.

Nonetheless, the joint chief of staff was called to explain what the deputies were already calling a 'security lapse.' The moment Fox had been waiting for had finally arrived, and it would not be the chief of joint staff who addressed the matter.

'Mister Speaker and honorable members, let me begin with asking for a minute's silence in memory of our departed citizens,' Fox began.

The silence was so deep that not even the ever-waggling window curtains swayed. 'Honorable members, allow me, on behalf of the House and, of course, on my own behalf, to send our sincere condolences to the families of our departed citizens. I find it incumbent upon me to personally tell the House the situation of our force. Dunia Modern Army, honorable members, needs recruiting, retraining, rearranging, reintegrating and renewing. The list is endless.'

The House booed.

'There is no way we can let this crime go unpunished. Of course, we all know who did this, and if we do not follow them, then we have turned ourselves into a state that is mindless and careless of its people. This takes me back to my campaign, and I shall not rest until it is achieved. But let me tell you that we are very weak indeed – as a result our enemy has entered our doors, striking at will. During the harsh weather, honorable members, Dunia Modern Army suffered the most. We need funds and we need them now. The army should once again be the pride it was if we are to overcome our enemy, who is getting more sophisticated.'

One of the deputies from Hollyfield rose and asked the president what he was going to do for the traumatized residents who were fleeing to nowhere. Fox answered that the army was working on it. The deputy rose again and asked whether the army was going to resettle these millions of city residents and where. Fox answered that resettling them wasn't the answer. The deputy then queried what the answer was. Fox replied, 'Tracking down the culprits.'

The legislature punched harder by asking why the incident had to coincide with the army camping in the area, and whether the constituency should prepare itself to receive uniformed bodies washing up on its shore again! As the exchange between the man and the president became nasty, the Speaker called for the House to close.

Full coverage of the exchange ran in the press. The question of the incident coinciding with the army's arrival in the area made people think. Those who had been optimist about helping the army joined ranks with those who were pessimistic about it. People began to reject what the army was telling them. The exodus to vacate the city changed course. People turned around and went back to their homes.

News of bombs going off in the center of Hollyfield was received nervously in the south. Most people knew that their army unit posted at the seaside had done it. The population began to fear the worst; that Fox's battle-hardened men would arrive at any moment.

David was fast to summon all senior officers of the army and civilian departmental heads, including his brother Fredrick, to the Covenant Hall for a meeting. The issue was what to do next. Questions like who, and why this act of all acts, were a waste of time, according to the Cicotaf and minister-president. He asked Colonel Mandark, the commander of Attack Brigade, to explain what had motivated him to provoke the north by attacking the city of Hollyfield.

'I swear to the living God that none of my men are responsible for that act,' said Mandark, looking shaky.

For a moment everyone just looked at one another in silence.

'It could be so, sir,' said Brigadier Muna (CoS), 'otherwise the press wouldn't have reacted the way it did.'

Mandark glanced at Muna and then put his head down. The silence continued.

David asked his brother to brief the meeting on the state of the bunkers, because, in his view, these were the only things that could minimize an attack by Fox.

Fredrick was very brief. 'The bunkers are a long way off if the entire population is to depend on them,' he said. 'The question now is how we can protect the people.'

Major General Knots rose. 'I think any state must defend itself, however weak. We have an army, and we must trust in it.'

'How did your recruitment drive go, chief?' David asked Muna.

'Well, sir, as you know, it was a vigilante force. The training is complete and they are ready, on call.'

'By the way, what is the strength of our force?' David asked.

Muna waited to see whether Knots would answer, but in the end he replied, 'Three brigades, sir – that is one division with about 10,000 officers and men.'

'Are all these men ready?'

'Not all of them, because there is always the sick, but most of them, yes, are deployable.' It was Muna who answered the minister-president again.

The meeting ended with the authorization of the evacuation of all urban areas. The army was tasked with helping to transport the population to the southern tip of the state, where the land was forested. People could camp there and observe lights out.

An order of no open cooking when an attack began was considered. The bunkers, since there were not enough for the population, were to be used by essential staff and the army.

# Chapter 64

The mayoral election was in its closing stages in Adam. Abraham was standing against a number of other candidates, but his strongest rival was Isacliot. Exit polls used a language of a sexual nature to inform the public the likely outcome: It appears the incumbent has got a dipper public screw, which leaves his closest rival, Isacliot wanting – was the article which appeared in the electoral publication.

Although neither candidate was allowed to campaign, on Sunday during her sermon, Ingrid blamed the language the exit poll had used for being immoral. The first lady priest used the moment to thank her parents for her good upbringing. Praises of many youths being like her, if people similar to her father were to be the nation's leaders, were noticeable.

A leading journalist interviewed Abraham and Isacliot in the Covenant shortly before a security meeting regarding an imminent attack. When Abraham came back home he looked unusually tired, and Barbara was concerned. She knew the meeting had affected her middle-aged husband, who had not been feeling so well lately.

At first there was an argument over why he had gone, but Barbara soon realized her husband needed care rather than curses. She remembered that he was meant to be having an interview where he was to announce his retirement from public duties.

The interview began with both men shaking hands, and the journalist sat in between them. Isacliot, who was asked to speak first, spent ten minutes outlining his proposals, whereby Adam would become modern, and electric transport would replace buses. His plan was largely about making the city greener.

Although not feeling well, Abraham preferred to stand while speaking. He got up and said, 'Fellow countrymen, I shall begin by thanking you for the cooperation you have given me as your first mayor of our fast-growing capital city, Adam. I shall also take this opportunity to thank my running mates for the spirit they have shown. Surely, the people to thank are too many, so allow me to just give a general appreciation.

'However, my wife and I have been doing a lot of thinking ahead of this day. By the way, greetings to my wife, without whom my task would have been more difficult. I take this opportunity to announce my decision to withdraw my candidacy. This I have done after consulting fully with my family.

'As you all know too well, our country is facing a war, and my family shall be highly involved in ensuring we emerge from this scare with the slightest harm possible. Without a doubt, my daughter and son-in-law will be working around the clock to ensure it. So, I think it is time I helped my wife with looking after our grandchildren. Thank you very much, and may God bless us all.'

=

In Northern State, the weather had once again deteriorated miserably. It turned the earth into a sheet of ice. For some time people enjoyed skiing, but as the trend persisted, the population began to stay indoors. The very young and old began to die as a result of the harsh climate. Factories closed down because the power plants could not cope.

The one thing that the people of the north had learned was not to bring their ships too close to shore. This time they hurried them out to sea where the water hardly froze. When it did freeze, some people ventured onto the ice and skied to the ships, which had their engines running. The middle of the sea resembled a city of ships, standing row after row. People hoped to stay there until the weather changed on land, after which they would return to their homes.

As people queued to reach the ships, President Fox announced the D-day for firing Lethal Weapon into Southern

State. The scientists were angry, as NEDO would be more catastrophic than the current problem, making the south equally environmentally unfriendly.

The Millennium Hatchet Man, the label that the media had given Fox, was undeterred – the missile had to be launched a fortnight away.

The debate in the Millennium was bitter until Fox's personal scientist confirmed that Lethal Weapon had been revised. When pressed how, he said it could kill all living things, but would not affect plants. The fusion would not affect things that gave off oxygen, by which he meant foliage. This, he claimed, was being done to find green pasture in the south.

The Archbishop called the president on the matter. In an hour-long conversation, the prelate humbly asked Fox not to make the move he was anticipating. The president didn't say no, but neither did he say yes. Instead he said, 'I understand, Your Eminence.'

The Archbishop then called his representative in Southern State and told him about halting the firing of Lethal Weapon. That was enough for all the houses of God throughout the south to ring their bells. A mass was said, during which Fox and David were simultaneously prayed for.

=

The next day, after challenging his scientist about NEDO, Fox warned of the political consequences of the phrase 'You're either with me or with the enemy.' The deputies were unmoved, thinking that Fox must be joking. Opinion ratings were at their lowest in his presidency, and any political move by him could backfire.

After a day of stalemate, Fox, with one year to go as president, stunned the Millennium by stating, 'I hereby dissolve the House. There shall be new elections in a few of months.'

According to the constitution, Fox was still president until after the new elections, but his announcement had effectively rendered all politicians ineffective. The salaries of the legislators had been halved and their allowances stopped.

═

The Lukiko in the south was doing things differently. Fox's intention was not a matter needing prayer, but action. A joint meeting of all people's representatives and councilors was called. The issue was about spreading the word of attack among the people. As always in these meetings, the first thing was to ask Fredrick about the progress of the bunkers around the townships across the state. There was some good news when he said they could now handle the state's essential staff and the army. He also said that places to accommodate the general public in concealment were ready.

Those listening exchanged glances, which seemed to ask how long the danger would last. Fredrick could not say whether the environment would get back to its former glory after what the meeting had come to call 'The Fox Fuss.' What Fredrick found incumbent upon him to tell, which he had learned from his earth science friends, was that Fox would pollute their atmosphere, but they, too, could not guess the extent of the damage.

Although some members were in favor of making this information known to the public through the media, Major General Knots cautioned that Fox might have moles around, so what was discussed at the meeting was off the record. Representatives would let the people know their fate without involving the press.

═

In Northern State, the issue of people registering themselves at their deputy offices for immigration had returned, but Fox slammed it aside. There was no time for it now, and people would travel across freely after the missile launch anyway.

The president had to tread very carefully. He knew there wasn't a northern army anymore, and the idea of some soldiers in the south surviving Lethal Weapon's onslaught gave him no sleep. The retired marshal spent his nights planning a conquest without troops, which he did by refreshing himself with his hobby game of robots. Realizing that surprise was his best weapon, Fox ordered the blackout of all media outlets.

The north was effectively under martial law. Life changed for the people, who were now sure that their leader was set to deliver his election promise. There were mixed feelings as the Southern State moved closer to being part and parcel of their land. The wait was an anxious one as the weather continued to unleash colder breezes and a thicker ice sheet.

# Chapter 65

D-day arrived and Northern State fired NEDO into the heart of Southern State. Although scientists had warned that the area would be a no-go zone for ten days in order to allow fission levels to recede, Fox dispatched a reconnaissance mission team two days after the launch. These scientists took photographs from the air; and upon detailed study of large-scale maps, they saw that the south of Dunia was green, still and vacant except for the impact area, which was blighted.

To most of the northern populace, who had had enough of the weather, Fox was a redeemer. Life had almost stopped and people no longer ventured outside. The situation was so dire that church leaders had started saying that the north was too harsh for human habitation.

The believers were against the idea of occupying the sister state. They continued to call for a negotiated settlement whereby the south would allow its vast uninhabited plains to come under the care of the north. However, the time had come where expressing one's views in public could be lethal. A number of believers had been attacked by angry mobs, and some lost their lives in the process.

=

Although NEDO claimed lives, the death toll wasn't as high as it could have been. Soldiers on patrol outside the bunkers were true martyrs in unlocking the secret behind the pollution. The drill was to keep as low as possible, actually ordered to crawl and observe only as far as possible, but some soldiers did not obey the orders and stood up in areas without vegetation. These men found it difficult to breathe and couldn't make it back to the bunkers.

Even then, the army did not know why some of its soldiers were dying and others were not. Speculation was commonplace, but there was one good hint: the pasture was green and healthy.

Thereon, all of the people were told to keep as low as possible when going outside for fresh air. It was also emphasized for them to keep close to vegetation. The people in the forests were enjoying life as usual.

At the bunkers nearly all of the casualties among the soldiers were former deserters with brown skin, no doubt the commanders with vision gadgets that had been charged with getting up to survey the horizon. The native dark-skinned men had taken it that Fox's poison was targeting those who had deserted him, and they had declined to take precautions.

The danger period of ten days as given by the scientists elapsed, and an announcement for the exodus to start to the south had to be made by Fox. The plan was simple: people were to ski to the boats in the middle of the sea, and row the vessels across the water to the southern shores. The sick, elderly and infirm would be taken by the few operating ships owned by the nation.

At the exact time that Fox wanted to announce the start of Operation Exodus, a strong storm with winds of up to 150 knots per hour blew across the sea. The initial plan had been for people to ski to the vessels waiting in deep water. However, secret trials by presidential men revealed that the ice near the vessels was soft, and any attempt to ski on them could be fatal.

The only option was to airlift people by helicopter, but that idea had its own shortcomings. Chopper fuel had been supplemented for lighting and heating ever since the electric power failed. Although there was enough fuel to fly to the marine vessels, if it was used up, roads in the south were known to be impassable in the rainy season, which was about now, and the task of transporting essentials was going to be daunting.

Fox therefore suspended Operation Exodus.

Day fifteen after launching NEDO saw the storm ease. Fox called the Speaker and asked him to call the House, as he had very important news to tell them. The president did not expect many deputies to turn up and arranged for the meeting to take place in his office. To his amazement, nearly all of them heeded the call.

The legislators looked tired, but willing to listen. They, too, were fed up with the weather in their land. Fighting Fox was now a lost cause, because the nation was firmly behind him. 'God is the villain for allowing nature to become so unfriendly' was a national phrase that even the believers could be overheard whispering.

The meeting, which had to be switched to the Millennium Hall, lasted less than an hour. Fox, after reminding the deputies that they were still on the payroll of the state, asked them to explain the procedure of Operation Exodus to their constituencies, as his office had arranged it.

There were, however, some changes to the arrangement. Some deputies volunteered to assist where help was badly needed, such as in guiding skiers to the vessels that would transport them. The meeting also resolved that the landing site be changed from the obvious one.

After careful study of the photographs brought by the research team, it was decided that the people would land in the delta where River Line entered the sea. Canoes and small boats were considered too dangerous and ruled out. It was also decided that people living far from the coastline would assemble at the nearest airport, from where they could be flown to Hollyfield airport near the sea.

The meeting ended with an agreement that Fox would make an announcement on the radio to kick-start the exodus.

Two days after the meeting, Fox went on air to speak to the people. 'Good evening,' he began. 'As commander in chief of your armed forces and president, I salute all of you for your understanding and patience. The day has finally come for us to start our journey south. As you know, this operation needs to be done efficiently, which the state has meticulously developed. It is my duty to ask you to be orderly and obedient. I shall therefore tell you how the operation will proceed.'

After explaining how the exercise would be performed, which prioritized the sick, elderly and infirm, Fox told the nation that volunteers, most of whom were well-known faces, were waiting to receive them at sea. He ended by wishing every citizen a safe journey. No one knew that Fox had no intention of taking the sick and elderly until the useful people were settled, if then.

The population set out as Fox had requested. It was true that there were people waiting to receive them who happened to be, among others, their deputies, designers from marine companies and church councilors. While the legislators did a lot in directing who should go where, the designers provided pump-up boats and handy skis, and church people helped care for the disabled, sick and infirm waiting to be helped to boats.

Amazingly, it was warm at sea and paradise on board the ships, whose engines had been running for days.

—

The statement from President Fox to start Operation Exodus made David's army treat the situation with extra caution. The soldiers in the bunkers were monitoring things on a minute-by-minute basis. They knew Fox's battle-hardened men would go ahead to secure the region before people landed.

Colonel Mandark began to send out patrols. He expected Fox's force to land right where his force was dug in, which did not happen for days. The sea was calm. At night the troops could see Hollyfield sparkle, but not as it used to. Electric lamps which used to line roads were something of the past. What Mandark and his troops saw on the other side of the sea was generator lighting, which receded as the days past.

Surging waves hit the coastline, but there was no sign of the marines. After three days of seeing nothing, Mandark sent a message to all units in which he warned of the enemy infiltrating from elsewhere. Night patrols increased throughout the south.

The fact of the matter was that Croks' regrouped force had succumbed to nausea. Those who survived just melted into the masses as ordinary citizens, unable to even talk about their past careers.

As for Croks himself, it was hard to live with what he had done to the people of Hollyfield. Whenever the man looked at himself in a mirror, he saw images of people asking him why he had taken their lives. It became too much for the general when he looked at his hands he saw innocent people's blood dripping from them. He began to talk to himself, trying to answer the spirits by asking for their forgiveness. Croks became very tense after such moments. The general took his own life with a shot to the head.

Wolf was perhaps the only surviving soldier, which happened because his family had threatened to kill themselves if he dared to take his own life. He was a man who loved his relatives dearly and so he accepted misery. Now and then too much frustration would set in, however, making Wolf hold his gun to his head, which he did after making sure that he was alone. Which wasn't so, because Wolf's five-year-old grandson asked his grandfather what he was up to. Wolf's frustration normally eased after looking at the blur of his smiling grandson. The boy thought it was some kind of game, and on one occasion he was caught holding a gun to his head with his forefinger in the trigger guard. 'I learned it from grandfather. He does it often,' he said.

The family decided to remove all weapons from the house and bury them.

# Chapter 66

The period of curious people coming in day and night saw the towns in the south fill with foreigners. Fox jetted in and established his headquarters at the airport. The first political act for him was to name the new nation. 'This land shall be called Dunia State and its capital New Eden,' he said upon stepping off his plane.

Ingrid asked her husband for leave, and decided to go and stay with her children and parents. She had always kept herself busy by reading. With her books packed together in a small chamber in the bunker, at times it took her hours to find a particular book that she wanted. One day she came upon the letters that her mother sent to her at college. She opened the bundle. The letter on top was telling her to abandon the search for her relatives and concentrate on her education, and that her family would trace her if she made her mark on Dunia. The need to know her maternal roots began to haunt her. She thought it would be a consolation, since the family history of her father made her sad whenever she revisited it.

Abraham became an orphan at a very early age. His father was said to be one of the very first traders across the water into the north, and presumably the most daring. When the sea claimed its first known victims, his body was never found. After his wife had waited for her beloved one in vain, she picked up her son and travelled all the way to the coast in search of him. While there she was told that the description she was giving matched that of a man last seen boarding a canoe bound for the north. She spent days trying to find out what really happened.

After understanding the wife's story fully, a fisherman told her that all of the canoes that made the crossing at the time she described had capsized in a strong storm, and there were no survivors.

The woman became so depressed that she jumped into the sea, leaving her child alone. This was a time when the number of missionaries there, travelling from north to south to spread the word of God was at its peak. A group of them came across the boy abandoned on the seaside and took him in.

While in the monastery, Abraham was amused by the way the missionaries talked about life in the north where they came from. Although he was being groomed to become a priest, the boy left after being baptized Joseph. He was fourteen years of age.

A year later he journeyed into Dunia's wonderland of the north. While there he bumped into Barbara, who was doing vacation work in a job center. Unwittingly, she led him into finding out who he was and where he belonged. That was how Abraham became a young man with political ambitions.

Ingrid's father told her that story the same day he expressed fear over Barbara being deported if she rejected marrying David. Since then Ingrid hated asking about her roots. She felt that her mother should have told her the story. After all, she was aware of Ingrid's failure to locate her relatives while at school in the north.

The letter and the looming war brought out a new feeling in Ingrid. It was time to learn about her maternal parentage.

Barbara had started calling her relatives without realizing that she was doing so. The woman said the initials 'SS' whenever she did something accidentally, like dropping a spoon or spilling a drink, which was happening more often. It seemed Barbara thought it was unlikely coming out of the bunker alive. The time came when she said 'SS' uncoordinatedly.

Then one day, Barbara cradled her grandchildren for well over an hour until they fell asleep on her lap. She called Ingrid over, asked her to sit next to her, and began to tell her a story. 'I wouldn't be what I am if it was not for him,' she began, looking unusually scared. 'He was a great father to me. He warned me of the dangers ahead, but I couldn't understand him. That led me into politics, after being persuaded by the local church at Lostsummer.'

Barbara paused, possibly wondering how her parents might have looked. She recalled the night at the dinner table when she made the pronouncement to 'SS Family' that she would be taking up politics for a career. The reflection didn't last and she burst forth, 'Maybe the spirit of my parents plunged me into this. Because, for sure, my parents both died instantly in a car crash that had politics to blame. I don't know why on earth I decided to take up a career that left me an orphan through and through!'

Ingrid looked her mother in the face and saw tears in her eyes. Barbara was unable to talk further. Ingrid, too, began to shed tears. Although she had known her mother was an only child, she thought she would get a chance to meet her grandparents one day. Ingrid had always believed it was Barbara taking a dark-skinned man for a husband that had separated her from her parents. As a mother and a believer, Ingrid looked forward to the day when her mother's relatives would come knocking on their door.

It was after those emotional tears that Barbara explained in detail about Uncle SS. After she said his full name, 'Simple Satan,' Ingrid hated every word that came out of her mother's mouth. She wanted to tell her mother to keep quiet, but something she could hardly explain stopped her.

Ingrid tried to stop listening, but the story had become such a part of her that she could hardly afford not hearing it. Finally, the part about Barbara's only surviving guardian throwing her out of the house because of her father was too much for the lady priest. Fury filled her heart and she yelled at her mother to stop talking.

Barbara went quiet and observed her daughter crying. She hugged her and said she was sorry. The two women stayed in each other's arms for quite some time, after which they sank to their knees and began to pray. They asked to see their loved ones again.

# Chapter 67

The new immigrants to the south needed to do a lot to overhaul their new homes to match their standards. Tales from the elders of what the north had been like before the weather changed made people collect in groups, lying on their backs in the scorching sun, listening and imagining how beautiful their old home once was. People seemed to like nothing better than to spend entire days in the sunshine, sunbathing.

The authorities were startled that the people were not doing what they should. President Fox tried to be rough, but the public did not mind him – 'It is his name, after all,' they said, and took no notice whenever the ex-marshal barked. Had the president forgotten that he had no army any more, they wondered.

Fox went around firing his pistol in the air and ordering his people to do something. As the president was the only one who officially owned a gun, the people thought he was just excited about his personal past. Many even ran after him, cheering him to fire. Finally, Fox ran out of rounds.

The president then talked of building a vigilante force, but no one volunteered. Not even the prison guards, who had ceased to operate during their work to clear dead bodies from the city streets due to the bad climate. They had been trained to handle criminals, a job that disappeared with harsh weather patterns, because people had to stay indoors all the time. Northern State had decided to turn its prisons into reception centers for the needy and homeless at the time. The guards were therefore retired, and some were still demanding unpaid benefits from the state.

The northerners now in the south were acting completely different from when they were at home. They would not listen to their idols, the scientists. As soon as they arrived in the warm part of Dunia, they knew that God, and neither Fox nor science, had answered their prayers.

Fox regretted the motion to dissolve the Millennium. His hope had been to guide the elections and get the people he trusted on the new political scene. His dream was failing. There was no way he could handle the current situation alone. Knowing how the public had trusted the scientists during the hard days back home, he asked them for help.

The scientists placed posters everywhere, warning the public of a deadly disease that could affect their skins due to staying under the blazing sun for too long. People called it wolokoso, but the combination of changes in skin tone, blisters caused by nasty flying insects, and deadly creatures creeping everywhere set them on their guard. The skin of the people was changing from clear light to spotty dark. Then a cloud appeared, and everyone sought shelter from the heavy downpour without much success.

When the rains stopped, people developed all kinds of sickness and their blisters became wounds. The only medical care available was in makeshift tents, and moving them around was a nightmare. People began to succumb. Children and the elderly were dying like flies. Death managed to collect them together as one family in search of how and where to inter their loved ones.

Southern State had no public cemeteries. The southerners buried their dead in family plots, and in most cases the earth claimed all traces of the graves. As the immigrants wondered where to bury the dead, bodies began to decompose. Another cloud of rain began to build in the sky, and people had to accept the inevitable – the bodies had to be burned.

==

Natives hiding in the forests found life difficult after the heavy rain. A rare type of mosquito was feeding on them and many, especially children, developed temperatures. It had been only days, but the situation was already pathetic and unbearable. Children cried and many succumbed.

Those underground, too, were finding it rough, as the bunkers had become a nightmare. The heavy rains had submerged big sections of the townships. A lot of garbage from days of litter by the new occupants blocked the drains. Water flowed into the bunkers via the ventilation above. In some places the bunkers were full of water, right up to the ceiling. The worst scenario now was drowning. A solution was sought. After confirming the absence of Fox's battle-hardened men, the Lukiko gave the order for the people to come out.

It was like a dream when the people from the north awoke to a morning filled with dark-skinned army personnel all over the place, ordering them to do all sorts of humiliating things. Fox and his hastily formed administration were taken underground.

The southern army seemed to be working with impunity, according to reports that reached Ingrid, who was in a conditioned bunker with her children, mother and father.

The natives arrived to find new occupants in their homes. Scuffles broke out, and in some cases they were fatal. Yet the only arbitrator, the army, was on one side – that of the natives. Those who had deserted the northern army were all out to settle old scores.

Ingrid could not let things go the way they were heading. She felt duty bound to pay back those people who had made her writing gain holy status and profitability. Ingrid went to meet her husband, but David was not well. Days of living in a poorly ventilated, hot bunker without any sleep had taken its toll on him.

'Take my place for now, I beg,' he told his wife.

Ingrid called for an emergency meeting of the Lukiko and told the House, 'After consulting with your leader, we have come to a decision that pushing people down must...'

She was booed even before she could finish what she wanted to say. The whole day was spent arguing the matter in a disorderly manner. Not allowing foreigners to take over their land changed from a slogan—no room for foreigners into a chant—south for southerners. Legislators that Ingrid had once respected were chanting the most, and there was hardly a member listening to her. Ingrid gave up when one senior member pointed a finger at her and called her a traitor.

When Ingrid arrived home she went straight to see her children, who were staying with her parents in their mansion annex they named Marlote. She felt worn out. Barbara asked Ingrid what the matter was, but before she could answer, her father asked whether David was all right. Ingrid only shook her head in the negative and turned her face away to hide her tears from her parents. The two elders, fearing the worst, looked at one another. Barbara went to her daughter and hugged her.

Ingrid burst out, 'Surely they cannot do this. There must be a way to stop them.'

'What do you mean, my dear?' Abraham asked.

'GOA – it is a vendetta,' Ingrid said.

'What's David's position?'

'He's sick, but, of course, against it.'

'Who is in charge now?' Abraham asked.

'Me.'

'Good, take up the matter with the Lukiko.' Abraham advised.

'I spent the whole day... nothing!' Ingrid said.

'Come on, talk to those you have confidence in, and then put the matter to a vote. I am sure you can achieve what you want, girl. You've come this far. You can't give up now.'

'How I wish you didn't retire, Dad.'

Abraham pointed at his grandchildren. 'Come on, girl, I had to look after them, as they needed us,' he said.

Ingrid took her father's advice and visited the representatives with northern education to ask for their support. When the Lukiko resumed, the matter of the army acting without causing body injuries upon northerners was voted on. The result was in favor of the motion, calling upon soldiers to treat what it called immigrants humanely. And the editor immediately wired the ruling over to the media and security heads.

That evening there was a phone call from someone wanting to speak to the commander in chief urgently. David's secretary, who had been living in the mansion ever since the underground operation began, told Ingrid, who said her husband could not come to the phone.

The secretary went away and returned almost immediately. 'It is the chief of staff, ma'am,' she said.

'I'll take it,' Ingrid replied while walking towards the phone. 'Ingrid, may I help you?' she asked.

'Ma'am, it is Brigadier Muna, can I speak with the minister-president?'

'I am afraid he isn't feeling well, can I help?'

There was a moment of silence. 'Well, it is the situation that I want to brief him about.'

'What is it exactly, colonel?' Ingrid demanded.

'Brigadier, ma'am...'

'Oh, sorry, forgive me, sir.'

Brigadier Muna continued, 'No problem, back to the matter. Anyway, there isn't much to report; otherwise, I think the army commander should be spoken to, because it appears the situation could best be solved by him. I saw the message about the way our troops are behaving and thought of replying to it, but I felt that calling was better. Well, some soldiers are, how can I say it, all out to demean our army. Anyway, I hope you can talk with the major general personally.'

Ingrid looked at the receiver in total silence and after exhaling a deep breath, she said, 'I knew. Well, thanks, Brigadier Muna, I'll take up your concern with the relevant authorities.'

Major General Knots arrived at the mansion late that night.

'The commander in chief is not well, but he told me what to tell you.' Ingrid told him.

'Yes, ma'am.'

'I think you know how crucial the union of the people of Dunia is.'

'Of course, ma'am,' Knots acknowledged.

'Sorry, but I'll be personal to you if you may; how would you feel if you came to learn later that it was your uncle or cousin being ill-treated?'

'I don't understand,' said Knots.

'OK, let me put it this way; do you think our parents were wrong to bear us as mixed races, or is the color of our skin a curse?' Ingrid spoke with her voice raised.

'Not true, of course, but, well, anyway, in my view black is black.' Knots answered.

Silence.

Ingrid bounced back. 'No one can doubt that, but I want you to forget what happened in the past. The future, which has already begun, owes us quite a lot.'

'I understand,' said Knots.

'And this should apply to all soldiers under your command. Let us make history by stretching both our hands towards our enemies. Remember they are not enemies anymore; it was Fox who wanted to be enemies. The people we expected aren't the ones that have come here. Have your men had any confrontation or any conflict of any sort?' Ingrid asked, looking relaxed.

'Not at all, ma'am.'

'Now let us settle all scores by healing old wounds. And please send my greetings to your men,' said the first lady with a smile.

—

There was an argument in the Lukiko over whether to send the northerners back home. After a day's wrangling, members considered voting on the matter. Ingrid's earlier appeal of not sending back the people she referred to as 'our cousins' had captivated most members, and the vote was in favor of them staying.

The immediate task was to list the newcomers according to their field of work. With the population far higher than the infrastructure could handle, intellectuals and technical persons were called upon to serve. This, however, brought about renewed wrangling in the House. Most members of the Lukiko felt that light-skinned intellectuals would sabotage the state infrastructure.

Ingrid, in rebound, insisted that the newcomers were in a position to understand that this was now a land for all. The issue was put to a vote, and this time the two top military commanders, Major General Knots and Brigadier Muna, were invited to cast their votes.

Pessimists were shocked. Northern-born Knots voted against, while native-born Muna voted in favor of allowing the immigrants to participate in building the nation. The new Lord Mayor Mr. Isacliot announced the ruling. But the House was not ecstatic. The differences between the resisters and modernists were showing signs of re-emerging.

# Chapter 68

Barbara went all over the state, searching for the SS family like someone possessed. Whenever she came into a new settlement, she yelled out 'SS.' People took her for someone looking for a missing kid or pet called Cicy, because she sounded this way due to her panting. Dogs went after her, barking and wagging their tails.

==

After days of fruitless searching, she returned home looking sunburned and sad. Either she'd had no time to apply her makeup, or she forgot to take it with her. Ingrid took up the matter since her mother had become so restless and stressed.

The village where people from Lostsummer had settled was finally traced. The community was living in the same way it did back home in the north with the church leader as the most prominent person. It was apparent that not all of the people had offered to leave the north for the south. Some, especially those opposed to dark skin, preferred to remain and even die. Although these northern light-skinned individuals were convinced that everyone in the south was dead, they were people who had sworn never to enter a house used by a dark-skinned man. They included the SS family and a few others. The state opted to abandon them.

Eventually, a youth with a story about the SS family showed up. 'Mr. Simple Satan, he declined, because he feared facing Barbara.'

Barbara cut in, 'No, that's misleading. No one ever expected to encounter a living soul here in the south. You took Fox's report for real, and even your scientists approved it,' she said, feeling agitated.

The young man did not reply and neither did any other person in the gathering. Barbara left the place with a broken heart.

Mr. Simple Satan, for one, had a different reason for his absence. He had dreamed of meeting Barbara and apologizing for everything that had happened between them, calling it the power of Satan, but Barbara would not listen to him. He had the same dream over and over again until he called his family together, and gave a ruling for his household not to cross over to the Southern State. SS nonetheless wrote a brief note in which he admitted being racist and asked for forgiveness. He then sent the brief to the local church in Lostsummer, but the church council chose not to talk about it.

=

Barbara asked her daughter if they could arrange to go to Lostsummer and find out the real truth.

Ingrid offered to join her parents on the special plane fitted with satellite imagery that Fox had flown in on. Notable scientists eager to know what was happening in the north were allowed to accompany them.

Lostsummer village would be explored exclusively until the SS family was found and brought on board. Unfortunately, the entire land mass had been buried under snow and there was no place for the plane to land. Even then, the aerial satellite search unveiled shocking results at every step. The onslaught of ice had left more than half of northern Dunia with temperatures as low as -250° F.

No human being could have survived, according to scientists, yet Barbara still hoped to find her relatives alive. Not anymore when the satellite revealed a thick, moving cloud twice the size of Lostsummer dropping right where the village once stood. Barbara collapsed. This tragedy marked the end of the search.

=

The task of the first family changed drastically after the failure to locate Ingrid's maternal relatives at Lostsummer. Building Dunia State would take years – everyone, including Ingrid, knew that, and most people thought the possibility of seeing Dunia's final glory a myth. Nevertheless, the spirit to work as one race was glowing like a burning ember in a gentle wind.

Twege had conquered people's minds and hearts such that color discrimination became a crime of conscience. In the eyes of many, Ingrid Ngobi was a saint. Light-skinned people accepted her in the same way as the dark and brown-skinned did. Her morale was boosted.

Calling the Lukiko members bricks, Ingrid reminded them that mortar was needed if they were to stick together and resist the powerful wind of change. Her allegory took no time to be understood. The lady politician-priest was calling upon the Lukiko to accept northern immigrants into active politics. Her idea was vehemently opposed, but after a long discussion, coupled with the general good behavior of the immigrants, Ingrid's opponents within the Lukiko could cite no reason to reject her notion.

Nearly all of the politicians from the north claimed to be political veterans, but if every one of them was accepted, overloading of the political arena was a possible scenario. To solve the problem the panel asked to see their CVs. That approach was impractical, however, as interpretation of what was written in them varied among the panelists.

To break the stalemate, politics had to be redefined. Professors of politics were given the task. The issue dragged on for quite some time as several scholars came up with varying views, some clearly erratic. After a grueling argument, during which they called each other names, the definition was narrowed with a mathematical formula ($P*3A$), meaning 'politics is allegory, allure and allusion.'

How the panelists were to know which politicians had the qualities in the formula was another issue. Elections were the best answer, it was decided. The members of the Lukiko were not ready to call an election, however. Instead, they made many suggestions, some as undemocratic as tossing a coin to choose between two nominees. The Lukiko had never had such fun until the Lord Mayor advised things be done in the same the way he was voted in.

In the weeks ahead, Politicians from the north were invited to attend open debates against one another. Many proved their potential and were invited to join the Lukiko with observer status. With time, though, the observer politicians felt an overwhelming need to represent their people, who they felt were unrepresented. Sending them back to campaign would not be good, according to most members of the Lukiko.

Those supporting the motion put up a matching argument. The immigrant politicians heckled every speaker, whether he or she supported them or not. Old intrigues among the modernists, resisters, believers and seculars returned, but this time under the same roof. The House came to blows.

When the Lukiko assembled after that nasty incident, Ingrid read out an order from the minister-president whereby the observer politicians had been allotted constituencies to represent. Murmuring was heard, but the lady priest would not allow it to rise. 'The state cannot afford the time it would take for successive campaigns one after the other,' she announced.

There was total silence in the House.

Ingrid resumed to talk, 'Soon, Dunia State will go to the polls, because what has happened here recently demonstrates the urgency of a balanced government.'

The House heckled.

'However, that government can come in place only when we have a parliament...'

Ingrid could not speak on, because the House was filled with the noise of table knocking, foot stamping, and yelling.

—

Elections for parliamentary seats took place sooner than expected. Electronic voting had been enhanced and most people participated from their homes. It was raining on the day of polling, and those with cyber connections in their homes invited their neighbors over to cast their votes online. At the end of the exercise the media reported a very high turnout.

It took a matter of hours for the results to come in. However, these were figures being collected from various polling stations. After twenty-four hours, the results that were claimed to be authentic and state-backed were read over the radio and on television. The figures agreed with those reported earlier.

With the political system well in place, the state invited anthropologists to try to merge the language spoken by the immigrants with that of the natives. The issue was not to make one language override the other, but to use words from both. In the meantime, parliament carried out its business in either language, depending on the subject being discussed. When the issue was to the benefit of the immigrants, the preferred language was that of the north, and the other way around if the majority beneficiaries were southerners. At the end of the day, it was the duty of the press to inform its readers accordingly.

Notable faces bounced back unopposed in parliament: Wood Tiger, yet again as Speaker, and Ingrid Ngobi, who was unanimously appointed as prime minister. Although the new state would not necessarily be a monarchy, parliament agreed to have a royal role, free of political decision making. The person who would take up the post was nominated without being consulted.

'Father, I have some good news for you,' Ingrid told Abraham, when she went to visit her parents in their Marlote annex residence.

'I hope it is to do with my grandchildren,' Abraham replied.

'Well, they are fine, of course, but it isn't about them.'

'What then?' Abraham asked.

'Parliament has unanimously chosen you to be our first king,' said Ingrid.

'Is that a wise idea?' asked Barbara from the far end of the room where she was preparing a cup of tea for her daughter.

'Yes, of course, Mother,' said Ingrid.

Abraham, after a moment of thought said, 'Well, I'll have to talk it over with your mother, I hope it can wait.'

'Yes, besides it is between me and you,' said Ingrid.
'Noted,' Abraham said.

# Chapter 69

A couple of years later, Dunia State was doing better than anyone had expected. The infrastructure was growing at breathtaking speed, and to other people, especially the natives, the growth rate was alarming. On the priority list had been schools, houses of God, roads, and the means to live, which meant agriculture, on which the state sustained itself.

Everyone was calling Twege a fortune teller. Schools and churches had become part and parcel of one another in delivering knowledge and spiritual guidance.

Light-skinned people began to view their names as truly reflective of deadly creatures to mankind, so many dropped them and took on new ones. Those who had decorated their bodies were in a relentless search for ways to erase the howling images.

The most remarkable episode of the merger was perhaps the marriage of Aan Savage and David's youngest brother, Fredrick. Besides one being light-skinned and the other dark, they were both ministers and members of parliament. The wedding was to take place in the gardens of the biggest cathedral, which had just been built on a hill overlooking the capital city of New Eden. A big percentage of the city population was expected to watch the momentous occasion.

The couple was both forty on the day of their wedding. Prime Minister Ingrid Ngobi, who was by now more of a spiritual leader than a political one, was to preside over the ceremony as chief priest. Twege, which was seen by the couple as clearer than the Holy Book, was to provide the readings.

The couple had endured many cancellations of their wedding, as Aan's parents were divided on it taking place. Her father was not against the marriage, but against her changing her last name. Yet Fredrick had made it clear to his fiancée that she would be called Aan Ngobi after their marriage. Aan and her mother had no problem with it, but her father was so advanced in age that decisions against his will could easily kill him.

Ingrid paid the Savages a visit in their castle home on a hill overlooking New Eden. She held a long, spiritual conversation with them until the legendary leader said in a shaky voice, 'I see that it is God's calling. Let good come out of it, and I offer my whole blessing.'

When Ingrid later broke the news at her family's dinner table that Mr. Savage had given the go-ahead, Fredrick was thankful, but he did not look convinced.

—

At eight sharp on a beautiful Saturday morning, mass began. The couple had arrived in secrecy, and the MC called upon the preacher to deliver her sermon before uniting the two people. At the altar, Ingrid put Twege aside and read a verse from the Holy Book. 'Thou sought, thou find. And in bondage neither thou can unbound. Surely, I say to ye, here sit a knot to tie!'

Many people questioned why she didn't read her own version. As if understanding her audience's dilemma, she resorted to Twege to unravel the verse of the Holy Book. 'A woman and a man become one once they decide to take on each other as wife and husband. No one should ever interfere, even if the row between them is worth intervening. They, together as one, should allow your intervention. Never should an outsider listen to either wife or husband before judging, and if the judgment is to hurt one of the parties, it is better not delivered. To you, Fredrick and Aan, I ask you to live with only three words – mistake, accept and forgive – for that is the formula for marriage.'

Everyone was silent and still throughout Ingrid's sermon. When she asked for forgiveness at the end of it, even arch enemies faced one another and shook hands. Then the moment to unite the couple came.

Instead of asking the congregation if anyone had a reason to stop Aan and Fredrick taking their holy vows, she asked the people of Dunia to rewrite their history: 'The age of agony has all along been referred to as dark,' she remarked and then quieted as the entire crowd murmured its approval. 'But let us know that period as Peoples in Darkness. For we were, ourselves, dressed in the darkness at the time.'

The entire hill was thrown into a frenzy of joy after the marriage. Then a dark-skinned man who had lost his wife to malaria during the hiding ran through the crowd, swearing never to speak with light-colored persons. 'Never, never, never – against,' he shouted while waiving a palm branch.

At first the people thought it was the excitement of the moment making him behave that way, and they did not give him much attention. The man then moved in front of a light-skinned couple who were holding hands and forced them apart. 'You shouldn't be doing this now, I beg,' he said in southern accent.

The couple did not understand and just stared at him, feeling scared and confused. The scene attracted a crowd. From the balcony of the mansion house, Ingrid saw what looked to be a scuffle. Surely, a happy day shouldn't end like this, the lady priest thought as she rushed outside.

Meanwhile, the man was still saying the same things in his native language. Ingrid translated his words to the frightened couple. On understanding, the pair, who was brother and sister, smiled.

One year later, the dark-skinned native man and the light-skinned woman got married in the cathedral.

# Chapter 70

Abraham's refusal to accept the role of monarch was a big disappointment to Ingrid. She tried to convince him, but he stuck to his guns, with retirement being his only answer. She reported the matter to parliament and a search for a royal leader began.

By this time, David had become so frail that Ingrid ruled him out as soon as his name came up in parliament. The name of Savage was mentioned, only for Aan Ngobi to alert the House that her father was too ill to take public office, suspending the idea indefinitely.

The most trying moment for the joint parliament was the case against Fox. It had been going on for years, and Corona Trots was to hand down his sentence shortly. The media had foretold the maximum penalty, which was death, but that had been when the case was still fresh. Lately, rumors were rife that the ex-president would spend the rest of his life in prison. Not that his sentence would be altered, but it was felt that to crucify him, as the press had started calling hanging, would dent Dunia's fragile racial integration, according to critics.

Since the marriage of Aan and Fredrick, one-and-a-half years earlier, many mixed marriages had taken place, but the current statistics gave a corresponding number of breakups. The situation was so alarming that parliament passed a bill banning divorce, which stated: 'There shall be no more official granting of separation between married couples.'

There was a protest outside parliament after the divorce bill was passed. Ordinary people ignored it, after realizing it was organized by people wanting to benefit from their rich former spouses.

Finding Fox guilty on three accounts of genocide, environmental pollution and acting outside the doctrines of God, Trots handed Fox the sentence of death by hanging, as expected. The corona, in announcing the sentence, said that although count three was viewed as counts one and two put together, the accused was a man who belittled his creator so embarrassingly that it became a count on its own. Fox was to be executed within twenty-four hours.

Fox had changed considerably while in jail. Beyond growing gray haired, he was now in his mid-seventies and had grown to trust in God. According to him, he had 'seen the light.' When the prison chaplain asked him to say something before the sentence was handed down, the former president and retired top soldier said he had done enough to qualify for the death penalty, but he stressed that it would have been so in the archaic laws of the past. He did not ask to be pardoned. Instead, he asked the prime minister, in her capacity as a priest, to pray for him before sending him to the gallows.

Ingrid heard Fox's message live, because she was following it on television. She felt extremely challenged. With David, who was the only person able to change a court ruling, still unable to leave his bed, Ingrid made sure the issue of Fox was discussed in parliament.

The Speaker made the issue number one on the agenda, as requested by the prime minister. The matter dragged on and parliament was split down the middle on it. Some members wanted Fox executed as a lesson to all, while others wanted the very opposite – the man had changed, they argued, and as such he should be given a second chance.

If the issue was not decided during the session, it would be too late, as Fox was to be executed the next day. The sitting went on until late in the night without a clear agreement. Votes were called and there was a tie in those as well.

A moment was granted for recess, during which Ingrid approached the Speaker and asked for his opinion. Wood Tiger said he was against the sentence. Knowing she had him on her side, Ingrid asked him what they should do. The Speaker thought for a while and then his cell phone rang. Totally confused, he glanced at Ingrid.

'Take it, please,' she advised.

'It is Mr. Savage, wanting to know how far we were on the issue,' said Wood Tiger.

'Good friends, are they?' Ingrid asked.

'I understand so,' answered Wood Tiger. 'But why don't you find out the position of your husband? His prerogative makes him the last man in this.'

Ingrid thought for a while, and then rushed to a corner to phone David. Afterwards, she asked the Speaker to call back the House.

'Prime minister,' the Speaker said as soon as the House resumed.

'Honorable members,' Ingrid began, 'after consulting our leader from his sick bed... and, by the way, he sends his greetings to the House and has praised your dedication. I told him how we are doing on the issue of Mr. Fox...'

'No, no, no! Marshal Fox!' murmured the House.

'Whatever you please,' Ingrid responded, and there was heckling, which eventually became noise.

The Speaker called the House to order, which took some time. By then it was midnight and one member asked for the matter to be closed, because the time was over. Everyone looked at the clock on the wall. It was a minute past midnight. There was silence in the House until a voice asked, 'Now what?'

'The prime minister is still holding the floor, please,' announced Tiger.

'As I was telling you,' Ingrid continued, 'the minister-president has cast his vote.'

'What is it?' the House roared.

'He is against,' said Ingrid.

'Against what?' one member asked.

'Fox shall not be executed,' Ingrid declared.

=

Dressed in the attire of priesthood, Ingrid began to say her prayer, 'We break the laws we make. Fox, you are no exception. Among the many evil things you did, you did one good thing. None of us ever expected to witness the people of Dunia share creed and cradle like today. Who of us can doubt the integration flourishing in a society that only a short while ago lived in the jaws of hate and jealousy and mistrust? You, none the less, used excessive force. That is true, though surely, you harmonized rather than harmed.

'But, even then, I take this opportunity to outlaw the institution that made you what you weren't, but what you became. From now on, I declare the army an institution no longer to be associated with man. As we embark on disbanding the army, we need you, for you know far more than any of us about this cruel institution. On behalf of Dunia, I do hereby pardon you, Mr. Shroud Rough Fox. Please enjoy your advisory role in retirement. May God bless our new generation under a harmonious natural order! Amen!'

Major General Knots jumped on his escort jeep and drove straight to the prison where Fox was being detained. Without returning the salute at the gate, he asked, 'May I talk with Fox?'

'I shall find out if he is still here, sir,' said a prison guard.

'Of course he should be,' Knots roared.

'Then you can proceed to the office, sir.'

Knots headed for the cells instead, where Fox was being led out to the release chamber. On seeing Knots, he tried to run back, but the two-star general drew his pistol and took a direct shot, which caught Fox in the neck. He staggered, but the loss of so much blood made him dizzy and he collapsed. Knots fired two more shots, finishing off Fox completely. He then turned and walked back to his Jeep and headed for parliament.

Technology had become part of the security apparatus, and the House in session had seen what happened in the prison. There was pandemonium when the security screens showed the killer storming inside.

Knots caught up with Ingrid in the corridor. 'I need to have a word, ma'am,' he said after saluting.

Ingrid wanted to run, but her legs could not carry her that fast, so she kept walking away from Knots.

'It isn't what you think,' Knots said, following behind.

Ingrid slowed. 'What is it then?'

'I have come to surrender myself. The army should also be disbanded. I actually have no objection about it now.'

Ingrid was startled. 'Why are you doing this?'

Knots pulled out his pistol and dropped it on the floor, where he kicked it towards her. 'They were never with you, and never will they ever be,' he said. 'They know people by skin color. They call themselves whites and called us blacks. They are the angels of God with a skin without color. That is why our color is associated with the most negative things you can imagine.

'We are nothing, and we will never be anything in their eyes. The coup was not about anything else; it was about Fox and Savage and, of course, a few others still there. But now the cult leader is gone, they will begin to fall like dominoes.' Knots saluted and walked away.

A moment later, Aan came running down the corridor towards Ingrid. 'My dear, my father has died. The old man couldn't stand the way that man shot Fox, as they were very close friends...'

Aan was cut short by Barbara, who came in panting and looking for her daughter. 'I have sad news, my dear, Moses the Shepherd has shot Esther and taken his own life.'

'They'll fall like dominoes,' Ingrid said, thoughtfully.

Abraham walked in, appearing calm. 'Well, it is not the end of the world,' he said amid silence. 'At least this is not as bad as the violence that shook Dunia and separated it in two. We are united now, after all.'

THE END

www.ingramcontent.com/pod-product-compliance
Lightning Source LLC
Chambersburg PA
CBHW070541260626
47161CB00002B/470